MASTERS' COUNTERPOINTS

MASTERS' COUNTERPOINTS

Larry Townsend

■ ■ ■

Boston ♦ Alyson Publications, Inc.

To Victor Terry, with thanks.

Copyright © 1991 by Larry Townsend.
Cover design copyright © 1991 by F. Ronald Fowler.
All rights reserved.

Typeset and printed in the United States of America.

This is a paperback original from Alyson Publications, Inc.
40 Plympton St., Boston, Mass. 02118.
Distributed in England by GMP Publishers,
P.O. Box 247, London N17 9QR England.

First edition, first printing: October 1991

5 4 3 2 1

ISBN 1-55583-189-3

PROLOGUE

It was a large, squarely built house set arrogantly on top of a hill, constructed upon ground that had been leveled and pounded until it conformed to the architect's design. Its white walls dominated the brush-covered slopes, permitting the occupants to look down upon the rest of the city, much as some medieval lord might have surveyed his subject domains. Originally built to satisfy the ego of a fading TV personality, it now belonged to a man whose passions far exceeded those of the original owner, and for whom the lofty prominence of his home, with its disregard for aesthetic effect, was merely an extension of his own attitudes toward the rest of humanity. During these last weeks of waning Southern California summer, he had been bringing a long-held dream into sharper focus, and with the completion of some basic modifications he perceived the house as ever more the castle it had appeared when the realtor had first shown him through the property.

"I think it's finally done," he said. He was a big man, aging, but still possessed of a powerful body and commanding posture. As he stood in the doorway, looking back into the basement room, his hand was on a dimmer switch, playing with the lights, watching them change from bright to dusky shadow. The floor was covered in latex sheeting, over a layer of foam — all tacked onto a carefully fitted plywood base. The walls and ceiling were Cellotex, double thick to muffle any sound. A few days before he had placed a tape player in the center of the room, set to ear-shattering volume, closed the door, and stood outside. Not a sound had penetrated. "Yes," he concluded, "I think we're ready to move the equipment in and christen the place."

A short, younger man stood beside him and slightly to the side, his solid, slender body in the shadow cast by his larger companion. He noticed and grinned to himself, silently aware of the symbolism. Both were stripped to the waist, sweaty from their unaccustomed exertions. Although they worked out in a gym to keep their bodies in shape, neither was used to hard physical exertion. It was therefore with an inflated pride that they surveyed the product of their labors. The most difficult had been the plumbing and the tile work around it. No way to hire that out — difficult to explain to some dim-witted Spic tool jockey why they wanted a sink and a toilet, with a double-headed shower stall in the corner of a wine cellar, no partition separating it from the rest of the room.

"I think we've earned a swim," suggested the youngster.

"Yeah, and a drink," agreed his companion. He draped a beefy, heavily muscled arm across the other's shoulders as they mounted the stairs. "Just you and me, Son," he said softly. "Just you and me against the rest of this rotten, disintegrating world."

The stairs ended in a short hall, which led in turn to a cavernous room, furnished in a spartan elegance: gleaming white marble floor, with several islands of gray-black carpeting where chrome-and-glass tables combined with sofas and chairs of modern design and monochrome simplicity to divide the great hall into a number of disjointed groupings. The overall impression was one of expensive aloofness, of a cold formality contrived to impress rather than render a sense of ease for any casual visitor.

The two men passed through and the senior touched a button that activated a motor-driven traverse. The heavy, hand-woven gray draperies receded, and the young man shoved back a sliding glass door. They emerged into fading sunlight, which glittered in ruddy brilliance against the choppy surface of a swimming pool. So high above the city, on a private road off Mulholland Drive — Los Angeles to the south, San Fernando Valley to the north, brush-covered hills in between — they enjoyed a view of both major sections of the sprawling metropolis. They also caught every breeze that passed over the basin. The pool was huge, almost Olympic size, lying between the house and a fifteen-foot wall that surrounded most of the property. Both men shucked their jeans and work shoes, diving naked into the coolness, assured of their privacy — as well as their ascendancy over the tiny creatures inhabiting the lower areas beneath them.

Later, reclining on a pair of chaise longues to watch as lights began to flicker on through drifting palls of smog, the younger man broached a subject that had been troubling him since the start of their project, a concern he had been able to suppress while the possibility of culmination lay in some distant future. Now his fears were about to achieve fruition, and he felt compelled to speak. "I'm worried, Dad," he managed at length. "What if something goes wrong?"

His father rolled his head against the padded back rest, pulling the terrycloth robe more securely about his body. His steely gray eyes fastened on his son's face for several seconds before he replied. "It's a matter of minimal risk," he answered in an emotionless tone. "We're the hunters, the masters. If we're stronger than they are, we have the right. If we let them stop us, well ... that would mean we weren't really the strongest to start with, wouldn't it?" When there was no immediate response from his son, he urged: "Wouldn't it?"

"Yeah, I guess so, Dad. But...?"

"Rights. You're worried about rights, aren't you? Everyone entitled to life, liberty — the usual bullshit, the kind of soft morality you read in almost everything they publish. That it?"

"Maybe ... maybe that's part of it, but mostly it's ... I just don't want to end up behind bars," he whined.

The older man sat up, dropping his legs down either side of the chaise. His robe parted with the motion, allowing his dark, heavy genitals to lie partially exposed against the white cloth. It amused him, flattered his ego, to note his son's glance drift downward. He was still a handsome man, and he knew it, had played upon his looks and taken advantage of others because of them — just as he had done with every other asset: wealth, social status, intelligence. Now, following up on his perception of the boy's response, he allowed one sinewy hand to slip between his thighs, cupping the powerful organs in his palm. "When's the first time you learned to worship these?" he asked.

The unexpected vulgarity of the motion caused the younger man to pause, to reorient his thoughts. "A long time ago," he whispered hoarsely.

"And when did you first learn to trust me?" pushed his father.

"Always, Dad. I've always trusted you. You know that. Even when you and Mom separated, there was never a question but that I wanted to stay with you."

"Then, as for the others ... we take our time; we do it right, not like some nigger deciding to rob a bank one day, and rushing in to do it the next. Never forget, the blood of several aristocracies flows in those veins of yours. Your forebears made this country, the same as they ran the ones they came from. We've always been the masters of the masses; we've always lived in our castles, miles above the flesh pots. We've always taken what we wanted, because it was God's will that we take it ... for the same reason that He gave us better bodies, better minds ... let us survive the plagues and wars that killed off the less well-equipped segments of society.

"We both know how they'd react to me if I published my convictions in the *Times* or some other stupid organ of the liberal media. They'd call me fascist, or worse, say I had delusions of being God. But in a sense we are gods, and you can't expect some asshole who was only born to do the dirty work for us to understand that he's exactly where he belongs in the greater scheme of things. I know you've read all the arguments, you know how they put down people who've thought as I do. But remember, most of these others were subsisting on delusions of their own grandeur. Their philosophies might have been right, except that the ones who dreamed them up also assumed that they were the ones entitled to the mantle of glory. That's where they missed the point. I mean, take the prime example in recent history..."

"Hitler," the young man responded. He'd heard this all before, but each telling seemed to strengthen his own resolve, to give him the courage and confidence he needed to perform the duties his father assigned him.

"Yes. Hitler," agreed the older man. "He was brilliant, but he was just a peasant who rose to the top of the dung heap, then eventually lost out because he wasn't intended to rule in the first place."

"Dad, I don't..." The youngster sighed, unable to frame his thoughts into the easy syntax of his father's arguments. "I mean, what if we end up having to kill someone? You know, I really don't want us to be another Loeb and Leopold."

The older man snorted contemptuously. "Those were a pair of smart-aleck Jew kids. And that's just my point. They recognized the existence of superior man; they made the mistake of thinking they fit the pattern." He leaned across the space that separated him from his son, seizing the other's shoulder in an almost painful grasp. "That's the difference," he continued. "The strong — the *truly* strong always prey upon the weak. You see it every day in business, or in Third World countries where they don't have some liberal establishment dogging the heels of every man who's powerful enough to take control. But this is different; it's a game, don't you see? A game of hunter and hunted, of Master capturing slave. If we play it correctly we'll never have to kill. That's the crux of it, really. If we need to kill it means we've lost. And you know I *never* lose!"

There was a fiery zeal in the older man's tone, seeming to project from his eyes, so that the final dayglow was reflected in them and for a moment his son perceived it as an inner gleam, a reflection of the power he knew reposed within his father's mind and body. "Well, it'll be fun, anyway," he responded weakly. "And if things get too hairy we can always hang back until it cools off."

It was not exactly the response the father had anticipated, but he nodded acceptance. His son lacked his strength. He knew that, and it troubled him. He was an unusually attractive boy, with his deep tan and sun-bleached hair. He was pretty, actually, maybe too pretty for a man. As the years passed he would change, of course, grow more mature, more distinctively masculine. He was still too young, too innocent. But if they shared this adventure, experienced together the sense of power as they stood over some groveling lesser being, perhaps he would begin to perceive the true potential buried within him. The proper qualities were there, he knew, and needed only to be animated.

ONE

Bruce MacLeod was a man of extremely diverse interests and abilities — a product of his time, one might say, but also an enigma. At thirty-eight he had already made a considerable reputation for himself as a therapist, commanding substantial fees from those of his patients who could afford them, but spending many hours in volunteer work, as well. He was also known within law enforcement circles for his ideas on criminal profiling, and for the contributions he had been able to make in several specific cases. He was a U.S.C. graduate, with additional studies at Stanford and Johns Hopkins — degrees in medicine, psychiatry, psychology, and computer sciences. As a professional his credentials were well established, irrefutable, and somewhat mundane.

As a man, he was considerably more interesting. A gymnast in college, he had been at some pains to maintain his bodily definition, although heavy workouts had made him considerably more bulky than he had been in his youth. Bright and handsome, with light brown hair and gold-flecked hazel eyes, his sexual attractiveness had always been an additional asset. While an undergraduate he had taken a constellation of courses in both music and mathematics at the university, as well as outside instruction in several keyboard instruments — acquiring a sense of musicianship and balance that he still enjoyed, although his later activities left little time to maintain his once considerable skills. As a sidelight to his extracurricular activities, he met and came to know — often in considerably more than the biblical sense — a number of men who were associated with the more esoteric side of sexual behavior, and through them he had received an early indoctrination in the finer points of male-to-male sadomasochism.

Bruce MacLeod's life had grown into a triple-tiered structure: a brilliant professional aura on top; an active and highly respectable social existence in the middle; and underlying it all, an equally intense involvement with the underground world of leathersex and the extremely interesting array of men who populated its space. Although very active in these circles throughout his twenties and early thirties, the last few years had witnessed a sharp curtailment in his sexual encounters — this due more to force of circumstances than to the factors of waning desire or age. His practice had become more time-consuming, especially with the many hours he felt compelled to donate as the AIDS crisis grew worse, and his close contact with so many victims only served to heighten his own fears to a point where extraneous contacts were few and far between.

His own intelligence assured that he was perfectly aware of all these subtle ramifications of his existence, and also permitted him to handle them without much overt conflict, as a skilled juggler keeps his multitude of ten pins spinning in the air, never allowing them to drop or collide. But Bruce was reaching a stage in life where the secret parts were pressing more stridently for expression, for acknowledgment. He was also finding his continued sexual denial more repressive — thus on a more covert level, he was not a completely happy man. *But I'm still HIV-negative,* he told himself. *Better a horny old man than a dead one. Still, all the academic achievements begin to pale when you're in bed at night and there's no one around to make it interesting.*

It was because of Dr. MacLeod's professional credits that, on this unusually warm June afternoon, he awaited the arrival of a scheduled client. Seated at his desk, he tried to push the intruding thoughts of his own condition aside, wondering about the reason for Rufus Wolfe's impending visit. The computer reference had identified him as a "major independent agent, specializing in the representation of stage and screen artists." But he was not coming as a patient, apparently; in fact, the notation on the appointment pad had indicated that it was an urgent matter involving one of the agent's clients. Dennie, who had taken the message, had also remarked that the man had sounded "agitated." *Interesting*, thought Bruce, *a flesh peddler who needs psychiatric advice, coming to see a psychiatrist who needs a warm body. Better cool it, Bruce baby, or you'll project your thoughts and shock your client.* He laughed silently to himself. *Good thing they can't read my thoughts sometimes — physician, heal thyself...*

"Mr. Wolfe is here, Doctor." Dennie's voice sounded strained over the intercom, as if he were suppressing a laugh.

"Show him in," replied the psychiatrist, intrigued by the undertone of his assistant's announcement. He allowed his strong, well-defined body to relax against the black leather of his swivel chair.

The door opened a moment later and the visitor was conducted inside by Dennie Delong — "Big Daddy D," as he was known to the inner circle. Dennie had worked with Bruce as receptionist-secretary for a little over five years. Although he looked more like a lumberjack than an office type, he was very good at what he did — at everything he did, professionally or otherwise.

"Dr. MacLeod, this is Mr. Wolfe," he said, giving his boss a quick wink over the other man's shoulder before he withdrew, closing the door behind him.

"Call me 'Rufus,' Doctor," said the newcomer. It was a booming Welcome-to-Hollywood entrance. A gross figure, despite the gray Gucci suit and conservative English public school tie, Rufus Wolfe weighed at least three hundred pounds, and spoke with a grating Bronx accent, projecting his voice at a needlessly high volume. The doctor guessed his age as "early forties"; he had curly, salt-and-pepper hair, rather heavy Semitic features dominated by a preposterous bushy mustache that almost hid his ample upper lip.

Bruce MacLeod, experienced practitioner that he was, found it difficult to suppress a surge of distaste. He also felt a nudge of basic, primordial uneasiness ... danger? ... something he could not quite place. Wolfe had called for an appointment the day before, stressing the tightness of his schedule and using the fact of his willingness to expend this time as evidence of his concern and the urgency of his mission.

"Nice that you can work out of your house, Doc," remarked the fat man, lumbering toward the wall of glass that overlooked Bruce's pool. "Guess it makes your subjects feel more at home."

"I moved out of my Century City office about six months ago," replied MacLeod, "and the patients do seem more comfortable here ... less intimidating atmosphere and all. Er, why don't you sit down?" He leaned back in his chair, waiting for the agent to settle his bulk, unaccountably eager — and strangely apprehensive — that the fat man get on with his business.

Rufus selected a large leather settee, poking at it with pudgy fingers before settling his buttocks into the center, nearly filling the space that was meant to accommodate two people. "I can see you're one of those nondirective therapists," quipped the fat man, "going to wait for me to do the talking." He grinned knowingly, twisting slightly as if to relieve some pressure on his back.

"You've been in therapy?" asked the doctor.

"Haven't we all? The Hollywood crowd's what keeps all those Wilshire Boulevard high rises in business."

"And your client? Has he — she — been...?"

"Frank? Nah, he's the All-American stud — pro quarterback before he decided to try acting. Frank DeSilva. You probably seen him on the tube."

"Maybe, but I don't recognize the name."

"Yeah, I suppose you might not know him by name, but you almost have to have seen him. He's a real good-lookin' guy: five-ten, straight black hair, nice well-defined body — slender, though, and a'course a very Latin type ... green eyes, kinda pretty face. He was one of the detectives on 'Washington Street Beat' — ran three full seasons on NCS."

"Oh," Bruce nodded his recognition. "Sure, I know who he is — very handsome man, and not too bad an actor."

"And a very straight guy," added the agent. "Doesn't play around much, no dope, no heavy drinking. Likes girls. Banks most of his money, or invests it in something solid." He paused thoughtfully, then continued. "I guess what I'm sayin' is the guy's real genuine — no flake, certainly no pansy. So, what happened to him — what he says happened to him — just don't make any sense."

"And what did happen to him?" asked the doctor softly.

The corpulent agent regarded him with a fixed gaze for several seconds. "This is strick-ly confidential, isn't it, Doc?" he asked seriously. "I want your help, or at least your advice, but I can't take a chance..."

"I won't compromise you," Bruce assured him.

"Okay," Rufus agreed. "Well, ah ... Frank ... he got raped — not just thrown down and fucked like a woman, but — oh, sorry about my language, Doc," he blustered.

"I've heard the word once or twice," Bruce assured him.

The agent glanced up at the other man's face, seeking reassurance, possibly a denial that Bruce's retort had been intended as sarcastic. Seemingly satisfied, he continued: "Oh, yeah ... sure ... sorry. But Frank, you see ... they kidnapped him, held him for two — maybe three days, did all kinds'a sick things to him — probably more than he's admitted to me. Then they let him go, and now his head's really fucked up. Says he feels dirty, and he's afraid he's going to get a disease, only he's embarrassed to go find out."

The agent's account had brought Bruce upright in his chair, and focused his interest for the first time in their exchange. "You say he was kidnapped. Does he know who...?"

"No, that's the crazy part of it. See, the way he tells it, he went to bed as usual, real tired because he was workin' on a new pilot, and he wakes up in this booby hatch. Says he's not sure, but he thinks somebody gave him a shot in the shoulder while he was asleep, but whatever they did it knocked him out so he never saw the bastards."

Bruce regarded his visitor thoughtfully for some seconds, not exactly doubting him, but wondering how much was being lost or distorted in this secondhand recital. "If all this is true," he suggested at length, "it seems much more a case for the police than for a shrink." He paused, watching Rufus carefully for whatever facial clues or body English he might reveal. Obviously, he realized, the man had come to him because he didn't want to go to the police.

Rufus Wolfe sighed and shifted his bulk on the settee. "Yeah," he replied slowly. "I tried to get him to do that, but he's scared shitless of the publicity. I mean, the guy makes his living by projecting the heavy stud image on the tube. Getting tied up and fucked in the ass — even if he was forced to do it — well, that isn't exactly going to help make him Macho Man of the Year."

"I can see that," Bruce agreed, "but it still doesn't explain why you came to me. What do you want me to do?"

"I got Frank to agree to see you," replied the agent. "He don't really like the idea, but I got him talked into it — 'least I did an hour ago. But he's really a basket case, Doc. Ya know, the Macbeth syndrome ... *not all the waters of the seven seas* business. Every time I call him he's in the shower, trying to get clean. No, this wouldn't be a problem we'd take to some hard-nosed cop, even if Frank was willing to go to 'em. What he needs is a shrink, or a good understanding parent. That's why I thought you might help straighten out his head ... you know, convince him he's still a man and all that."

"If he really wants to see me, okay," MacLeod replied cautiously, "but I haven't the time or patience to try working with a man who is going to resist me — who's only coming to me because he's been coerced into it. I don't take court-appointed cases for that reason. In fact, I only take cases, now, that are interesting to me."

"Huh," grunted the fat man. "And does this one sound interesting enough for you?" He peered up again into Bruce's face, with the trace of an indefinable expression that made the therapist wonder how much this deceptively crude man really knew about him.

"It might," Bruce replied cautiously, although in truth he was already more than a little intrigued. "Tell me, Rufus, why did you pick me instead of some other therapist?"

The fat man seemed surprised by the question, blinking his little piggy eyes before a grin contorted the heavy flesh of his face. "Well, you're famous, Doc. You done all that stuff for the cops, scientific papers for the FBI training school. You gotta be the right guy to handle this ... as long as you can keep it on the Q.T."

"All right, I'll speak with him," said Bruce. "There's one patient scheduled in a few minutes, but I'm free after that. Why don't you have Frank come by at five?" Bruce suppressed the urge to question the man further. He'd speak to the actual victim in a couple of hours, and already — in their brief exchange — he realized that Rufus Wolfe had a far better mind concealed within his overweight body than he allowed most people to recognize. Bruce's papers, while not secret, were certainly not widely circulated. A man would have to do a lot of reading to come across them.

The agent left a few minutes later, after making a phone call to Frank DeSilva and arranging for him to come by that evening. "Thanks a lot, Doc," he said in parting, "'specially for seeing him right away ... before he gets buyer's remorse, if ya catch my drift."

■ ■ ■

The young actor arrived a few minutes after 5:00 p.m., dressed in Levis and a plaid sports shirt. In person, he seemed smaller than he did on the screen, but — if anything — even more handsome. He was also extremely agitated, and understandably hesitant. Bruce seated him in an easy chair, and took a similar seat facing him.

"I understand you don't drink very much," said the doctor, after some initial pleasantries, "but you've arrived at the cocktail hour, and you definitely look like you could use something."

"Doctor's orders?" He forced a smile that revealed a set of perfect, white teeth.

"I think it might help relax you," replied the therapist.

"Yeah," he sighed, "maybe it would. Vodka-tonic, not too heavy on the vodka," he added.

Bruce went into the small bar, which connected through to the adjoining family room, where he could see that Dennie was also having a drink as he watched the evening news. Bruce pulled the panel shut, winking at Dennie as he closed the opening between them. "Rufus tells me you had quite an unpleasant experience," he said over his shoulder, trying to sound as casual as possible. It disturbed him to realize that he was more than clinically interested in the tale this Hollywood Adonis had to tell, and he was afraid his own sense of discomfiture might be forcing him to appear more coldly clinical than he did with most patients.

Frank had not answered by the time Bruce returned with the drinks, so as he handed the young man his glass he made firm eye contact and added: "You know, at this point in my practice there isn't much I haven't heard. And, from the little Rufus told me, none of this was your fault. You don't need to feel guilty about it."

Frank looked down at his glass, took a sip, and pressed his large hands together after setting his drink on the coffee table. "I know all that," he sighed, "but it's so ... so goddamned embarrassing! And I feel..." He sighed again, and seemed almost on the verge of tears. "I'm so dirty!" he blurted. "I can wash the outside of my body, but how can I ever get clean inside? I feel like their ... their jism's still churning around in my guts!"

"But you know it isn't." Bruce answered him softly, trying for eye contact again — failing, because his patient was refusing to look up at him.

Then Frank did look up, tilting his head abruptly backward so that the deep green of his eyes caught Bruce almost by surprise. "I know ... intellectually, I know. And I also know that eventually I'm going to work out of it, emotionally anyway ... physically, too, if they haven't infected me with ... something. And I know I should talk it out with someone — probably with you." He dropped his gaze again as emotion distorted his features. "But it's so fucking hard to admit to ... anyone, that my body — *ME, don't you see?* — that this ... this *being* that's me could have been treated like this, used like it was."

"I can only try to imagine how miserable it is for you," Bruce replied, knowing that anything he said at this juncture was going to be woefully inadequate. He wanted to get up and go to this tortured man and put his arms around him and somehow reassure him by a sincere physical contact. But he knew this was impossible. Not only might the attempt be misperceived; the act would be totally unprofessional, probably damaging to any further therapy. He therefore continued in as encouraging a tone as possible, but forced himself to remain within the limits of acceptable therapist-patient utterance. "I'm here to work with you," he continued with as much encouragement as he could force into his tone. "I'll not only try to help you get your thoughts in order, but I'm a doctor in addition to being a shrink. I can understand your concern about some possible infection and I can take a blood sample if you want, and have it tested — all under a phony name, so whatever the results no one else will know."

That seemed to strike exactly the proper chord, because his visitor nodded gratefully and some of his tension dissipated. He leaned back in his chair, resting his head on the riser and staring at the ceiling. "Yeah," he said softly, "I'd like to be tested, after what those bastards did to me..."

"Do you want to tell me about it?" urged Bruce.

He nodded without changing his posture, and after a few more words of reassurance he sighed again and nodded agreement. Bruce moved behind his desk, tapping his toe against a concealed switch to activate his tape recorder, feeling a surge of guilt as he did it. *Standard ... do it with all my patients, but he's so concerned with secrecy...*

■ ■ ■

CLINICAL TAPE #1: DeSilva, Franklin Robert

Client: I'd gotten home late from the studio, because we'd just put a "wrap" on the pilot, and I was planning to sleep in the next day. I was really bushed. You see, my part was pretty physical, and I did most of my own stunts. I just had a bowl of cold cereal, watched the late news, and dropped into bed. I've got a small house in the hills, up above Studio City — vacant lots on both sides, so it's a real quiet neighborhood.

I'm not really sure, but I think someone got in while I was asleep — or maybe was already in the house when I came home. Anyway, I sort of remember a needle going into my left shoulder, and when I started to wake up a hand coming down on my face. Whatever, I must have conked out again right away. The next thing I remember I'm coming to with a leather hood over my head, and my wrists strapped to either side of a collar around my neck. I knew I was naked, and lying on some kind of a padded, rubbery surface.

The room was very warm, and I'd been sweating. I could feel my skin sticking to the rubber, or whatever it was underneath me. I guess I groaned, because someone says, "Master, he's awake."

Of course, I couldn't see anything, because the hood didn't have any eyeholes. But the mouth was open. Someone lifted my head and shoulders and poked a glass or cup against my lips. "Drink this," he whispered. "It'll make you feel better." I was so thirsty, I did as he told me. It seemed like just plain water, but it might have had something else in it, 'cause it did help bring me around.

I tried to act like I wasn't scared, but I don't think I fooled anyone. There were two of them...

Therapist: You're sure there were only two?

Client: I think so, but it's possible there could have been someone else watching and never saying anything. Anyway, no one ever spoke except in a whisper, and the one called "Master" explained what he called the "rules."

"You're my prisoner," he told me, "and you're going to stay here for as long as it pleases me to have you. I'm going to enjoy using your body, and I'm going to cause you some pain. But I'm not going to do you any permanent injury, and when I'm finished with you I'm going to let you go — unless ... unless you're stupid enough to work that hood off your eyes. If you see me ... well, we won't go into that. I think you get the picture."

Now, Doc, I gotta tell you ... I'm straight. I really don't get off on having sex with men, although ... well, Rufus doesn't know anything about it, but I did a couple of things I'm not too proud of in order to survive in Tinseltown, before I got my first part. What I'm trying to say is, I know the score, but it's really not my bag. And being tied up, getting my ass whipped — all that S&M shit, that really isn't for me. Still, there are times — and this is something I didn't tell Rufus either — there are times when a guy can't help responding to things that are done to him.

Anyway, I'm lying there on the floor on this rubber sheet, and the "Master" says to the kid — I guess it was a kid — something like: "Get down there and put my new slave in the proper mood" — or words to that effect, and the next thing I know the punk's got my cock and balls in his mouth, and he's tonguing the hell out of me. I guess I yelled at them, calling them cocksuckers and assholes, but the kid never let go of me, and after a while ... I couldn't help it, I started getting hard. Then he backs off, and takes just the head of my dick in his mouth and starts working his tongue up under the foreskin until I'm standing up stiff as a board.

I was pissed off at myself, but there wasn't anything I could do about it. And the bastards really knew their business, because the kid stopped just before I would have shot my load, and they lifted me up onto my feet. I was still a little wobbly, but they looped a couple of chains around my neck and attached them to a pair of hooks or something in the ceiling. "You better stand up straight," the "Master" tells me, and I do the best I can. I'm still right on the verge of being choked, but I managed to stand, because if I didn't the chains were going to strangle me.

Now, when they did this, it took both of them to get me up, and this gave me the first real clue about how big they were, or how they were built — body size, I mean. The smaller one, the one I've been calling "the kid," was completely naked, and he couldn't have been too tall, because he had to stretch up, leaning against me, when he fastened one of the chains. The other guy was bigger and a lot stronger. He was dressed in leather, or something that felt like it. Anyway, I could feel it rub against me, both on the legs and the side of my body.

He broke off, here, and sat forward in the chair. His glass was empty, just the melting ice swirling around in the bottom as his long fingers toyed with it. MacLeod took it from him and made them both another drink.
"Feel like telling me the rest?" he asked.
Frank nodded and took a swallow from his glass.

The "Master" gave me a good going-over, running his hands all across my body, making comments about the firmness of various muscles — all this in a whisper; he never let me hear his real voice, just the whisper. He felt my chest and belly and back, then down onto the hips and ass. Finally, he took hold of my cock and balls, started squeezing them, playing with me until I yelled something at him ... called him a "queer" among other things, and he just suddenly let go of me. He didn't say anything for a few seconds, but I could hear him doing something behind me, and then it all came down, man; I mean, he smacked me across the ass with some kind of a keen switch! Hurt? Jesus, it was a sudden, unexpected, blinding pain like I've never felt in my life!

"Now let that be your first lesson," he tells me. "While I've got you strung up naked in my dungeon, you will speak respectfully. You'll call me 'Sir,' and you'll only do that when you have permission to speak. Just pretend you're a Spic peon, back on the rancho and your patron is working you over." The whip came down on my ass again, and he whispered: "Understand, Spic?"

I didn't answer him; I was so pissed off at this point I just tried to defy him. It didn't do any good. And this "Spic" shit, it didn't make any sense to me. I'm Spanish descent and all that, but I didn't grow up in a barrio, and I don't speak the language — just the little I learned in high school, so — you know — I've never really identified with being anything but a plain American, Anglo despite the name and background. Anyway, he kept working me over with that whip, mostly on the ass but twice on my back, each time demanding that I answer him until I finally did it ... called him "Sir," and stood quiet while he went back to playing with my dick. I'd gone soft, of course, and he started giving me a hard time about this, started working me over with a flat strap and telling me to "get it up," which he must have known I couldn't do.

Finally, they took me down and made me kneel on the rubber matting. He made me crawl around on the floor, shoved my face down on his boot and made me lick it. Kept calling me "greaser" and "Spic." Then he makes me ... orders me to suck off the kid, who grabs my head and forces it against his groin.

I tried to buck him off, but the "Master" just started whipping my back until I took the kid's cock in my mouth. I was fighting mad again, and I could feel the salty tears against my face, inside that fuckin' hood. But I didn't have any choice, and once the kid poked his dick into me, he grabbed hold of the hood and never gave me a chance to dislodge him ... just face-fucked me till he shot, then shoved himself as deep as he could ... damn near throttled me, 'cause my face was pressed up tight against him. I was struggling to breathe, and the kid was still holding his cock inside me, when the "Master" asked if I was a good cocksucker.

"Not too bad," says the kid, "not very experienced, though, Sir. I don't know if he's skilled enough for you."

"We'll see," he whispers. "Just watching him struggle has me turned on enough — he's going to get it in one end or the other. In fact, I'll give him a choice." His hand closed against the back of my head, and he pulls me free of the kid. "Okay, greaseball," he says, "do you want it in your mouth, or up your ass?" He kinda laughed, then, and gave me a soft slap across the back with his leather strap.

I was still gasping for breath, and I wanted to spit out the little bit of cum that I hadn't already been forced to swallow. And I was scared, of course, more so because of the racial slurs and name calling. You know, I figured the guy for a real nut case. I didn't want anything else stuck into me at all, but I sure as hell didn't want to get cornholed. When I didn't answer right away, he let me have a blow with that strap, right across the shoulder blades, that almost knocked me off balance.

"I asked you a question, punk! Answer me!"

"I ... I don't want to get fucked ... Sir," I told him.

At that, he took hold of my head, and he stuck a couple of fingers into my mouth. He kinda reamed them around for a few seconds, mumbled something about his "better not feeling any teeth." Then he stuck his cock head between my lips.

Now, the kid had been hard to start with, but this guy wasn't. Still, I could tell right off that he was built a lot bigger. He wasn't circumcised, either, and I could taste, or smell that odor a guy gets under his skin when he hasn't washed for a day or so. It wasn't real strong, but just enough that it made me want to retch. He didn't give me a chance, though — told me just what he wanted ... tongue up under the foreskin, then take it slowly into me. I could feel it growing, getting bigger and harder, until I started to choke when it was only halfway in. Before he was finished, I was coughing up phlegm, gagging, trying my best to do what he wanted, because he'd told the kid to "use the crop" on me if I didn't "do it right."

It took him forever, but he finally shot his load and made me swallow it, telling me, "You show promise, but you still have a lot to learn."

After he'd caught his breath, he had the kid guide me over to a toilet, where he shoved me down and told me to take care of myself, because it was the last chance I was going to get for a while. Now, Doc, I'm not usually piss-shy, or especially sensitive about having to take a shit in a public toilet. But this was really humiliating. To make it worse, I really did have to go ... both ways, and I didn't have any choice. I took care of myself, and the kid wiped my ass when I finished.

I thought they were through with me for the time being, then, but the "Master" had a couple more things to do. First, he ordered the kid to throw me down on my belly — which he did, and before I knew what was going on, he poked some kind of lubricant into my rectum and shoved in a big wad of some kind of rubber. This was fastened in place by a strap that went around my waist, and down between my legs. Then they flopped me onto my back and after some preliminary fooling around with some kind of liquid, they worked a tube up my dick. It was a regular catheter, I guess. Anyway, I suddenly felt myself starting to piss, except they somehow clamped the line shut and stopped it.

They moved me onto a table of some kind, also padded with rubber, or vinyl, and strapped me down on my back. "Get some rest, beaner," says the Master, "you're going to need it." He gave me another drink of water, letting me have all I wanted, before telling the kid they'd "given me enough for the first night."

With that, they must have left, because I couldn't hear any sound of movement. I was alone, strapped down naked on a table with some kind of a plug shoved up my ass, a catheter in my dick, my hands still locked onto a leather collar, a hood over my head. It was the first time I'd been left alone — given a moment to think — since I'd come to, and I realized how helpless I really was. I didn't know what they were eventually going to do to me, but I knew they'd only started. I was so fuckin' scared I wanted to cry, but that wasn't going to do any good. Then I was mad again; but that didn't help anything, either. Finally, all I could think of was the "Master's" promise that if I left the hood in place he was going to let me go ... eventually. There wasn't anything I could do but wait.

Bruce could see that his client was emotionally near the end of his rope, just from recalling this much of his experience. He suggested they might have a bit to eat, after which he could continue if he felt like it, or they could pick it up again later.

"That's a good idea, Doc," Frank agreed. "But, I'd like to get it all off my chest as soon as I can. Then, maybe, I'll be able to sleep again."

Bruce stood up, stretching as if to relieve some kink in his shoulder, but actually to delay a moment before he spoke. There were several intuitive strains of thought coursing his mind and he was trying to frame them into a proper *Gestalt*. He did not exactly doubt the story Frank was relating, yet there was something that didn't ring quite true. Had he given up too easily? Hard to say, since fear can render such diverse effects on different people. Or was it his own attraction to the young man who now rose slowly from the other chair to join him? Bruce shrugged. *Plenty of time to sort it out at my leisure. For* the moment, best to keep the momentum and the story flowing.

"Let's go in the other room," he said easily. "Dennie can probably whip us up a snack." He grinned reassuringly, placing his hand on Frank's shoulder and guiding his client toward the door. The contact, casual as it appeared, and as Bruce had intended it to be, was electric, like the meeting of alternately charged particles in a vacuum. The warmth of the younger man's being seemed to flow into him until Bruce had a momentary flash of guilt that he should be so strongly attracted to a client.

But Frank appeared unaffected, merely responding to his therapist's guidance. He paused in the doorway, however, when he saw Dennie comfortably ensconced on the sofa, drink in his hand, half-eaten sandwich on the coffee table. The big, bearded man looked up, and seemingly aware of the visitor's unspoken response, shifted his muscular body into a less slovenly position.

Taking in the silent exchange, Bruce laughed and moved past Frank, into the room. "Dennie lives here," he explained offhandedly. "He not only keeps my office in shape, he makes sure there's food in the frig and booze in the cupboard."

Frank accepted the comment without question, but it was obvious to both the other men that their living arrangement at the very least puzzled him, maybe disturbed him. At a nod from Bruce, Dennie gathered up the remains of his meal and moved into the kitchen. The large TV was still turned on, displaying the last of MacNeil-Lehrer on PBS. Otherwise the room was illuminated only by fading sunlight that filtered through the heavy exterior foliage. Although the house was small by Beverly Hills standards, it was still a substantial residence — rather too large and too obviously well tended to pass as the typical bachelor's pad.

Bruce could see that all of this was causing his patient to have some second thoughts, and he quickly moved to remedy the situation — to *make it or break it*, he thought to himself. "I won't try to deceive you," he said easily, motioning Frank to a seat. He hesitated another moment, perhaps to summon his own courage, but also to gauge the reactions his words were producing. "This is an all-male household," he continued tentatively.

He could see the look of puzzlement on Frank's face devolve into a blank acceptance, then a nod, and finally a shrug. "Are you telling me you're gay guys, then?" he asked softly.

"Both Dennie and I are gay men, although we aren't involved, except as friends," Bruce explained cautiously, and when Frank still gave no indication of distress, he added: "This may have been the reason Rufus sent you to me — I assume he's aware of all this. I'm certainly going to be more incisive — and even more on your side because of my own orientation than otherwise," he continued, keeping his voice soft and even, eyes searching his companion for whatever responses might show on his face or in his bodily movements.

To his surprise, Frank suddenly regarded him almost in alarm. "Jesus, Doc," he said apologetically, "I didn't know ... I mean, I hope I didn't offend you by some of the things I said in your office." He stood up abruptly, wringing his hands in one swift motion, then rubbed his palms on his pants as if they were sweaty and he was trying to dry them. He moved to the window, looking out on the dense growth of plants surrounding the pool. He took hold of the door handle, glancing back at Bruce. "Mind if I open this? Go outside for a minute?"

"Help yourself," Bruce replied. He tried to sustain the casual tone he had set since the beginning of their exchange, but he could feel the adrenaline surge through his body, sensed that he might have opened himself up too soon ... frightened his client, or worse. He tried to examine his own motives. Had he dropped the curtain so suddenly because of his own attraction? Of course, he made it a point with his gay patients to let them know the truth, but...

Frank was standing outside, thumbs hooked over the back pockets of his jeans. As Bruce moved a few steps closer, the other man turned halfway toward him. "Sorry, Doc," he said softly, "but you shook me up for a minute."

Bruce moved through the opening, sliding the glass panel all the way back to permit his passage without actually touching the other man. A cool evening breeze brushed his face, and he could hear the distant rush of traffic on Sunset Boulevard. "I didn't mean to cause you any distress," he said gently, "but it's much better if you understand my situation right from the start. I mean, if you get into therapy with me, I don't want you to suddenly find out a couple of months down the road."

As if sensing Bruce's discomfort, Frank turned fully toward him, holding the other's gaze with his own. "I understand, Doc," he said, grinning suddenly in another blaze of white dentition. "It *will* make it easier to tell you what happened and ... maybe to describe how it affected me." His grin broadened. "And maybe it'll make it easier for you to tell me why."

"It could also make it more difficult," Bruce suggested more seriously.

Frank seemed puzzled for a moment, his smile fading. Then he shook his head. "Not really, Doc," he replied at length. "I've been going through a period of ... what you might call 'indecision' for some time. This whole thing might serve as an excuse to get it all aired out."

"So do you want to get back to work?" asked Bruce.

"Sure, but ... do you suppose your helper might get us something to nibble on? I haven't been very hungry since all this happened, but all of a sudden I'm starving."

TWO

While Dennie busied himself in the adjoining kitchen, Frank resumed his place on the leather sofa, but this time he appeared much more at ease, as if a terrible burden had already been lifted from his shoulders. "I guess I should correct a couple of things I told you, Doc," he said. His voice was even, now, and apparently as relaxed as his posture.

"Whatever you feel comfortable with," Bruce replied, "and by the way I really don't object to being called 'Doc,' except it makes me feel like an old man with granny glasses. 'Bruce' will do fine, unless it's too informal for you." *I'm doing this badly,* he thought, *letting down the barriers of professionalism ... because it makes it more comfortable for him? Easier for him to unburden himself? Or because I like what I see, and have my own agenda. Jesus, Bruce, get hold of yourself!*

"Okay by me, D— ... Bruce. But what I meant was my remarks about being such a straight shooter." He hesitated a moment, as if gathering his strength, or collecting his thoughts, then continued in an even tone. "I'm not really what I guess you'd call a 'compulsive heterosexual,' but I'm certainly not gay either. I've never really done anything with a man, except for a couple of times I let some guy blow me in order to get into the right producer's office. My real sexual experiences have always been with girls, but some of that's because I'm afraid to get it on with a man, what with all this AIDS crap. And I sure as hell don't want to fuck up my acting career by getting my face on the front page of some supermarket rag: "Frank DeSilva's Queer Relationship." But there have been times when I've felt attracted to another guy, and wondered what it might be like to have sex with him. And to some extent I guess that's why I was so pissed at what these assholes did to me."

"You mean because it was forced," suggested Bruce.

"Well, yeah, that, too. But what I meant was that some of it turned me on, even when I didn't want it to. They went way too far with all the S&M shit, but there were a few times when ... you know, the mind was fighting them, but the flesh was weak."

"Or hard," suggested Bruce, grinning in his turn.

Frank laughed for the first time. "Yeah, hard — that's for sure — and don't think they didn't react to it."

Dennie came in with a tray of sandwiches and coffee, which he placed on the table in front of Frank. He was about to withdraw again, when the young actor looked up at him. "Listen, there's no reason for you to have to hide in your own house. Bruce's told me that you're his ... assistant, so I guess there aren't many secrets between you. I don't care if you hear whatever we have to say."

Dennie glanced at Bruce, who nodded, and the big man settled into a chair across from their visitor. "I couldn't help overhearing some of your conversation," he admitted. "And whether you enjoyed some of it or not, it was a really lousy thing for those guys to do. I'm for everybody getting it on however he likes, and with anybody he wants, but it's never right to force someone, even if they're able to make the guy respond eventually."

"Well, I didn't mean to make it sound like a pleasure trip," Frank replied bitterly. "I only meant that some of the things they did forced a response from my ... my body."

"So, you got a hard-on when they sucked you off. That could happen to anyone."

Frank did not answer immediately, and Bruce leaned forward in his seat, reaching for a coffee cup. "And you're afraid that some of the ritual, the lighter parts anyway, were things you secretly, or subconsciously, wanted to do?"

Frank shrugged, spreading his hands. "Oh, I don't know. I've never played any of these kinky games, and I've never really thought much about them. I know they go on, of course, and I don't much care what other people want to do. Except so much of it seems silly, all those costumes and attitudes — the stuff that comedians make fun of. I certainly couldn't see myself involved in any of that."

"*Chacun à son goût,*" said Dennie, smiling. "Everyone to his own taste — as long as it's with a willing partner," he added grimly.

"That's the whole thing," said Bruce, directing his remark to Dennie. "You didn't hear all of Frank's story, but they actually kidnapped him from his house and held him in a dungeon for several days..."

"Jesus, I thought he'd just gotten roughed up by a couple of oversexed punks."

"Frank," continued Bruce, "like many psychiatrists, I tape most of my sessions, especially if they involve a crime victim." He watched Frank carefully for any indication of dismay. Finding none, he continued: "I later have Dennie transcribe them if I think it's going to help me put some pieces together. I did this with our discussion. Do you mind if Dennie goes into my office and plays it back? If he's going to sit in with us, he might as well know as much as he can."

Frank shrugged again. "No, fine with me. He'll hear it anyway if he's going to type it out."

Dennie left the door open when he entered the doctor's office, permitting all three men to hear the contents of the tape, although Frank carried a sandwich and cup of coffee to the open glass doorway, and seemed oblivious to his own voice floating in from the other room. Whatever emotions he felt were unspoken, nor did his posture betray his thoughts. When Dennie finished and returned to his previous place, the young actor turned toward him, assuming a seemingly casual stance with his coffee cup still in one hand. "No matter how many times you hear your own voice on a recording," he said, "it always sounds like it has to be someone else."

"Guess so," Dennie agreed, "but, shit, you were lucky to come out of that in one piece. A couple of maniacs like that..." He stroked his well-trimmed beard, looking at the other man with obvious consternation. "Christ, there's no telling what they might have done."

"And I have a feeling that Frank hasn't told us the worst of it, yet," Bruce agreed. "They held you for what — two days, three?"

"They grabbed me last Thursday night," Frank replied, "and I woke up in my own bed about noon on Sunday. And this time, I know they gave me a shot." He unbuttoned the top of his shirt and shoved it back to reveal a small puncture mark on his left shoulder.

"So you really have no idea where you were, how far they took you, or anything?" asked Dennie.

Frank shook his head. "Not a clue," he said. "I've tried to remember anything that might identify the surroundings, but the room I was in must have been soundproofed. I never heard anything from outside. They played music a lot of the time — kind of contemporary stuff, a lot I didn't recognize, but I think one of the pieces was *The Planets,* you know, Holst; and then some I think were Bartok, or at least that kind of sound."

"All classical?" asked Bruce.

Frank nodded. "Yeah, except for some really weird stuff that was sort of a mix — and then something that sounded like Tomita. Whatever, it was enough that I couldn't have heard even a loud noise from outside."

"And when they talked to each other? No names dropped?" asked Bruce.

"No, the kid called the big guy 'Master' or 'Sir,' and the big one never called the kid by any name."

"You say 'kid,'" Dennie remarked. "Are you sure he was really young?"

"He just felt that way," said Frank uncertainly. "He touched me quite a few times, and I'd say his body was young ... slender and solid. I guess he was fairly short, maybe five-eight or -nine, not much hair on his body, but medium long on his head. I could feel it brush against me at times. And his cock always seemed to be hard, about average size, circumcised."

"And the 'Master'?" Dennie urged.

"He was a lot bigger, for sure taller than me, and I'm a couple inches short of six feet. He was heavily built, but I don't think he was fat. I couldn't really be sure, because he always wore leather and I never actually touched his skin ... except his cock, the son of a bitch!"

"And he was uncircumcised," Bruce added.

"Yeah, uncircumcised and big — not real huge, but certainly bigger than average. He seemed to have some trouble getting it up, but once it was hard it was like a piece of cloth-covered steel. I've ... well, I haven't had all that much experience with other guys, but he sure seemed more solid than I thought a man could get."

"Do you want to tell us what else they did?" asked Bruce cautiously.

"Just about everything you can think of," said Frank. For the first time in several minutes he relinquished control of his feelings, and an angry expression contorted his handsome features. "They kept me plugged up, both ass and cock, whenever they weren't using me. I could only piss when they released the catch on the catheter. Then they..." He gritted his teeth and emitted a little groan. "They kept giving me enemas — hurt like hell sometimes, because they pumped so much water into me. Then, once I was empty they'd whip me and the big guy'd make me crawl around at his feet until he got tired of it. Then he'd just fuck the hell out of me, calling me every racial slur he could think of. He really seemed to get off by humiliating me. Even made me beg for water to drink and the few scraps of food they gave me.

"And into the second day, they started really playing rough. They took out the catheter and sewed my foreskin shut, poked needles through my nipples, and roped all three points together. My hands were strapped up against my throat most of the time, but once in a while they'd string me up by my neck, put some kind of irons on my ankles, and let my hands loose long enough for me to rub back some circulation. I couldn't fight them, though, because I was otherwise locked in place. I also took the big asshole seriously when he said he'd kill me if I saw him. So when they pulled my hands together behind my back, I let them do it. They used handcuffs, then, and once while I was standing up like that — this was after they'd taken the needles out of my tits and the stitches off my cock — then they roped my balls and hung a weight from them, made me swing it back and forth, whipped my ass if I let it stop moving. I'm still sore from it."

"Have you seen a doctor?" asked Dennie.

Frank looked at him questioningly, then glanced at Bruce. "I thought I *was* seeing a doctor," he replied, the trace of a grin back on his lips.

"I think what Dennie means," Bruce answered softly, "is to ask whether anyone has examined your wounds."

Frank shook his head slightly. "No," he said, "but I don't think I've got any infection, although I'm still a little sore. They always used alcohol or something when they pierced my skin. But ... do you ... want to see?" he added uncomfortably.

"Not if it's going to upset you," Bruce assured him. It was now the psychiatrist's turn to suppress any evidence of the surge he felt gripping his body. Dennie, he noticed, had shifted uncomfortably in his seat, almost embarrassed by the young actor's apparent willingness to display his body — yet surely as eager for the sight as Bruce, himself. *God, I bet he'd be in a snit for a month if I asked him to leave,* Bruce thought.

Frank remained in place for several seconds, looking from one man to the other. Then he gestured open-handedly. "Fuck, you can't be a movie actor without being an exhibitionist," he said cynically. "Here," and with that he stood up, stripped off his shirt and undid his belt, then shoved his Levis and shorts down from his slender waist. A sizable, uncircumcised penis flopped from the enclosure, hanging loosely above proportionately large testicles. He watched in almost quizzical amusement as both men seemed momentarily at a loss. "See," he continued easily, "I don't think I've suffered any permanent damage, not unless they gave me AIDS or the clap."

Although he felt painfully self-conscious doing it, Bruce moved to his patient and examined his nipples. He could see the tiny scabs where they'd been pierced, but there did not appear to be any inflammation. "Looks okay on this side," he said as lightly as the constriction in his throat would permit. "Let's see your back." Although there were numerous reddish welts crisscrossing his patient's torso, and some fairly colorful bruises on his buttocks, Bruce could not see any evidence of the skin having been broken. He ran his hand along one particularly angry welt. "You seem to be healing up without any problems," he muttered. He touched the back of his hand to the worst bruise on Frank's left buttock, feeling the warmth. "This must be sore as hell, isn't it?"

"It only hurts when I sit," Frank said, turning toward the doctor, trying to force another display of casual indifference, but not succeeding very well. He turned farther toward the other man.

Hesitantly, Bruce reoriented his attention to the genitals, trying to force his mind into a proper attitude of clinical disinterest. Outwardly, at least, he projected the proper image, although it was with some effort that he kept his fingers from trembling. Without apparent hesitation he took hold of the penis, lifting the end to examine the stitch marks. Frank started involuntarily at the contact, but otherwise remained still as Bruce gently maneuvered the foreskin, again forcing himself to maintain an outward appearance of detached professionalism. "This looks to be healing up without any problems," he said casually, but even as he spoke he could feel a subtle stirring in the flesh and sensed a slight, building tumescence. At the same moment he realized that Frank had a raw abrasion at the top of his scrotum, almost concealed by the pubic hair.

"I think we'd better put something on that," he said. "Dennie, get some Merthiolate from the office." He had retained his hold on the cock, although it was no longer the focus of attention. The crusty laceration on the sac would probably have healed on its own, he thought, but it was best not to take any chances.

When Dennie returned with the ointment, Bruce rubbed a bit onto the wound, only then releasing his grip on the patient's penis. He handed the jar to Frank. "Take this home with you," he told him, "and put a little on all the wounds until they're completely healed."

Frank's cock, as he shoved it back into his jeans, was decidedly enlarged.

"Okay," Bruce said, when they were all settled back into their respective places, "what else did they do to you?"

"Oh, they dribbled hot wax — candle wax I guess — on my nipples, then used a switch to crack it off once it hardened. A couple of times they hauled me into a tiled area, where they had a shower set up, and both of them pissed on me."

"Did they make you take any urine into your mouth?" asked Bruce.

Responding to the note of alarm in the doctor's tone, Frank shook his head. "No, but once they splashed some on my chest and it hit my lips. I could have swallowed a drop or two; at least, I know I could taste it." He looked up abruptly at Bruce, a worried frown creasing his features. His bright green eyes seemed to flash concern. "You are going to check me for AIDS, aren't you?" he asked.

"For sure," Bruce told him, "but it's too soon. We have to wait for your system to produce antibodies, if it's going to. Of course, taking urine isn't very likely to transmit AIDS — less likely than semen, it just seems nastier."

"What would you think, though?" he insisted. "Didn't they do about everything they weren't supposed to do?"

"It sounds like it," Bruce admitted, "although the anal sex is the only real cause for concern. But I wonder if they didn't pick you because they felt you were safe ... figured a straight man wouldn't infect them. If that's the case, they may well be HIV-negative."

"Are you just trying to make me feel good, or...?"

"I'm trying to be realistic," Bruce told him honestly. "In truth, I'd be surprised if they infected you. Even though they kidnapped you, forced you to have sex and all that, they seem to have used proper antiseptic techniques when they catheterized you and when they pierced you. And by the way, we'd better take a urine sample and have it checked in case you've got a bladder infection. I don't expect you will, since you didn't mention any pain. Your urine isn't cloudy or discolored, is it?"

"No," Frank assured him. "It just burned a little when I pissed the first few times Sunday. But what about the AIDS thing? That's what really worries me. How soon can I be tested?"

Bruce sighed, leaning back in his chair and crossing his feet at the end of his outstretched legs. "I'm afraid we won't be able to tell anything for at least six months ... twelve, maybe. And then, according to some of the latest theories, the virus can hide for several years before it forces the production of antibodies." Seeing the expression of genuine fear on Frank's face, he hastened on: "The really best bet we have is to catch the bastards and test them."

"Except they can't," said Dennie from across the room.

"What does that mean?" asked Frank.

"It means," Bruce explained resignedly, "that a man who is just a suspect in a criminal proceeding can't be forced to take the AIDS antibody test against his will. But I think there's some legislation pending to change that," he added.

"If I get my hands on the bastards, there'll be enough blood around for several tests," Dennie growled.

Frank had been silent through this last exchange, but now slipped to his feet again and walked with an agitated stride toward the outside doors. "But that's exactly what I don't want," he said miserably. "Bad as I'd like to see them caught and punished, I just can't appear on the witness stand as a ... a rape victim."

The weight of concern seemed to have fallen again, like a dark cloak over Frank DeSilva's shoulders. Bruce stood behind him at the window, tentatively placing a hand on his patient's shoulder. "We'll figure a way around this," he said with more assurance than he felt. "For you, it's all over. I'd almost be willing to lay odds that you're okay healthwise, and remember — if they did this to you, they're probably doing it to other men. Some of those are going to be willing to take the stand, if it comes to that."

Frank had made no move to displace Bruce's grip, and he now spoke without turning and thus dislodging the contact. "And you won't do anything ... I mean, there isn't any way someone could discover what I've told you?"

"No way in hell," Bruce assured him. "Look, it's gotten pretty late and I can see you're bushed. Why don't we call it a night, and Dennie can schedule you back in a day or two ... that is, if you want to come back."

"Oh, I want to come back!" he said. "And ... if there are other guys, do you think you'll get to hear about them?"

"Probably," Bruce replied thoughtfully. "In fact, I'll try to make sure I do ... without making any waves about it."

■ ■ ■

He was driving his "second car," his favorite really, because it was the last of the full-size Cadillac convertibles ... big, powerful, in perfect condition. Metallic gold with black leather seats, so much more comfortable and spacious than the damned Jap wagons most people were driving these days. The top was down, but the evening air was warm enough that he had the air conditioner turned on. He loved that sensation, cool air blowing up around his body. He was dressed in a dark brown jumpsuit, Rolex watch glinting on his wrist. He laughed to himself, remembering how this little gaudy display of wealth had once attracted the young men to his vehicle, back when it was safe to pick them up off the streets. It had been so much easier in those days. On a nice clear evening like this, just grab a hustler off the boulevard, convince him that getting tied up was one way for a man to prove that he *was* a man, to show what he could take ... then do whatever came to mind, and as long as you paid the punk enough he was happy.

He'd never involved his kid in these sessions, and he wondered how it would have worked out. Probably not too well. He would certainly have been apprehensive, fearful ... like now, worried that one of the slaves would do something to force the ultimate choice. But that was the real challenge, wasn't it? Do your thing, as the hippies used to say, but play the game correctly and it'll never come to that. Of course, if it did ... *kid would never be able to handle it ... I'd have to tell him to stay home, take care of it myself. What would it feel like, this ultimate act, this final condemnation of the soul ... if we really have souls. So far, in all my adventures I've never taken that irrevocable step ... never done anything that couldn't be repaired by human means. I've stolen when I had to, cheated, embezzled, robbed hell out of the tax man. But I've never experienced that ... what? Greatest sensation? Or to castrate one of those proud motherfuckers. That'd take the smile off some wiseass kid who thinks his youth and beauty make him superior to an older man. But that would create even more problems, if he lived through it. Sure to be reported — have to be reported if the fucker wanted medical attention. No, if I ever climb that top step it'll have to be for the big one, not some halfway mutilation that's just as irreversible, but impossible to conceal. To actually take some punk's life ... tighten a rope around his neck and watch the life drain out of him...*

Wonder if I'd really enjoy it. Problem is, if I didn't feel good about it afterward, I couldn't go back and make it right. It's about the only power I don't have — I can't buy off the Grim Reaper. And would I fear for my own death then, wondering what was waiting for me in the Great Beyond? I wonder...

There was a sudden, long blast on a horn, some kid in a yellow pickup coming up on his right side. The Cadillac's tires were just touching the broken divider line between the lanes. He pulled over a bit, startled by this abrupt shattering of his reverie, laid on his own horn as the pickup pulled past him. *Good-looking kid, redheaded, slender, real slender, but arms like a laborer.* The pickup swerved sharply into his lane, and the kid looked back, out the open window. "You need the whole road, asshole? Just 'cause ya got an old man's barge." He sped up, then, dodging into another hole in the right lane.

The Cadillac picked up speed, following the truck. *License plate. Let me get that wiseass bastard's number. No rotten punk calls me an asshole...*

■ ■ ■

Dennie had set up an appointment for Frank on the Thursday following his first session, which gave him a couple of days' break — placing the second interview exactly one week after the kidnapping. "I want to make a list of details to get clarified next time," Bruce remarked as the two friends sat together following Frank's departure. "I've already made some notes on our conversation — the part that didn't get taped. Be sure to append it to your transcript, plus anything you remember that I forgot. My first concern has to be the patient," he added, "but I'd really like to zero in on the perpetrators, the fucking bastards!"

"Do you think Frank could be their first victim?"

"I doubt it. But regardless, I'm sure he won't be the last."

"We've got to do something to stop these creeps," Dennie remarked. His tone was determined, despite the softly spoken words. "If we don't they're not only going to kill somebody, but in doing it they'll create an uproar that'll make SMers the target for every Bible-thumping nut in the country."

"You're right," Bruce agreed, "but we aren't going to get enough information from Frank to do any good. Their whole scenario worked too perfectly with him, and he simply doesn't know. And don't forget," he added, waggling a finger at his companion, "I can't betray a patient's confidence. That means neither of us can go around asking provocative questions."

Dennie grunted his agreement. "But that doesn't mean I can't keep my eyes and ears open," he added defensively. "If these fuckers are involved in the Community someone must have an inkling of what they're doing — who they are."

"Interesting pattern though, wasn't it?" Bruce interjected.

"How so?"

"Didn't it strike you as a little ... pat? Maybe too orchestrated? Almost like they were following the format of an SM guidebook? It was all very structured, almost formalized ... studied. Costumed Top, naked bottom assisting his Master. Apparently lots of equipment. A special room all set up for their games."

"So you think it might be someone in the regular scene doing this?" Dennie looked truly distressed at the idea.

"No, just the opposite," Bruce replied. "The 'Master' could almost have been following a recipe. And the wounds on Frank's body. From what he told us, they used several different scourges on him, including what he called a 'keen switch.' You know, if you don't hold back when you use that kind of thing you can cut the hell out of someone ... and I couldn't find any place where they'd broken the skin. No, I'd say there was considerable restraint used in the beatings. And Frank was right when he said their main purpose was to humiliate him. It's very strange."

The two men sat together in silence for several more minutes. Finally, Dennie got wearily to his feet. "It's been a long day," he said. "See you in the morning." With that he lumbered off to his own wing of the house. Bruce watched him go, thinking as he often did that Dennie's was an amazing intellect, housed in the body of a linebacker. A couple of years older than Bruce, Dennie had been brought up in southwestern Texas, and had not been exposed to anything more intellectually stimulating than a Bible tract until Bruce had met him some ten years before. Now, he mused, the guy had read — and retained — much of the contents in his own fairly extensive library.

He was also an attractive man, in a very rugged way, but gentle as a kitten until someone riled him. Bruce knew he had nearly killed a black punk who had attempted to roll him a couple of years before. *Probably cost the taxpayers a quarter of a million, before they finished patching the son of a bitch up,* he thought, amused at the idea of anyone trying to rob Dennie. You might as well try to rip off Fort Knox. In sex, Dennie was a classic Top, but he never abused his M's. In fact, his greatest problem was to disentangle himself later on, since more than one bottom had decided he was in love with his big bear of a Master. *And that's the whole crux of it,* he thought. *SM sex is all based on consent. A Top might seek to expand his partner's horizons, but even that has certain limits ... common sense sometimes, rather than anything spoken or agreed upon. These kidnappers are operating well outside the mainstream. Yet they are playing by some set of rules ... their own rules, to be sure. It's their game, but a game nonetheless ... or so it seems.*

He went to the sideboard and made himself a light Scotch and water, then carried it into the darkness of the patio. The ivy-covered hillside rose steeply in the darkness at the rear of his property. There were gentle sounds of nightlife, a cricket, the soft rustle of leaves as some small creature scurried away at his approach. He sat on the diving board, sipping his drink. *What sort of men am I up against? I am up against them, no doubt of that. Somehow, I've got to find them. I can bullshit my patient all I want, trying to alleviate his anxiety, but what if they did infect him? Big guy might be a doctor, though. Seemed to use sterile technique on the catheter, but that's no guarantee. I need help ... more than Dennie and I can handle on our own. Shit, I'm like a priest bound by the confessional. Can't make a move that might jeopardize Frank ... Frank ... another problem. Nice guy, physically exactly my type ... know just the kind of therapy I'd like to give him. But what if he's infected? Does he go down the tubes like all those kids I've worked with at the Center?*

He got up and walked to the far corner of his yard, where a short flight of flagstone stairs led to an ornate wooden gazebo that was built high enough to provide a view of the distant ocean. The house had been cut into the hillside, in the best Frank Lloyd Wright tradition. "Cozy," the realtor had called it when she first showed the property to Bruce. But the word as applied to a Beverly Hills home was a comparative term. Built in a soft "U," the single-story structure was deceptively larger than it appeared from the street. Bruce owned the entire slope behind his house, in addition to a big enough piece of flat land above it to prevent anyone from ever building directly on top of him, intruding on the privacy of his backyard and pool.

He sat down again, breathing in the cool night air, slightly moist from his neighbors' sprinklers. He could hear the soft hiss of misting water, but darkness obscured the spray. *The only way I'm going to find the answer to this will be when the bastards hit someone else and I get a chance to interview him. Wonder if the cops have anything on file? And how did they start? Did they always have an elaborate setup like Frank described, or was there some kind of earlier activity that might give us a clue? Computer. Wonder if my access codes are current enough to get me into the files? But if I do get in, where do I look? Under "M"?* he thought with grim humor, *"M" for "male rapist" or "M" for "maniac." Fuck! So what do I do? Sit and wait for some other poor bastard to get his ass worked over? What other choice do I have?*

He sat fidgeting with his drink for quite a long time, trying to sort his thoughts. *Why am I so concerned? Do I feel an obligation to the Community? Is it a matter of self-protection, not wanting to see the media tar all SM people with the brush of these criminals? Or is it Frank? God, I'd like to have him here right now. Beautiful man, physically perfect, like a sculpture. And stripping like he did!* A warm rush of excitement coursed his being, and despite his trying not to think of a patient in sexual terms, he was unable to detach himself from the unwanted flood of arousal ... *lust. That's what it is, just plain lechery. And the guy isn't even gay. It would be the height of unethical behavior to try converting him. And if I take him on as a patient, which I've already done ... Jesus, I wonder if my poor, aging cardiovascular system can stand the strain.*

THREE

An oppressive dry heat had drifted up from the valley floor, making the air feel warmer at midnight than it had in late afternoon. On the North Hollywood side street, a light blue van was parked in the shadow of an overhanging eucalyptus. Inside, a young man shifted uncomfortably in the bucket seat, sweating less as a result of the heat than from the internal pressures of his own body. His back was starting to ache, but again this was not so much from his enforced lassitude as from fear, which gathered as a tight lump in his belly. At the moment this was the foremost of his sensual responses, but there was also the element of sexual excitement. In fact, the two conflicting emotions now seemed almost an inseparable pair — the one blending into the other, as if neither could exist alone.

The object of his attention was across the street and down several doors, a small clapboard house with a low rise of untidy, nondescript hillside separating it from the pavement. The bedroom light had gone out almost half an hour before, but the thump-thump-thump of a teenage disco party continued to resound from across the way, on the same side of the street where the young man sat impatiently, wishing the neighborhood would settle in for the night. He felt the van stir, as his companion shifted position in the back. "Party's still going," remarked the driver.

"I can feel it," replied his father. "Shakes the ground like a goddamn nigger war dance."

"I don't think we'd better stay here too much longer; someone's going to spot the van."

"Not likely. We're just one in a row of cars, and no one can see through..."

His son motioned him silent, a nervous, needless gesture as a police cruiser approached from behind, passed, and began to slow when it approached the source of disturbance.

"Dad, let's get out of here!"

"Easy; don't panic." The older man came forward on his knees, grasping his son's hand to prevent his turning the ignition key. "Slip back here with me," he whispered. "No one's going to see us."

Obediently, the driver edged off his seat, onto the floor. Both men eased back onto the carpeted surface, keeping their heads just high enough to watch the police car double-park in front of the disco house. Two uniformed men got out, one of them fumbling a long baton into its waist holster before joining his partner, both of them mounting the cement steps to the door. It was a poorer, ethnically mixed neighborhood only a few blocks from the Ventura Freeway, the sort of place where residents were likely to respect a policeman's orders, but where there was little danger of an officer's facing a loaded weapon at someone's front door. The older man slid farther into the darkness of the van, reclining backward and pulling his son down beside him. "The cops'll take care of it," he said softly. "Relax, now."

The occupants of the house seemed to accept the policemen's request without argument, and the party broke up less than an hour later. The kids drove off with little dallying or conversation in the street. Within a few minutes of their departure, the neighborhood was silent, and the lights had gone off even in the party house. The van was not alone on the street, however, as several older vehicles — including a battered yellow pickup truck — remained parked at intervals along the curbs. On the floor of the van, the older man cradled the younger one in his arms, feeling the tension and fear that his son was unable to control. He had also felt his own sexual arousal increase during the moments that their bodies had remained in such intimate contact. It was a pleasurable sensation; he could not deny that simple fact. Yet, it bothered him, as it always had — this uncontrollable attraction — not only to his own son, but to young men in general.

Inevitably, the active awareness of this dichotomy distressed him, formed a seething anger just below the surface of his consciousness. In every other aspect of his life he was a proper, upstanding citizen, a conservative businessman who supported all the right causes, who held a position of respect in any society. Yet he could not suppress this unnatural love he felt for his son — a love that had expressed itself in many ways for all the years of the youngster's life, physically as well as otherwise. Lying in the warm darkness he thought back with a mixture of loathing and hard desire to the moments when — during his marriage — he had taken the boy into one or another of their "secret places." Like an alcoholic who could not refuse a drink, he had possessed his son with a loving passion that he had never been able to display toward any woman.

He knew what the others, the outsiders, would have to say if they could fathom the depths of his mind, if they could have witnessed his unrestrained behavior with the boy. Child molester, at the very least. But he'd never possessed the receptive, willing body with less than love — more love, certainly, than he ever felt for the mother. And now ... what? Psychopath? Nihilist? Sociopath? Sex criminal, homosexual rapist ... them for sure. What "they" could never understand was that his desires were different, just as his very existence was different. There was no way he could be compared with some silly, costumed faggot. He was a man, like those rare and respected men all through history who were able to satisfy the cravings of their loins only with another male, but who nevertheless were real men who accomplished real, often earth-shaking things, just as he — in his own way — had done in business and through his support of the social causes that interested him. The modern world left no opportunity for the emergence of a Frederick the Great, a Caesar, a man who might dominate the world while enjoying the bodies of the young men around him ... yet still be a person of stature, even greatness. Instead, he was limited to this game he'd elected to play, bound by its rules, abiding by its restrictions ... and winning, always winning.

The do-gooders would never understand any of this, naturally. There was no organization to lend support to the truly unique, no one to defend his civil liberties, because there were so few who shared these qualities. So what? They had to identify him first. They had to hunt down the hunter. That meant they had to outwit him, and that they'd never do. He gazed at the dark outline of his son and felt again the need to draw him close, to share as much as could be shared ... and to continue hoping that this youthful flesh-of-his-flesh would one day inherit the essence of the father.

I love you, really love you. But I've never said it to you, have I, not like this, not when I'm holding you like a man holds the object of his devotion. He increased the pressure of his grasp, pulling the boy more tightly against himself. *I know exactly what I'm doing. I'm about to commit a capital crime. By the power of my own mind and body I am going to assert my right, this time with even more justification than before — if any justification is needed. This bastard, tonight, he asked for it! Dumb shit never knew how surely he'd receive retribution.*

Outside, a seed pod dropped onto the roof of the van, caused the boy to start at the sound, forcing but a moment's break in the father's reverie. *A man gets what he is able to take in this world — no more, no less. If my intelligence and imagination permit me to have more than the next man, so be it. If the kid would only understand this! He's weak, but he's young. At his age, would I have dared the things I'm doing now? He's afraid; I can feel it. But he's never failed me. It's as if he draws on my strength. I've made him what he is, molded his life. He's passed every test so far, but ... something more difficult, maybe.*

He maintained his hold on the boy, pressed his mouth against the willing lips and kissed him. For a moment he felt the urge to hurt him, to cause him physical pain. But the image of the youngster's face, blurred and indistinct because of the darkness and the closeness of their position, was clear only in his own thoughts. He could not bring himself to cause those trusting features to contort, even in the emotional pain of censure or displeasure. Just as in their private sexual games he found it ever more difficult to give his son the punishment he knew the youngster wanted. The boy was part of him, an extension of his own being ... stood with him against all the others. "Power," he whispered.

"Dad?"

The big man laughed softly. "Just thinking out loud," he said. "Ready to go?"

■ ■ ■

Frank DeSilva came to startled wakefulness. He'd been dreaming, but he could not precisely remember the content ... something complicated, involving his agent and a contract, and a woman who somehow had seemed to be living with him. But it wasn't the dream that had brought him up breathless, sitting sweaty and naked in his bed.

Ah, the dog, he thought. After his experience several weeks ago, he had decided he needed the company of an animal in the house, and he'd answered an ad in the *Times* — "Free to a good home. Loving Labrador, male, housebroken, obedience-trained, etc." And Rudy was all that, except the ad had neglected to mention that the damned beast had nightmares, kicked the side of his box in his sleep. Every time he did it, he scared Frank into full, heart-fluttering wakefulness. Rudy looked up from his cushion, tongue out, tail wagging, all innocence and anticipation. *Really a nice dog — exuberant as all hell, but that's because he's only a little over a year old, I guess. Obeys pretty good ... knows his commands ... follows 'em if he knows you mean it. Likes everybody.*

Frank stood up, feeling a chill from the air conditioner against the moistness of his skin. He rubbed his sides, spreading the sweat like alcohol during a massage, enjoying the sensation of firm muscle beneath his palms. *Horny,* he thought. *Tired of sleeping alone, but shit, do I want to go through it again? The where-have-you-been?'s, the where-are-you-going?'s ... stockings drying on the shower curtain rod. Then after a few months the I'm-too-tired's when you've got a boner a dog couldn't chew. And what did Rufus tell me? "Palimony. Watch out for palimony. In this state they'll stick it to you like you've signed the book."* He sighed and opened the door to the small balcony off his bedroom. As he stepped through, letting the warm air and darkness caress his moist nakedness, he heard Rudy panting up behind him, cold nose probing his butt until he moved aside and let him through. "No, I'm not taking you out, you little shit. If I do it once, you'll start that kicking on purpose every night." Idly, he stroked the furry head, leaning forward, gripping the iron railing with his free hand.

Other than a pair of streetlights across the canyon, the entire hillside was in darkness. A chorus of crickets was clacking away about the base of his house, and far in the distance a dog was howling ... or a coyote. Rudy pricked his ears and emitted a soft growl to let his new master know he'd heard it. Frank tweaked his ear, then set both hands on the cool metal railing.

Another appointment with Bruce tomorrow ... fourth? Fifth? I'm getting so used to them I don't know what I'd do if I weren't sure they had me down for the next one. Nice man, sharp ... always a step ahead of me, never surprised no matter what I say. Sexy guy, too. If I were going to get it on with another man ... gay guy, but he's never made any mention of it again since that first night. He let one hand slide across his thigh, touching himself. *The way I jumped when he touched my prick that time ... Wonder what he thought ... what he thinks? Never seems to get that "lean and hungry look" with me. Wonder if he's afraid I might infect him? Still says it's too early for the test. Bastards! If I could get my hands on them right now!*

With his anger came the familiar tingle between his thighs, the sharp little twinge in his prostate. *Standing out here naked, getting a hard-on over ... over what? Memory of having my hands tied to my neck ... ass whipped ... cock shoved into me ... I've tried to talk it out with Bruce, but something always holds me back after a certain point. Because I know he's gay? He's too ethical, too professional ever to make a pass. Huh! Wonder what he'd say if I came in tomorrow and told him I was standing out on my balcony at three in the morning ... naked, jacking off thinking about him.* He laughed to himself as he tried to picture the expression on Bruce's face. *Might finally shake him up — surprise him for once.* "Come on in, Rudy. Back to bed. Daddy's got to get his Z's."

■ ■ ■

"So what you're saying," Dennie suggested, "is that this guy has to be completely lacking in superego."

Bruce responded with a slight shake of his head. "As far as we know he hasn't killed anyone. In fact, we don't know for sure that he's done this to anyone other than Frank. And despite everything he did with Frank, there were some elements of restraint — not the least of which were all the precautions he took so as to avoid killing him."

"Couldn't there be more than simply moral restraint holding him back?" Dennie insisted. "Certainly in Frank's case he knew — or had good reason to suspect — there wouldn't be any police involvement. He didn't have to kill him."

"He might have supposed that Frank wouldn't report the incident, but he couldn't be completely sure, could he?"

It was Dennie's turn to shake his head. "What if he didn't care? I mean, what if he thinks he's smarter than the cops and wants to beat them at their own game — figures to sit on the sidelines and laugh at them while they chase their tails trying to catch him?"

"I don't know," Bruce replied. He was sitting on a beach chair beside the pool, looking down at Dennie, who perched on the edge, legs dangling in the water. "To assume this would be to assign him the kind of pathological personality that would be the most dangerous to deal with." He shifted his position, spreading his hands as he tried to explain his thoughts. "According to the book, rape is not really a sex act ... psychologically speaking. It's an act of aggression. In effect, the penis becomes a weapon. Conversely, a Jack the Ripper–type killer *is* committing a sex act — even if he never sexually assaults his victim — because his knife becomes his penis."

"But what if this guy is just hot to get it on with good-looking studs, but he's too ugly or too closeted to be able to do it. In a situation like that, couldn't a cock be just a cock?"

"Like the times when a cigar is just a cigar?" Bruce leaned back and stretched. "I'm afraid it has to be more complicated than that." He looked at his wrist, forgetting he had left his watch inside. "What time is it? Frank ought to be arriving about now, shouldn't he?"

"Yeah, I thought I just heard your little mantel-dinger go off in the living room. You'd better pull on a pair of shorts or you'll scare your patient." Then, in response to Bruce's sigh as the therapist stood up to follow his suggestion, he added: "When are you going to give the guy a clue?"

Bruce lifted his sunglasses to give his friend a properly raised eyebrow.

The doorbell sounded and Dennie hurriedly stuffed himself into a pair of jeans. "You could always give him another physical," he added as he beat a hasty retreat.

■ ■ ■

CLINICAL TAPE #5: DeSilva (excerpt)

Therapist: What I meant to ask you concerned a couple of terms you used in our first interview.

Patient: Did I say "fuck" too often?

T: (Laughing) No, I meant your use of the word "girl" when you referred to a female sex partner, but "man," not "boy," for a male. Does this have any significance for you, now that I point it out?

P: Huh! I never thought about it, but I guess it's a reflection of the way I think. I mean, I can have sex with a woman I think of as a girl — maybe because we call young women girls a lot of times, but a boy implies a kid, someone who's underage. Guess that's kind of sexist, isn't it?

T: Not necessarily. I think it projects the realistic use of language, and it might be more reflective of the company you keep, or have kept. But what about men? You really ought to face that issue head-on, not keep trying to pretend it doesn't exist.

P: (After long silence) You know, I do sometimes think about other guys — not just guys in general, like I might with girls — women — but sometimes a specific man.

T: When you do think of another man — and by this I mean in a sexual context — in what relationship do you see yourself?

P: Do you mean, what would I like to do with him ... sexually?

T: No, not precisely. But in general, do you see yourself as the aggressor, or do you visualize this other man in that role?

P: Well, I guess he'd have to make the first move. But as far as the actual sex went, I guess that would be pretty mutual ... and pretty much dependent on the situation.

T: Do you think you feel any differently about this now, after your experience of a few weeks ago?

P: I don't know. Everything that happened to me sure made me think about things I hadn't thought of before. And a few times ... at night, when I'm by myself ... well, I guess the ... images, whatever you want to call them ... maybe they're not all completely negative.

T: So, in this respect, the experience may have altered your perspective?

P: Yeah, maybe. It's, like I said, it's made me consider some things I hadn't really thought about before. I ... I...

T: Go ahead, Frank. Say whatever's coming into your mind.

P: You and Dennie. You're into S&M, aren't you?

T: Yes. Does that bother you?

P: No. I kind of suspected it from the start. In fact, when we finish the therapy ... I mean, I know you're very proper and all...

T: Well, that's not exactly what I meant to get into right now. What I was after was to make sure my particular ... er, interests weren't inhibiting you, or forming a barrier to our counseling relationship.

P: You're saying you're not interested?

T: No, I'm only saying it would be improper for me to take advantage of a patient.

P: You wouldn't be, Bruce. But like I said, I think the other guy would have to make the first move.

■ ■ ■

Bruce sat behind the wheel of his Mercedes two-seater, unwilling to turn the key in the ignition. It had been years since he had been beset by such conflicting, nearly destructive emotions. He was only a few car lengths from the door to the Center, where he had just finished a "People with AIDS" group session. These always upset him more than he was willing to admit, but tonight had been especially bad. One of the kids with whom he had established a particularly tight rapport was in the hospital — not in good shape at all. He'd watched him growing steadily thinner and weaker over the last several months, and now — when the kid desperately needed help — there was absolutely nothing he could do. He was totally helpless. He was also physically in good shape, uninfected, and he felt this was driving a wedge between his other patients and himself.

Somehow, it makes me an outsider. First time in my life that I'm not fully integrated into the gay group that I'm with ... socially, professionally. I try to help these kids ... kids — men, even the youngest of them. Facing death when the most they should be worrying about is the mundane crap of job and friends and sex ... of life. And here I am, panting over one of my patients ... questioning my ethical standards. Even starting to lose sleep over it, and right now it all seems so petty.

With a sigh of resignation he reached for the key and started the engine. One of the guys from his group was passing at that moment and glanced over at the sound. He paused, and for no reason Bruce could readily name, he touched the button that lowered the window on the curb side. The young man leaned into the opening.

"Nice car, Bruce," he said. One hand stroked the leather upholstery, an almost loving touch. "I'd always thought that one day I'd have wheels like these." His tone was plaintive, the unspoken thought implicit in both their minds.

On impulse, Bruce motioned him inside. "Have you had dinner, Tommy?" he asked.

The youngster shook his head.

"I thought I'd stop by the French Market on the way home," said Bruce. He could see the other's discomfort, knowing that even the small price of a meal in this popular gay coffee shop was probably beyond his means. He hesitated, not wanting to patronize him, but knowing that he wanted to make this little gesture. "Not only could I use the company," he continued, "but there are a couple of things I'd like to discuss with you ... if you have the time," he added with an uncertain grin.

"You don't have to..." The young man groped absently for the door handle.

"No, really," Bruce assured him. "You've been in the group for a while, and I'm having some problems I'd like your opinion about. Come on, it'd be a big help to me."

"Okay," agreed the youngster, settling back in the seat. "I *am* hungry," he added weakly.

As the car pulled away from the curb, both men found themselves reflecting on the vast difference between the present situation and what it might have implied a few years before — two attractive guys getting into a car together, driving off for some erotic adventure. Tommy Sims had been "on the street" until a few months before, when he had first noticed the purple spot beginning to grow on his right leg. He'd gone out that night and tried to hustle along Santa Monica Boulevard. But every time a car slowed in front of him he'd turned away, leaving the guy to stare after him in puzzlement. Others he'd known had been aware of their infection and continued as if nothing were wrong. Tommy couldn't do this. He felt it was wrong, although that alone might not have stopped him. It was the fact the disease had resulted from sex, and somehow the very thought made his cock shrivel in his jeans. He'd gone to the Center the next morning, and he hadn't hustled since, although he was surviving on the ragged edge of nothing.

He looked over at the handsome, well-fed man sitting beside him, feeling a sexual attraction that had evaded him for months. He wondered what had prompted this act of generosity, knowing that it wouldn't be for sex. Bruce was fiddling with the stereo as he drove, not speaking, *seems to be deep in thought. Really nice guy ... trying to help. Sure different from the last bastard who picked me up in a Mercedes — what? Three years ago — four? ... asshole conned me into letting him tie me up, then just beat the shit out of me. Put me out of commission for a week. Gave me two bills, though ... more than anyone else ever paid me. Worth it, maybe. Didn't do any permanent harm, but sure pissed me off...*

Bruce was turning into the parking lot, waiting as a car pulled out, leaving a space. "Want to sit outside?" he asked. "It looked like there were some vacant tables."

"Sure," Tommy agreed. He looked around the lot, almost wishing some of his buddies could see him in the car, arriving in style — almost like the old days. Of course, he was thinner now, and he knew he looked ten years older than he had only a few months before.

They sat on either side of a table beside the railing that separated the dining area from the sidewalk. The place was well maintained — neat brick walls with posters of the French countryside, tables covered in pink linen under thick plastic tops. Originally a branch of the infamous hustler coffee shop on the edge of Hollywood, it had now outlived its predecessor and attained its present respectability.

Because they had arrived during a lull between the dinner hour and the later period when guys stopped by on their way home from bars or theaters, there had been no wait for a table. The place served wine and beer, so Bruce ordered them each a Heineken and leaned back in the white garden chair as Tommy lighted a cigarette with a battered Zippo. "So Bruce, what advice can the patient give his doctor?" he asked. Just being back in this moderately priced establishment seemed to make him glow, as if some fresh sense of life — or belonging — had suddenly renewed his self-confidence.

"I've just been wondering how the guys are reacting to me," he replied honestly.

"Oh, I think everybody likes you," Tommy assured him. "In fact, I think one or two would like to offer you some personal ... ah, expressions of gratitude." He grinned, ignoring the frosted glass that had arrived with his beer, and taking a gulp directly from the bottle.

"I'm not as concerned with their liking me," Bruce replied, "as I am with their responses to the things I have to say. Sometimes I'm a little uncomfortable trying to help someone handle his anxieties when I'm somewhat of an outsider. Or at least I sometimes get that feeling."

"You mean because you're negative?" Bruce nodded and Tommy continued: "I don't think it matters that much. All the doctors we go to are negative, too, as far as any of us know, and most of them are really decent people. 'Fact is, you understand things, like the real problems most of us have ... outside of being sick, I mean. Like we know about the fundraising stuff you've done, trying to get us places to live and money to buy food and pay for the drugs."

"Those are all things that have to be done," Bruce said, "and if we don't do what we can within the Community it's hard to make a proper argument for government or private outside funding."

"Yeah. They talk about 'human dignity' when it comes to the dole for unwed mothers and such, but for gay men it's a different ball of wax. People don't think we got a right to feelings, too. Like, you know, I'm living in the hostel and I'm getting my meals there. But just scratching up the price for a pack of cigarettes can be a bummer. You can't hold a decent job, even if you can find one, feeling so shitty half the time, and having to take off to see a doctor every few days. And most people — straight people — they just don't give a shit. But you *do* care, Bruce. I've seen it, like tonight, when you heard about Manny being in the hospital. That really shook you up, didn't it?"

"Yeah, it did," Bruce told him. "He's a nice kid, and bright. There was so much he could do with his life."

"He died, you know," Tommy said unexpectedly.

Bruce started, staring in disbelief. "How...?"

"After the session, just before I came outside. The night guy called the hospital for us, and they told him."

Bruce sat back thoughtfully, trying to suppress the lump rising in his throat. Tommy reached across and patted his hand. "See, Bruce, you are part of it," he said. "That's the difference between you and a lot of the others. You care. That makes you part of the group."

FOUR

Bruce had finished with his two early-morning patients, and was at his desk. It was the day after his session with Frank, whose file now lay open in front of him. He sat in deep thought for a long time, finally forcing himself to concentrate on his own situation, and to relegate the problems of the Center and of his other patients into the background of his thoughts.

Having Frank sit across from him as he had the previous afternoon, practically inviting an advance, was more disturbing than he could have imagined. There was no denying his own desires, but he simply could not break his ethical code by having a sexual relationship with a man who had come to him for help. He also had a lingering doubt in the back of his mind, about Frank's remarks. Had they been a momentary lapse, or did they mean he had given some real thought to the possibility of something happening between them? And if so, did he think of it as a passing fling, a one-time occurrence, or was there the possibility of something more?

He knew that Frank's residual anxieties were now minimal, and that he properly should be discharged. Yet he couldn't bring himself to terminate the relationship, maybe never see him again. And how ethical was that? Of course, the payments weren't coming out of Frank's pocket. The agency's insurance company was footing the bill. Somehow, that made it less improper ... or did it? Whichever way he turned, he was going to do something with which he did not feel completely comfortable. *Oh, the games we play ... the games we have to play ... always rules to follow — rules of law, rules of ethics. And then there're the rules we make up for ourselves. Sometimes it's tough to keep them all. Guess I'm just becoming a compulsive old fart — game player; that's me. Always try to play by the fucking rules, and suffer the guilt if I don't.*

In the midst of his reverie of self-recrimination, the phone rang, and Bruce reached out abstractedly to answer it. "Dr. MacLeod? Please hold for Commissioner Javits," said the silky female voice, and a moment later Bruce's friend Abraham Javits was on the line.

"Bruce," he said enthusiastically, "sorry not to have gotten with you for such a long time. How are things going?"

"Fine, Abe," Bruce replied warily. "It's good to hear your voice."

"I suppose you're up to your neck in work," returned the caller.

"I should probably say I am," Bruce replied. "What horrible mess have you got to drop in my lap?"

"Actually, it's a rather interesting situation." Abe's tone was almost questioning. "And it's one that I think would be quite ... er, aligned with your special interests."

"Which interests would that be?"

"Both your clinical and your recreational. I'd like to have Pete Jackson bring someone by to see you. It seems this kid was kidnapped by a pair of SM nuts, and got raped."

Bruce's heart seemed to be thumping in his throat. "Jesus, Abe, that's pretty wild!"

■ ■ ■

Lt. Peter Alfred Jackson was a slender, rather handsome black man in his midthirties. Bruce knew him only casually, although he had worked one case with Jackson a year before. He suspected that the detective was aware of his sexual proclivities, although nothing had actually ever been said. Still, he had sensed a mild disapproval in the other's attitude during their past association. But the detective was reasonably bright, and obviously realized that there were times when these very qualities were the key to an insight he had been missing. For Bruce, it was an "iffy" relationship, and he was therefore surprised when Pete Jackson arrived at the house later that afternoon, greeting his host like a long-lost friend.

"Dr. MacLeod," he said after the initial niceties, "this is Charlie Stuart, the guy the commissioner called you about." The young man who had accompanied him was in his early twenties, blond and blue-eyed, with a surfer's tan and a lithe, slender build. He was about five-nine in height, with a fresh, clean-cut look about him. His rather long, sun-bleached hair was arranged in casual disarray, which made him look somewhat out of place in an expensive gray suit with a red-and-blue paisley vest and conservative blue knit tie.

"You look very familiar," Bruce remarked as he shook his hand — warm, moist palm, firm grip. "Are you a TV type?"

The young man grinned, seemingly pleased that the doctor had implied a partial recognition. "I was on TV during the Olympic ski trials," he said, "got interviewed a couple of times, but didn't make the team." He took one of the large chairs facing Bruce's desk, and despite the forced smile and studied casual manner, the psychiatrist sensed his nervousness ... fingers never still, several times plucking at his tie or jacket.

"Try to relax," Bruce said, waving Pete into the other chair, and settling himself behind the desk. He was wearing a shirt and tie, but no jacket. "We're here to try and help you," he added, and with that he poked the floor switch with his toe.

■ ■ ■

CLINICAL TAPE #1: Stuart, Charles I., IV (excerpt)

Therapist: So, tell me, Charlie, when did all this happen to you?

Patient: About a month ago. I wasn't going to say anything about it, but I can't get it off my mind. It's causing ... problems for me, so I finally told my dad, and he took me in to see Mr. Javits.

Officer: Mr. Stuart is a business associate of the commissioner.

T: You say "problems," Charlie; what sort of problems?

P: Uh, well, uh, sexual problems.

O: Bruce, maybe I ought to step outside and let you guys discuss things between you.

T: If you like. Dennie's in the next room. I'm sure he'd be happy to fix you something to drink. (Sound of door closing as O leaves)

P: Thanks, Doctor MacLeod. The lieutenant's a nice guy and all, but he's still a cop, and all this is new to me. I don't usually discuss my sex activities with strangers, certainly not cops.

T: Do you feel comfortable talking to me?

P: I think so. They said you were a psychiatrist, so you've probably heard it all before, anyway.

T: I've heard a lot, but just when I think I've heard it all, someone comes up with a new wrinkle.

P: Have you ever heard of a guy being kidnapped and raped, like happened to me? I guess Mr. Javits told you what happened.

T: No more than you just said. This isn't something that's happened with any frequency since the Dark Ages.

P: But you have heard of it happening ... I mean recently?

T: No, I can't say that I have. Why don't you tell me about it?

P: Well, I was down at the beach. I ski in winter, surf in the summer — as much as I can, anyway. So, after spending the day on the sand I was sleepy, but these chicks had invited me to come by later for a cookout. I was supposed to be there at seven, and I live up above Bel Air, so it didn't seem worthwhile to drive home. I showered in the public john, and sacked out in the back of my van. I had a change of clothes, so I figured to catch forty, and pop by the chicks' pad later. And that's all she wrote, man. I corked off and the next think I know I'm trussed up like a hog for slaughter, with this leather hood over my head.

T: You have no idea what happened? Were you drugged, or...?

P: When they finished with me, I know they gave me a shot in the ass to knock me out. I guess they must have done the same to me in the van.

T: You say "they." How many were there?

P: Two, I think.

T: Can you describe them?

P: No, they kept this hood on my head the whole time.

T: And how long did they keep you?

P: Well, they snatched me sometime after 5:30, because that's when I went to sleep. That was a Friday. I woke up in my van again about midnight on Saturday.

T: And you have no idea what they looked like, how big they were, how old, or ... maybe some accent in the voices, even if you didn't see them?

P: Well, it's really hard for me to tell. I'd guess both of them were fairly good-sized, bigger than me. They always spoke in whispers, you see, and they tried to make me ... have sex with them.

T: Tried to have sex with you. Then, they didn't actually do it?

P: Oh, they did it all right, except that I wouldn't cooperate with them. The goddamned bastards tried to make me ... make me ... I don't know the polite words for it, Dr. MacLeod, but they tried to make me suck their cocks, and I wouldn't go for it. When one of them actually got his penis into my mouth, I bit him. They just whipped the shit out of me for that, but it was worth it. But then, they ... they fucked me in the ass!

T: After you bit one of them, they both sodomized you? Hadn't you damaged the guy's dick?

P: Yes, well, I guess I didn't do too much damage, because they forced my mouth open almost right away. I don't think I drew blood or anything.

T: Okay, Charlie, just ... try to relax, now. We're getting everything a little jumbled. Let's try to get a picture of the room you were in, if you can. Then we'll go from there.

P: Okay, Dr. MacLeod, but I can't tell you much about the room, because I never saw it, of course, and I was never left in it so I could move around and get an idea of how big it was, or anything. They just had me buck naked, hands strapped down at my sides, attached to a belt around my waist. I was on a table of some kind, with a surface that felt like rubber, or maybe vinyl. This hood they had over my head didn't have any eyeholes, but it ended just below my nose, so my mouth was exposed, and I think there was some kind of padding over my ears, because I couldn't hear very well. When they whispered, I couldn't understand them if they got too far away. I know there was a bathroom off in one corner, because they took me there several times.

T: Then you walked on the floor. What was it made of?

P: It was covered with some kind of rubbery stuff, too, and parts of it were padded. Oh, and there was like a shower over by the john. I know that for sure, because they took me into it and put a chain around my neck, fastened to something in the ceiling. They took off the belt and unstrapped my hands, then cuffed them in back of me ... not until I'd had a tussle with them, though. It took both of them to force my wrists together so they could put on the cuffs. They whipped my ass again for that, and then they shaved my balls, and my groin ... everything. One of them said something about my not having any other hair on my body, so this ought to go, too. When they'd finished doing that, they showered the soap and stuff off of me.

T: But the hood stayed on all the time?

P: Yeah. One of them had told me he'd kill me if I managed to get it off so I could see them. I might have tried to pull it off, anyway, but I was so busy trying to fight them off I didn't get a chance.

T: I was just wondering about its getting wet in the shower. What was it made of?

P: It was leather, but the shower spray didn't hit it. The nozzle must have been set low on the wall, because it only hit me from about the chest down.

T: Then, as to the men. Could you differentiate between them, tell which one it was who did one thing or another to you?

P: One guy called the other one "Sir" most of the time, and he might have been a little smaller, because the one guy was pretty big. But even that was hard to tell. The bigger guy wore leather all the time, but the other one was naked, and that might have made him seem smaller than he really was. Oh, and you asked about age. I really couldn't tell, except that the naked guy was hairy. I had the feeling that both were ... you know, mature men. I mean, they acted real confident all the time, never seemed to hesitate when it came to doing something with me.

T: So, they shaved you and they sodomized you ... whipped you. Did they do anything else?

P: Well, they tried to make me get a hard-on. They tied my cock and balls up with rawhide, and kept wrapping it around my scrotum to force my nuts down as deep as they could. Then one of them ... the naked one, tried to suck me off.

T: How did you respond to this?

P: I didn't. The bastards did everything they could, but I just stayed soft. Of course, I wanted to stay soft, and I never got over being mad the whole time I was there. The more they

did to me, the more determined I was not to give
them the satisfaction of seeing me do anything
they wanted me to do. The only thing I couldn't
stop was what they did to me, when they tied me
down on that table and both of them just fucked
my guts. And, man, did that ever hurt! See, Dr.
MacLeod, I just don't go for queer sex. I never
have, and just the idea of it makes me sick to
my stomach. So when they greased me up, I made
everything as tight as I could, and I guess that
made it all the worse for me. But I can't tell
you how furious-mad I was, and I never stopped
fighting them.

T: And the problems you're having now, that's
part of this?

P: Yeah, I guess it must be. But the last time —
the only time since this happened to me — but
the last time I tried to get it on with a
chick ... well, I couldn't get it up, Dr. Mac-
Leod, and that's never been a problem for me
before. Anyhow, it scared me and after thinking
about it for a couple of days I told my dad.

T: How did he react?

P: Well, you gotta know Dad to appreciate it,
but he just about threw a fit! See, he's even
more down on queers than I am, and the idea of
having this happen to me, well, he about had
apoplexy. Didn't blame me, of course, but he's
been after me for a long time to start working
at the office with him, and maybe I should,
but ... well, I'm spoiled. I know that. I'm a
playboy, I guess you'd call it. But the old man
blamed me only in the sense that if I hadn't
been sacking out in my van — like a beach bum,
he put it — the whole thing wouldn't have happened to me. And maybe it wouldn't, but it's

done now and I'd like to forget about it, except I can't. What do you think?

T: I don't think you've got any permanent problem with this. A lot of men experience what we call transitory impotence from time to time, and for a lot of different reasons. Unless there's a physical cause, which seems unlikely in your case, it's simply a matter of working out the emotional crisis that brought it on.

P: Do you think you can help me with that, Dr. MacLeod?

T: We can try, but I think we have to clarify your situation with the police, first. Up to this point, everything we've discussed is more or less open to them, because they brought you here and I'm acting as their consultant. If we were to establish a therapeutic relationship, that would be completely confidential.

P: Oh, I don't think Dad would like that — having everything I've told you put into some police file. We haven't filed a formal complaint, you know.

T: Why did you go to the police, then?

P: We didn't, not officially. Dad knows Mr. Javits, so he called him and Mr. Javits said for me to come in ... that he'd keep it unofficial for the time being. Dad's thought — and mine — was that if these guys had done the same thing to other people, we might be of some help, or at least let the police know that there had been another victim.

T: And did they indicate that there had been other victims?

P: They didn't tell me, but I don't think so.

■ ■ ■

Pete Jackson was slumped in a big leather chair, watching an afternoon talk show, when Bruce and his client entered the den. "This guy's a nut," the detective said to no one in particular. "He claims that beating your wife is okay, so long as you don't do her any permanent harm."

To Bruce's surprise, Charlie answered him. "He's probably right," he said. "Most women would be better off if they'd been whupped a little more when they were kids."

"That's enough of that," said Dennie, zapping it with the remote control.

Pete stood up and stretched. "How did you guys make out?" he asked.

"Okay," Bruce told him, "but I'd like to know the department's position on this. If I'm going to work with Charlie, here, we're going to get into areas that don't belong in a police record."

"Oh, this is all very informal," Pete assured him. "There's nothing on the record at all, so far. I'm just acting as chauffeur and bodyguard."

As they spoke, Charlie had wandered outside through the sliding glass door, and was standing by the edge of the pool. "You're welcome to take a dip," Bruce called to him.

"No swimsuit," he answered.

"You don't need one," Dennie told him. "No one can see in."

Bruce turned his attention back to the policeman. "So, Pete, did Abe give you any idea what he wants me to do?"

"The kid's old man is a big mucky-muck political contributor," he explained in a hard tone that expressed his contempt. "He's kind of an asshole, you know ... Mr. Conservative, and I wouldn't be surprised if he wasn't slipping a few bucks to the Aryan supremacist shits. Anyway, he's got enough political clout to make some serious waves, and Javits's just playing it cool ... figures by sending the kid to you, it'll show we were concerned, and if you choose to take him on as a patient, it'll take the pressure off the department. Last thing Stuart Senior wants is for it to go on record that his kid was forced to take it up the ass. I don't think Javits really likes the old man, but he's too rich to ignore."

"Tell me," said Bruce with carefully feigned thoughtfulness, "have there been other cases like this?"

Jackson pursed his lips and shrugged. "Not that I know of," he said. "You get any vibes that this might be a serial thing?"

"It just seems to me that someone who'd do it once might very well have done it before," he replied evasively.

"Or might do it again," suggested the lieutenant.

Bruce was just nodding agreement, when a loud splash sounded from the pool, followed almost immediately by a shrill shout: "Jesus, it's cold! Don't you guys ever heat this thing?"

The two men looked out to see Charlie Stuart gripping the side of the pool, blond hair plastered against his head. "Whew!" he gasped. "Now I'm getting used to it, 's not so bad." And he started doing a lap down the forty-foot length.

"What do you think of the kid?" asked Jackson.

"Spoiled rotten," Bruce replied. "Probably hasn't done a good day's work in his life, and I'd guess he's as bigoted as his father."

"Do you buy his story?" asked the detective unexpectedly.

Bruce regarded him curiously, shrugging now in his turn. "Sure, why not?"

"I don't know. Whole thing sounds kinda strange to me. Why would a pair of S&Mers go after some straight kid and rape him ... in this town, when you can find it in God-knows-how-many bars, or buy it off the street, for that matter? Doesn't make sense."

"Most sex crimes don't make much sense," Bruce replied, "except to the people who perpetrate them. In this case, it could be any of several things: someone who knew the kid and resented him, someone who just likes the thrill of the hunt. Hell, it could even be some misguided fool who thinks he won't get AIDS if he makes it with a straight partner."

Pete Jackson stood in front of him, absently shaking a cigarette from a pack he took from his inside pocket. His gaze wandered absently toward the pool, where Dennie was just handing a towel to the naked visitor. Bruce could not help but be impressed by the tight, well-defined body. The pubic hair had partially grown back, but he could see that the kid had been telling the truth about being shaved. As he dried himself, Charlie took no pains to cover his body, and Bruce was amused to watch Dennie's eyes as they followed the recovery of the kid's genitals from their pool-shrunken state to a more respectable normalcy. After hearing about his father's right-wing attitudes, Bruce had half expected the kid to be uncircumcised. But he was neatly clipped, he noted absently. *Nice, nonetheless.*

"So, where do we go from here, Doc?" asked the detective. "Do you want to take him on? As a patient, I mean," he added with a knowing but friendly leer.

"I don't know," Bruce said honestly. "I'm not sure I can handle the holier-than-queer bullshit. Besides, he's so shallow, I don't think his problem is going to prove as serious for him as it might for someone else. He got raped by a pair of loonies and claims to have experienced one instance of impotence. Hopefully, he'll get over it in a few days without any help from anyone."

"Yeah, but you know he's got more problems than that. With a father like his, who wouldn't?"

"I'm not sure those are areas I'd want to get into with him, in any event," Bruce said. "Ingrained bigotry isn't something to be easily worked out, especially when the patient doesn't see it as a problem."

"For him, maybe it isn't," returned the detective.

"That's pretty insightful for a cop," Bruce told him.

"Comes from hobnobbing with the Beverly Hills intelligentsia," he replied lightly.

Then Charlie came back into the room. He'd put his pants and shoes on, carrying the rest of his clothes in one hand, still using the other to towel his hair. "That's a nice pool, Dr. MacLeod," he said. "It's long and deep like ours ... gives you a chance to really swim." He glanced at Jackson and Bruce in turn. "You guys come to any decision?"

"Like what, Charlie?" Bruce asked.

"Like are you going to give me a shot in the ass to cure my problem, or do we talk it out?"

"I'm afraid there isn't any medication I can give you," Bruce told him evenly, "and as to talking it out ... why don't you discuss it with your father? If he approves, give Dennie a call and we'll set up an appointment. I can't promise to take you on as a regular, but if you keep having problems ... well, we'll see."

Charlie started putting on his shirt, quiet and thoughtful for a few seconds. "You don't like me, do you, Dr. MacLeod?" he added unexpectedly.

"I don't like or dislike you, Charlie," Bruce assured him, then added: "At this point I don't really know you. But as I told you in the other room, I don't think you have a problem that's going to be serious or permanent. I'm also just about booked up, right now. I'm doing a lot of volunteer work, in addition to my regular practice, and it all keeps me pretty busy."

■ ■ ■

A cooling breeze came in off the ocean as darkness fell, and the traffic noises receded from the distant boulevard. The visitors had long since departed when Bruce and Dennie settled into the gazebo for one of their frequent end-of-the-day discussions. They had carried up a tray of drinks with some send-out food from the local Italian deli.

"That kid's a cocky little shit," Dennie remarked as he spooned a generous portion of ravioli onto his plate, "but just my type. Did you see those tight buns? Um!"

"Yeah," Bruce agreed, "but he's certainly not very *simpatico*. Now, after what's happened to him, he's going to be more homophobic than ever."

"I don't know," Dennie replied. "He sure shucked his clothes in a hurry when you invited him to use the pool, and he didn't seem to care who was lookin'."

"I doubt he thought much about it," said Bruce offhandedly. "I'm sure he didn't realize the effect he was having on some horny old lecher lurking around poolside. I notice, though, he was telling the truth about getting shaved."

"Was it the same pair of assholes as snatched Frank DeSilva, do you think?" Dennie asked.

"It almost has to be," Bruce said. "I can't imagine there'd be more than one pair of nuts out there doing this."

"Did his impressions jibe with Frank's?"

"More or less. He got the needle the same way — in the butt instead of the shoulder; but then he's smaller, so maybe they wanted more muscle mass to take the injection. The only real point of departure had to do with the second man on the team. Frank described him as small and hairless. Charlie thought he was bigger, and with lots of body hair."

"That's not uncommon, though," Dennie observed. "Every time you have more than one witness at a crime scene, you always come up with discrepancies in their observations."

"True," Bruce agreed, "but it makes me wonder if we really are dealing with just one pair of perps, or whether the 'Master' has more than one helper."

"Did the physical setup sound the same?"

"Yeah, it did. You'll have to play the tape," he told him. "I'd like it transcribed anyway ... Frank's last one, too, while you're at it."

Dennie nodded. "First thing in the morning," he said. "Oh, by the way, Abe Javits called back while you were in with Charlie. He said he'd like to stop by tomorrow evening after dinner. Wants to talk to you in person. I guess Jackson was in the office when he spoke to you before, and there were things he couldn't say in front of him."

■ ■ ■

Abe Javits was probably the most genuinely compassionate man Bruce had ever met, and someone whose friendship he greatly valued — despite the fact that they had lately seen very little of one another. As his name would imply, Abe was Jewish, the second son of an orthodox family. Although they had originally lived in Boston, they had moved to Cleveland when Abe was still a baby. Brought up in any setting other than the very patristic structure of a kosher household, he might well have come out early as a gay man. Instead, he had allowed himself to be pushed into an extremely unsatisfactory marriage when he was twenty-three. This ended in divorce two years later, and Abe moved to Los Angeles.

By this time, he had learned the investment business so well that he became a highly valued member of the Beverly Hills inner circle of financial advisors. He also became very rich. At thirty-two, he married for the second time, much to the distress of his parents. The bride was a younger, gentile woman named Alice, who was the epitome of graciousness and beauty. When Bruce first met her, his impression was of a younger Rosalind Russell. But she and Abe shared a secret that was the cause of his coming to Bruce for counsel. Alice was a dominatrix, a fact known to Abe before their marriage, and in truth the principal reason for his loving her.

"I looked you up in the yellow pages," he announced at their first session, "and I picked you because of your name. Out of all the long list, you were one of the few who I assumed couldn't be Jewish."

That remark took Bruce so by surprise that he could not help laughing — a very unprofessional reaction, of course. "What difference would that make?" he asked. "I hope I'm not dealing with a closet Nazi."

This brought an answering chuckle from his patient, and after that they developed a friendship that quite transcended any professional relationship. In fact, it was Abe who guided his therapist's investment program so well that he was able to move his practice into his home — or really, to afford the house at all. His concern not to engage a Jewish shrink was best summed up in his own words:

"Listen, any Jew would consider me a complete schmuck for what I've done. My father won't speak to me, and every time my mother sneaks a call to me while the old man's out, she starts to bawl and can't understand why I married a *shiksa,* when there have to be so many nice Jewish girls in Beverly Hills. If she knew just half the truth, she'd probably end up in an early grave."

Their friendship burgeoned quickly after this first session, with the agreement that each would apply his expertise for the other's benefit on an even-exchange basis. At this time — the early seventies — Bruce was still very active in gay SM circles, while Abe was being pulled into a clique of his wife's kinky, heterosexual friends. In a sense they were both leading double lives, and as such they were natural soul mates. Once all their respective cards had been tossed onto the table, they really became "best buddies." In 1981, when Abe was first appointed to the police commission, he immediately began channeling a number of consulting jobs to Bruce, who liked the work, and was lucky enough to strike a couple of the right nails on the head early on, so that his reputation within the department became nearly legend.

A year Bruce's junior, Abe was still a strikingly handsome man, with a small, wiry body and black curly hair just tinged at the temples with a "touch of experience," as Alice called it. He had light hazel eyes that sparkled within the swarthy setting of his well-proportioned features. He was witty and fun to be with — a condition that he attributed to his psychiatrist's guidance, as he had been depressed and withdrawn when they first met. He was also completely satisfied to be "straight," but equally accepting of his friend's orientation — one that he admitted he might have shared, had Alice not come into his life and offered him something "even better."

■ ■ ■

Dennie had taken off to the movies with a friend, leaving Bruce alone in the house. Abe arrived shortly before nine, parking his Rolls under the *porte cochère*, walking around to the side gate, and letting himself in. He knew Bruce would be in the den, the same room where he had spoken with Pete Jackson the day before. "You're going to have a nice crop of avocados," he said, as he pulled the sliding glass door aside. "Your trees are loaded."

"Maybe I could get 'em to tax the place as a farm," Bruce suggested.

"Fat chance. They'd probably turn you in to the IRS, to see if you'd made a buck selling 'em."

"So, how's it going in the big world, out there?" Bruce asked. "Got some hot ideas to make me rich and you richer?"

"Wish I did," he sighed, going to the bar and making himself a drink. "How did you make out with the Stuart brat?"

"He's a mixed-up kid, but I don't think the rape experience is going to have any serious consequences..." And then it struck him. "You know," he said, thinking aloud, "it completely slipped my mind, but we didn't discuss the possibility of his having been infected ... AIDS, I mean, or anything else. I should have arranged a blood test for him, and made sure he knew to get an HIV test six months from now."

"It'd be a little soon, wouldn't it?" asked Abe, settling into the chair across from his friend. "I thought nothing would show up for at least a year."

"I still should have thought of it, and I didn't."

"Little bugger shake you up ... or turn you on?" he asked slyly.

"Not that, although I think he made a conquest of Dennie," Bruce told him. "He's a little young for my tastes, and not much upstairs," he added, touching his forehead, "...and unassailably straight, or so he thinks — which is much the same thing."

"Well, you know about his father — Charles Iverson Stuart, the .Great. I had to do something to keep the son of a bitch from beating down the mayor's door."

"Upset?"

"That's putting it mildly. The idea that any no-good, queer, et cetera, et cetera ... I'm sure you get the picture. The man's a maniac on the subject, anyway ... thinks anyone who's not a straight WASP belongs in a concentration camp."

"I thought he was a friend of yours," said Bruce, grinning.

"Listen, friends like him I don't need. But he's got a lot of political contacts where it counts, especially on the judiciary. He's a lawyer, in case you didn't know ... not in practice anymore, but he's bought the bench for half a dozen judges. He's also got a direct line into the governor's office, so when he gets pissed everyone jumps. He's a big blustery bully of a man, goes back to his days as some kind of secret intelligence officer in the army. Anyway, Bruce, how did the kid's story strike you? Is it for real, or is he having some kind of a sexual fantasy?"

"Oh, I think it's real, all right. I couldn't say anything to Pete, but I've got another patient who tells just about the same story. And this has to stay just between you and me; I can't go around telling tales out of school, but Charlie's version and my patient's are too close to be coincidental."

"Shit! So, we've got ourselves a pair of serial homosexual rapists — kidnappers, to make it worse. Wonder what the media would call it if they got their mitts on it — the Bel Air Buggers?"

"Two instances doesn't make a series," Bruce observed softly.

"Humph! Every rapist we nail for a dozen crimes has at least five times as many we can't prove he did. And a brutalized woman is going to be lot quicker to come forward than some guy who gets buggered and doesn't want the world to know how thoroughly his manhood's been compromised. How are we going to handle this, Bruce?"

"I don't know that either of us can do much of anything, yet," Bruce told Abe unhappily. "Neither victim is willing to stand up and be counted. My patient's whole career could go down the tubes if it became public, and Charlie's father isn't going to want his son on the front page of the *Times* as the poor, sodomized victim."

"So far, then, you're the only one who's talked to both of them. Is there any clue, any common thread that might give us a lead?"

Bruce shook his head, biting his lower lip. "No," he said. "I'd be willing to give you transcripts of both sessions to show to one of your hot-shot detectives — minus the names and other data that might identify the victims, of course — but I don't think he'd find much to work on."

Bruce continued, then, to outline the stories he'd gotten from Frank and Charlie. In this discussion, he referred to Frank as "John." Beyond that, he identified him only as a "performer." When he finished his account, Abe sat back in his chair, sipping thoughtfully at his drink. "You know, if we don't stop them I think they're going to kill somebody, don't you?"

"That possibility had already crossed my mind," Bruce agreed. "But even just the things they've done so far — assuming there isn't already a corpse or two hidden out in the desert somewhere — is bad enough. We're all aware of the psychological repercussions a rape can have on a woman, but for a man..."

"Are you trying to tell me it's worse for a man?" Abe asked, an almost adversarial tone in his voice.

"In certain respects, it could be," replied the psychiatrist. "Remember, in our society at least, the male is perceived as the aggressor. Being raped has to be a very castrating experience. I don't know that it's necessarily worse than for a woman, but it's got to be different. There are lots of therapists working in crisis clinics and the like, who are trained to help a female victim. I doubt many are equipped to help a man in similar circumstances."

"And you ... do you think you could help them?"

"I don't know," Bruce admitted. "My own peculiar background might give me some insight that others would lack, but it could also distort my perspective. You know how disturbing it is for me to read accounts like the Freeway Killings, or the Trashbag Murders. I feel the same way here, as if I should somehow share the guilt, because I dig some of the same things these guys are forcing on their victims. I wouldn't admit this to anyone else, Abe, but I think you know me well enough to understand what I mean. It's not kind, I know, but whenever a gay man commits any kind of sex crime I can't help but think what the Falwells of the world will make of it. When the evening news gives you one of their precommercial teasers about some kind of sex-related crime coming up in the next segment I almost hold my breath, then sigh with relief when the victim turns out to be a female."

Abe nodded his understanding. "I know what you mean," he said. "I feel the same way when they bust a Jew for insider trading, or just recently that doctor in New York who beat his adopted kid to death. It makes you sick no matter who does it, but all the worse if it's a member of your own minority."

"All of which leaves us where, Abe? We can't very well put an ad in the paper asking victims to come forward; yet short of that, we've got no choice but to wait until another guy gets it and has the guts to report what happened to him, then hope he's observed something the others haven't."

"Your SM contacts wouldn't be any help, I don't suppose?"

"I don't see these rapists as belonging to the Community as I know it," Bruce told him. "They have to be outsiders ... loners, guys who aren't getting it through the usual contacts. In general theory," he added, "rape isn't really so much a sex act as an assault ... an expression of hostility. But even that definition doesn't fit here. The bastards are kidnapping their victims and having extensive sexual relations with them. It's strange. I just don't know..."

"So, let's add up what we *do* know about them." He took a notebook and pen from his pocket. "First, there are at least two of them, maybe three. One is a big guy, uncircumcised — at least that eliminates my tribe." He forced a grim smile. "What else?"

"They must have a house, as opposed to an apartment, and probably something like a van or at least a large vehicle of some sort, even if they're stuffing their victims into the trunk to transport them. They, or at least one of them, is probably well heeled in order to afford all the space and equipment."

"Go on," he urged. "I can see you've given it some thought."

"Well, in keeping with their having some money to play with, they have access to medical supplies. I guess you can get hypodermic needles on the street. But the shots they've given both victims aren't things you can pick up in a pharmacy — and it isn't a street drug. Either one of them's a doctor — or nurse — or they have the money to buy supplies they couldn't get legally. Then, they also had Foley catheters, and from John's description they must have had an anal Bardex. But again, there're a few places that sell them on the kink market — assuming, of course, they didn't all come out of a doctor's office."

"Confusing set of 'ifs' and 'maybes,'" Abe agreed. "But what about the way they find their victims? They could have just staked out the beach where they nabbed Charlie, picked off the first easy mark they found. But what about John Doe? You say he was snatched from his house. How did they know about him, where he lived? Was he a neighbor? Did they follow him from the studio, or wherever he works? And how did they get in?

"Then, they have to have bought the clothing and equipment — the furnishings of the room. It sounds like the floor must be covered in rubber sheets. I know these are hard to get, because Alice spent a whole couple of days trying to buy some. Shit, if we just had a case we could put on the books I might get a couple of investigators assigned to run down the various potential suppliers."

"You'd probably end up with a list of names that wouldn't do you any good. Hell, I'd probably pop up, and so would Alice — or you, if you've bought any goodies for her."

Abe sat thinking for a few more minutes, then suggested: "You know, both victims indicate an absence of clues, like sounds. So, instead of looking at this from a negative standpoint, what if we turn it around? What I mean to say is, if they didn't hear any extraneous noise, then maybe they were being held in a place outside the city, or at least away from any highway or airport."

"That still leaves a lot of territory," Bruce observed. "I wonder, though, if there might not be another path we could follow to get a little closer to them."

"How's that?"

"They snatched John Doe in North Hollywood, and Charlie up in Malibu, or more precisely Zuma Beach. These areas are fairly distant from each other. Wouldn't it be a fairly safe assumption that the center of their operating radius was somewhere in between?"

"Sure, but that would include the whole west side, plus a chunk of the San Fernando Valley," replied Abe, unenthusiastically.

"That's true," Bruce continued, "but it's a starting point. It eliminates downtown, East L.A., all the area south. I might even hazard a guess that they got out to the beach through one of the canyons, which means they came from the west end of the valley."

"So you're projecting that they live, or have their playroom, in the valley?" he said dubiously.

"I'd say somewhere in the hills, either side. Again, we'll probably have to wait for another victim, but I'd almost bet he gets snatched somewhere in between the other two."

"And if you're right?" he asked.

"I'm not sure yet," Bruce admitted, "but maybe we'll figure a way to tether a goat out there to trap our tigers."

"That would certainly be a hit-or-miss proposition. There are so many good-looking people in this town, how could you make them zero in on our bait?"

"It's too soon to tell," he admitted unhappily, "but both victims have been on TV. If the next one also fits the pattern, we might see if there's any common thread — time slot, channel they appeared on. It would be a long shot, again, but ... who knows? As you say, it's too early to tell."

"Or too late, if a body turns up. What do you think they'd do if one of their victims *did* manage to get the hood off and caught a glimpse of them?"

"I really don't know," Bruce admitted. "They've taken such elaborate precautions to protect their identities ... but also, in a sense, to protect their victims. Like you say, there are too many loose ends to form a proper pattern."

"I find it hard to believe that men as callous as this would really be concerned about protecting the victims," Abe replied. His facial expression reflected his distaste. "As I see it, they just don't want to commit murder. I think they assume — and at this stage they're certainly right — that their subjects aren't going to make waves, aren't going to file formal police reports. This leaves them pretty much free to keep going. If a body turns up, all hell is going to break loose. That's what they want to avoid. I don't think they give a shit about their victims' welfare."

"You're probably right," Bruce agreed. "I just hope they haven't already slipped up and hidden the evidence under a pile of rocks in the Mojave Desert."

FIVE

Lt. Pete Jackson stood up and did a couple of hard twists, listening for the satisfying little cracking sounds in his lower back. It had been the kind of day he really disliked, sitting at his desk catching up on all the paperwork he had been avoiding. At least the new office plan gave him a room with a door, not a very large room, but private enough to permit his being partially removed from the constant chaos and banter.

He was silently congratulating himself for having completed every last shred of busywork when Sgt. Holmes poked his head in the door. "Cap'n wants to see you." Newly promoted, Sergeant LeRoy Holmes had attached himself to Jackson as if the black lieutenant had been his big brother or favorite uncle.

"Do you know what it's about, Sherlock?" he asked.

Holmes beamed at the familiarity implied by the nickname. "He has a young white gentlemen in with him, suh," he replied in his best attempt at an English accent, "and the fucker's mad as hell!" he added, slipping back into his more accustomed South-Central Los Angelese. "I couldn't hear what they were sayin', but I know the kid was kicked upstairs by the detectives and it's all very hush-hush."

Jackson groaned, massaging his face with both hands, long fingers pressing on his eyes as if the contact might help them regain a proper focus. "Okay," he said. "I'm on my way." He was already intrigued, but also a little apprehensive, wondering if he was about to face some citizen's complaint.

But it wasn't unusual for the captain to call him in like this. Jackson had been a street cop, and had a well-deserved reputation as a competent, if not brilliant, investigator. Captain Marcus Fullbright was an outstanding administrator, and would probably end up commanding the Public Relations Office some day. Around forty-five years old, with silver hair and black eyebrows that gave him a senatorial appearance, he was great at placating the local citizenry and resolving the day-to-day problems of his subordinates. When it came down to the nitty-gritty of police detective work, he leaned heavily on Pete Jackson — which was fine with Pete. He liked his boss, and he suspected that Fullbright had pulled a few strings to get him assigned to this station, maybe even with the promotion board a few years back.

When he entered the captain's office, however, he immediately realized that something out of the ordinary was taking place. The young man seated in front of the desk was red in the face, sweat stains showing under his armpits and down the back of his blue work shirt. Even the captain's usually placid features were strained, and his tone was unusually curt. "Lt. Jackson," he said, "this is Harvey Simpson."

The two men nodded acknowledgment, neither extending a hand to the other. At a wave from his superior, Jackson took a seat next to the visitor — a slender, red-haired youth with a mass of freckles covering his handsome, well-proportioned features.

"Mr. Simpson has been telling me a story which..."

"It's no story!" snapped the young man. "I don't know what you..." he fumbled for a properly derogatory adjective "...you ... cops," he finally said, "...why none of you want to believe me!"

Captain Fullbright picked up a pair of reading glasses from his desk and went through the little ritual of cleaning them that Jackson recognized as one of his ploys to delay an answer. "Mr. Simpson," he said at length. "It is not that we disbelieve you. I'm sure it must have taken a great deal of courage for you to come here. It is simply that your ... your complaint is unique. Lt. Jackson is one of our most experienced investigators, and he has also dealt with many cases that were ... er, somewhat related to the type of complaint you wish to make — that is, as close as any other case is going to come."

He raised his hand to silence the objection that his visitor was obviously about to make.

"Now hear me out, Mr. Simpson. Let me try to encapsulate your problem for Lt. Jackson. Then let's hear what he has to suggest.

"Pete," he continued, swiveling his chair more directly in the lieutenant's direction, "Mr. Simpson claims that he was kidnapped from his home and subjected to an incredible sexual assault ... the details of which I shall leave for him to explain when you do a formal interview..."

"I've already explained what happened — to you and to the two others." The rage was again twisting the young man's features into a mask of unrestrained fury.

Fullbright raised his hand to silence him once more. "And you may have to tell it to several more people before we get a handle on the problem," he replied firmly. "And Lt. Jackson, here, is the best man to get an investigation under way. Pete," he continued, "I'd like you to take Mr. Simpson aside and go over the facts with him while everything is still fresh in his mind. Let's do an informal report on it for the moment. I don't think any of us wants the story to hit the media just yet."

"You're not going to shove this thing into some file cabinet and forget about it!" blurted Harvey Simpson. "I want those fuckers caught and put away!"

"I understand that, Mr. Simpson," said Jackson, speaking up before the captain could reply. He felt a tickle of excitement at the back of his neck, remembering Charlie Stuart. "Ah, Captain," he added, trying to phrase his request in a way that would not tell the kid that there had been another similar case, wondering if Fullbright might have heard a rumor. "It occurs to me that this might be a ... delicate enough situation to justify a consultant." He glanced at Harvey. "I'm sure Mr. Simpson doesn't want his face on the evening news as a rape victim, at least not until it's going to help identify the perps."

Fullbright was watching him closely, obviously trying to pick up some between-the-lines meaning. Finally he nodded. "I'm going to leave it to your own best judgment, Lieutenant," he said. "I want you to do everything you can to help Mr. Simpson, and I want you to keep me informed." He stood up, obviously relieved to be terminating the conference. He extended his hand across the desk. "Mr. Simpson, I want to thank you for having the ... er, wherewithal to come in with this."

Jackson timed his exit so that Simpson was already outside the door when he reached it. Lifting a finger as if an extraneous thought had just struck him, he asked the young man to wait a moment. He then pulled the door closed. "Captain, I think you ought to give Commissioner Javits a call. Tell him I'm taking Simpson to see Dr. MacLeod." In response to the look of consternation on his superior's face, Pete added: "Javits'll explain the whole thing to you." With that, he swung himself around the edge of the door and flashed his companion a smile that was supposed to convey both concern and friendliness.

■ ■ ■

```
CLINICAL TAPE #1: Simpson, Harvey Nicholas

Officer: I just want to set the record straight
about why I brought Harvey here to see you. Al-
though we don't have any official police com-
plaints of a similar nature, I am personally
aware that you have treated at least one patient
who reported a situation that was somewhat akin
to the story this man gave us. I know, and I
have so advised Mr. Simpson, that you are ethi-
cally bound not to discuss your other case, just
as you will be unable to discuss his with anyone
else.

Patient: I don't give a fuck about your telling
anybody what happened to me. Those assholes
broke into my house, doped me and my girlfriend,
and hauled me off to some torture chamber ...
here, look! (Patient strips off shirt to reveal
severely lacerated back and chest.) I want 'em
caught, and if I have to go on national TV to do
it, that's what I'll do!

Therapist: Let me see those wounds. (Pause)
Jesus, they really worked you over ... cut the
```

skin several places, but it all seems to be healing all right. (Pause) Okay, now I understand — and appreciate your willingness to do whatever you have to do to get these guys, Harvey. Both the lieutenant and I want to do exactly the same thing, but each of us is bound by the rules of our respective professions. If you'll cooperate with us, we'll do everything we can to help you! But making a public statement probably isn't going to do that — just the opposite. If the men who did this know that there's an active police investigation, they will make themselves even harder to find. And Harvey, have you had medical treatment for those wounds?

P: Yeah, Babs took care of it. She's a nurse. Did I tell you? She took blood, too, so it could be tested. If those bastards infected me...

O: Harvey, why don't you get ahold of yourself, and try to cooperate with the doctor. He's the best bet you've got right now.

P: All right. I've told this four times already, so I might as well do it again. And by the way, don't call me "Harvey" — makes me sound like a fuckin' rabbit. My friends call me "Harve" or "Red," because of my hair.

T: Before you tell us about the night in question, I'd like a little background on you ... your work, living situation — household, that sort of thing ... as well as your general statistics: age, education, so forth.

P: (Audible sigh and spoken in singsong tone) I'm twenty-four, white male, red hair with freckles — Irish descent. I'm five foot nine, a hundred forty pounds. I graduated high school, went to trade school and learned to be an electrician. I went into business on my own last year. I rent a house in North Hollywood — live there by myself, except that Barbara — that's my girlfriend — she stays over most of the time. I'm not a doper, and I mostly just drink beer. Uh, by the way, you wouldn't happen to have a brew, would you? I'm kinda dry.

T: Sure. Pete, would you mind? I'll take a Perrier while you're at it. Okay, now, Harve. As I understand it, you were home, asleep in bed when you were ... abducted. What do you remember about this?

P: Well, it was a hot night, so all the windows were open. Babs, she don't like air conditioning to sleep. We were lyin' there in bed, both of us bare naked on the sheets. I was out like a light, but she musta been maybe half awake, 'cause she hears something and comes to just in time to see a guy all dressed in black, with like a ski mask over his head. She got just enough of a scream out that I start to wake up, too. One of them — there were two altogether — clamps some kinda cloth over her face, and the other one jabs me in the chest with a needle. I'm up and outta the sack before I really know what I'm doing, but this big guy standin' over the bed just steps back, and as I get to my feet, man, it's like dreamtime. I'm dizzy and stumbling, and the whole place is in slow motion, and I'm gone.

Babs is out, too, except they didn't use whatever they used on me, on her. It was like chloroform or something. Anyway, they tie her up and gag her, and tie a piece of sheet around her eyes. 'Fact, they used strips of sheet to tie her up with, so I think maybe they didn't know she was going to be there. Whatever, she comes to enough to hear 'em just before they leave, and she thinks that they're ... you know, like going to rip off the TV and stuff.

O: But she didn't make a police report, did she?

P: Naw, she left that to me. See, they tied her neck to the bedpost and she was still there when I got back. She's a nursing supervisor, so she really didn't want to have it spread all over the place that she was sleeping with somebody.

O: You know, of course, that she'll have to be a witness when this comes to trial?

P: Well, let's worry about that when it happens.

O: Okay. But what did she hear? What did she tell you?

P: She said they'd driven their car up the driveway, and they carried me out to it. Then she heard them drive away. That's about it.

T: Did she hear them speak?

P: Yeah, she told me she heard one of them tell the other one to close the door. That's about all — oh, she did say that it sounded like a sliding door closing on a van — not a slam, though. They musta eased it closed so as not to make much noise.

O: Did they speak in a regular voice, or did they whisper?

P: I'm not sure — regular voice, I guess. She didn't say. 'Course, they went on like a pair of spooks with me.

O: You mean you think they were black?

P: Huh? Oh, no; I mean they talked in whispers all the time — like a pair of spooks, you know, like spies or something.

T: Interesting. So what's the next thing you remember?

P: I come to on the floor, with some kinda rubber padding under me. I'm lyin' on my back — still buck-ass naked, and they got my eyes taped shut with big pieces of — I guess — adhesive tape. They got some kind of shackles on me, so my hands are cuffed together in front of me, and there're chains connecting them to my ankles. The whole place is hot, and I'm sweating up a storm. I guess they don't know I'm conscious, 'cause I can hear 'em whispering together, but I can't make out what they're sayin'. At first I can't figure out what the fuck they're up to, kidnapping me. I haven't got any money, and there's nobody gonna pay a ransom for me. 'Course, that's before I find out they're just a couple'a queers.

O: Can you describe the shackles? Were they regular handcuffs with chains locked onto them?

P: No, I think they were made that way. 'Least I didn't feel any padlocks. But they never took 'em off my wrists, so I'm not sure how they worked. Weren't regular cuffs, though. I think they had like a cylinder on one side and a smooth curved piece that went around the wrist.

T: So you came to on the floor, and you heard them whispering together. Are you sure there were only two?

P: Yeah, just two. Anyway, I laid there for a few minutes, gettin' pretty hot under the collar — if

I'd had a collar. And finally, I yell at them. Something like: "What are you bastards doing with me?" Something like that. Then one of them, the bigger one it turns out, comes over to me and starts giving me a load of bullshit about me bein' his slave, and he's gonna to do whatever he wants to do with my body ... all that kinda crap. It's about this time I realize what their story is, and suddenly I remember Babs.

"What've you done with my girl?" I yell at 'em, and the guy smacks me across the mouth ... starts giving me some more shit about how I have to speak respectful to him. And he keeps calling me "asshole" — seems every other word. I tell him to fuck off, and ask about Babs, again. He tells me she's still back at the house. Then the other one says — all this in whispers, like a pair'a creeps — that if I don't obey them, they can always go get her and maybe me hearin' her scream'll make me behave. I tell him to keep his fuckin' hands off her, or I'll break his fuckin' head.

That's when the big guy hauls me up to my feet, and locks a chain around my neck so I have to stand up or hang myself. Then they do lock a chain onto the cuffs on my wrists, and while one of them unlocks the shackles on my ankles the other one pulls on the upper chain, so my hands are pulled up high in front of me, and the ankle cuffs are swingin' in the air — hit me in the face a couple of times.

T: Did he touch you in doing this ... more than just his hands, I mean?

P: Yeah, his whole body rubbed against me ... sweaty, like rubbing up against a slimy wall'a beef.

T: Was he dressed?

P: Naw, he was naked as me.

T: How big would you guess him to be?

P: Bigger'n me — six feet or more, and heavy.

O: Fat?

P: I'm not really sure. He felt solid enough, but he mighta been a little soft in the gut. Whatever, once he gets the chains set he gives me more gobbledygook about teaching me my "place," and he just starts whippin' the livin' shit outta me. And then I'm really mad, callin' him every name I can think of, tellin' him I'll kill him when I get loose, and he just keeps whippin' me, calling me "asshole" still, like every time he hits me — "How does that feel, asshole?" Finally, I can hear him puffing, out of breath, and he stops ... whispers something to the other guy. Then one of them, the smaller guy, I think, comes up to me and starts rubbing his hands all over me, smearing some kinda salve on me, 'specially the places where he's whipped me. But pretty soon he's playin' with my dick, rubbing the crap all over my balls and stuff. I hadn't said much at first, but now I tell him to get his fuckin' queer hands offa me, and I try to pull away, but of course I can't. He keeps playin' with me, and I just go bonkers, ya know, so fuckin' mad I guess I don't know what I'm doin', 'cause I'm choking myself on the chain, but I can't stop, and if I hadn't been steadied by having my hands chained up like they were, I'd probably've choked myself.
 Then the big one whispers something and they leave me alone, stand watching me for a couple'a minutes, I guess, while I get my balance back. One of 'em adjusts the neck chain so it's not

pressing so hard on my throat, and they go off and leave me.

T: You're sure they left you?

P: Oh, yeah, I could hear a door open and close, and they weren't there anymore. And they left me for a long time, man; I was really gettin' tired, and my arms ached from being pulled up like that. I was scared, then, I guess for the first time, 'cause I'd been so pissed off up to that point I hadn't had time to think about bein' scared. And I was worried about Babs. The thought crossed my mind that they might really'a gone back for her, and I didn't want that. Bad enough they had me.

O: Could you hear any sound, like from outside?

P: No. They had some shitty music playing, classical crap I didn't recognize, lotsa violins. Then the one comes back, the small one. He comes up to me and stands in front, takes hold'a both my arms. I think he'd been in a pool, 'cause his skin felt real cool and he had a kinda chlorine smell about him. He whispers to me that "the Master's very unhappy with you, and if you don't start to cooperate you'll just make it harder on yourself." Then he starts stroking me, again, and I'm holding back as best I can, mostly 'cause I'm thinkin' about Babs, and how they might go get her. So I just stand still until he bends over and starts to go down on me. And I can't take that, so I pull away from him and start yellin' again.
 He lets go'a me, and he says somethin' funny, then, about how "the Master gets more turned on if the slave fights him, and how I'm doing just what he wants." I calm down, I guess, and I stand there tryin' to think, and he goes down on

me again. Well, I'm so mad through all this I'm
actually outta breath. I don't try to pull away
this time, but I sure don't give him any satisfaction. Finally, he's tryin' like hell to get
me up, sucking on me and playing with me, but it
doesn't work. I stay soft. And sometime during
all this the big dude's come back, 'cause all of
a sudden, while the small one's still got hold'a
my joint, I feel a big meaty hand on my shoulder.

   This startles me, and I jump, and that starts
it all up again. I call him a "fuckin' queer"
and tell him he's the asshole and all. I feel
the small one let go'a me, and it all starts
again. They haul my hands back down, so they're
in front of my crotch again, and they relock the
shackles around my ankles. I put up some fight,
but my arms were so sore I couldn't do too much.
Then he's got that fuckin' whip, and he's
smackin' my ass and back, and when I try to turn
away he gets me on the chest and belly. I don't
think I ever stopped yellin' at him, and once
when he came near to hitting me on the cock I
got hold'a the whip and tried to hang on to it.

   I guess that did it for him, 'cause he
dropped the whip, unlocked the neck chain, and
made me hobble over to a table ... a padded
thing, and the two of them lifted me onto it,
belly down. They roped my neck to the edge, and
my ankles. One of 'em starts playing with my asshole, rubbing something into it, and I know what
they're after, and, man, I just about lose my
mind. I'm screamin' and tryin' to get loose, and
I can't do a fuckin' thing to stop 'em. The big
sonovabitch just climbs up and sticks his cock
in me. I'm still thrashing around as best I can,
but I can't move very far. He gets in and drops
his whole weight down on top of me, and humps
the shit outta me.

   Jesus, I never felt such pain! Not only is he
reaming my asshole with that barber pole'a his,

but he's thumpin' down on me and pressing the chains into my thighs and all along here, where the legs connect to the body. I think that hurt worst of all, and I'm still sore from it. But the small one was probably right, 'cause I never stopped fighting him, and he just took his time ... fucked me and slammed his hips down on me, then pulled back and lifted up a little so's I could squirm around ... laughed at me, whispered things that I'm sure, now, he just meant to goad me with ... to make me fight him all the more.

   He finally finishes, and the little one takes his turn, but he don't last very long. Then, funny, the two'a them whisper some more together, and one of 'em takes a belt to my ass, just pulverizes my butt. And without warning they jab a needle into my ass and when I come to I'm back in my own bed, my hands free, and Babs's on the floor blubbering in her gag.

O: She must have heard them come back, then?

P: Yeah. She said one of 'em crept into the house, so quiet she hardly knew he was there till he touched her ... scared her shitless, checked to make sure she was still tied up and all. Then he went out, and they came back with the car — or van, and carried me in. They never said anything, just dropped me on the bed, went out, and drove off. She said I was there better'n an hour before I came to, just as it was getting light outside.

■ ■ ■

"From what Fullbright told me, the kid's a cocky, hostile little shit," said Abe Javits, "and he's got a record — two assaults and battery." He was standing behind the bar in his Malibu condo, where an expansive wall of glass looked out across an incredible ocean vista. He had just turned off the blender, and started dipping long-stemmed margarita glasses onto a bed of rock salt. His wife, Alice, reclined in the corner of a massive white linen sofa, her ankle-length green dress and severely drawn-up hair giving her the appearance of a well-groomed Victorian lady. Bruce MacLeod was sitting at the other end, wearing gray slacks and a royal blue sports shirt. His handsome, even features were almost in silhouette against the fading spectacle of a Pacific sunset.

"I guess you'd be hostile, too, if you'd gone through what he did," Bruce replied. "But clinically — yes, I'd agree with the captain. Harvey Simpson is a basically hostile kid, but gutsy. He seems to understand exactly what's going to happen to him if he follows through on this, though, and he doesn't care. He wants to nail these bastards' asses to the wall. In a way, I'm relieved he didn't indicate wanting to work with me. He'd be a very difficult patient. And since his girl's a nurse, she's taken care of his wounds and knows when he should be tested."

"And what's happened with the other two?" asked Alice. She kicked off her sandals and drew her feet up under her, smoothing out the fabric of her skirt as Abe approached with her drink.

Bruce rubbed his chin in a moment of reflection, sighed, and shook his head. "Two very different situations," he said softly. "Charlie Stuart's about as shallow as a tide pool, but I have the feeling he could have the clue we're looking for."

"How so?" asked Abe, settling into a lounge chair facing his wife.

"He's not telling me the whole story," Bruce replied thoughtfully, "but I'm not sure just why. He's maybe embarrassed, or could be he's so intimidated by his father he's afraid that somehow I'll let something slip to him. Or, maybe he just doesn't realize that he's observed something — it doesn't occur to him to mention it. I'm really at a loss with him, and he's not on a regular schedule — won't book his next appointment when he leaves from the last one. I suspect it's the old man, again, probably thinks psychiatry is akin to some kind of liberal witchcraft."

"This sounds more like intuition than fact," Alice suggested.

Bruce grinned at her. "That's what a shrink's supposed to do, isn't it? Psych out the answers. Trouble is, other than money, this kid doesn't have much going for him ... spoiled, filled to the eyeballs with all this ultra-right-wing crap his father keeps feeding him; marginally intelligent, but repressed. You know, he doesn't even read very well — moves his lips and runs his finger down the page. The kind of help he needs would involve a lot deeper therapy than I want to get into with him. As for his aftereffects from the rape and kidnapping — well, I think they're a minor trauma, compared to all the mess that's been building up for years. But, strangely enough, all his previous defenses seem to have insulated him from the standard problems that most rape victims seem to have."

"And your other patient?" Alice urged. She took a sip from her glass and dabbed the salt off her lips with a dainty lace napkin.

Bruce sighed, leaning forward with his elbows on his knees. It took him several seconds to reply. He looked up, finally, with a boyish grin. "I'd only admit this to my nearest and dearest," he said, "but I'm ... in love with him."

"But that's wonderful!" Alice set down her glass and moved close enough to squeeze his hand.

"It might not be all that great," Abe interjected. "Didn't you tell me the guy was straight?"

"That's not the problem," Bruce assured him. "He's AC-DC — at least on an emotional level — and he's hinted around that he probably wouldn't be averse to a little game playing. Trouble is, I can't keep treating him, and right now we're on the edge of some fairly heavy things, or would be if I wanted to continue therapy with him. And these 'things' have to do with his basic sexual orientation. It's what I should steer him into, and try to help him gain some insight. But I'd feel guilty as hell doing this with him. There's the ethical implication, you see. If I hadn't been his therapist, would he feel toward me the way he does? Am I taking advantage of him when he's emotionally dependent on me? The same old problem — dates back to Freud."

"Well, of course! You know these relationships pop up all the time between shrinks and their patients," Alice insisted.

"Why worry about it? You're two people who fancy one another. You've got to give it a try, or five years from now you'll never forgive yourself."

"That's true," Bruce admitted. "He's got one more session, and then I'm going to terminate them."

"You'll accomplish more with pillow talk than you will in a formal interview, anyway," Alice assured him. "Believe me, I know."

"I hope so," Bruce replied. "I've just never been able to accept sex therapy as anything more than a doctor taking advantage of his patient."

"So where does that leave the investigation?" asked Abe, grinning as he made an obvious attempt to change the subject. "Do you think we ought to take a formal complaint from Harvey What's-His-Name? If we do that, I can get Fullbright to put a couple of men on it."

"At this point, I don't know what they'd do," Bruce told him. "You gave me the access codes, and I've been pulling up a bunch of crap off the computer. Nothing very promising, although there is one area that might be promising."

"So tell me," said Abe.

"Well, Dennie put me on to it, actually. You know I read the riot act to him about going around asking too many questions. But he has been trying to keep his ears flapping in the bars and at the various club events he goes to. Seems there was a string of quasi kidnappings about three years back — all hustlers getting picked up, then one way or another being tricked into a bondage situation. Once they were tied up, the guy did whatever he wanted to do. A couple of them got pretty well roughed up, but the perp always paid them well, so no one did anything about it. There was a write-up in one of the gay papers at the time."

"Never made official, and never picked up by the major media," Abe summarized.

"No, just some amateur detective work by a couple of gay reporters. They staked out a spot on Santa Monica Boulevard, watched their suspect pick up a hustler ... followed the guy to a house out in Silverlake. They waited outside until the two men came out — they'd tried to peek in the windows while their subjects were inside, but couldn't see or hear anything.

They tried to talk to the kid after the guy dropped him off, but he wouldn't tell them much — did admit that it got a little out of hand, but said he was happy with the bread. Anyway, they filed their story, and just after it got printed they broke into the house one night when they knew it was empty. Place had been stripped, and the owner was not cooperative, so they never knew who leased it."

"So, did you find anything in the police records? You mentioned the codes..."

"Not the police records, but the reporters had gotten a license number on the car the guy used. It was in their news story, but the plates were apparently stolen."

"Well, that didn't tell you much, then," said Alice.

"No, except that they were stolen in Bel Air. And this set me to thinking. You know, we've assumed from the start that this perp has money. I think this just confirms it. He must have felt comfortable in that area. Stop a minute to consider. If you were going to cop a set of license plates, would you go to Bel Air, of all places ... with all those big houses with walls around them, the extra security patrols?"

"You may be grasping at straws," replied Abe ruefully, "but I have to agree with your thinking. It also goes along with our assumption that he — they — come from the west side."

"Then you're looking for a big, rich guy who lives somewhere in the Bel Air–Westwood area," suggested Alice. She crossed her ankles delicately and reached for a cigarette from the mirrored box on the table before her.

"We can also assume that he's living as a single man — maybe divorced or widowed, but living alone at the moment, or maybe with a boyfriend," Bruce added.

"And he has a van," Abe continued. "But if he's rich he probably doesn't use it except during his hunting trips. What about the doctor angle? Have you had any more ideas on that?" He gathered up the glasses on a chrome-edged tray and returned to the bar.

"I don't think he's a doctor," said Bruce. "I listened to the tape of my interview with Harve Simpson a couple of times, and Pete Jackson told me about his interview with the girlfriend. They definitely knocked her out with chloroform, not ether or some other more commonly used anesthetic. Also,

Pete saw the strips of sheet they tied her with. The kid had cut them off, so most of the knots were still intact. He says they weren't what you'd expect a doctor to tie."

"That's sort of thin, isn't it?" asked Alice.

"True," Bruce admitted, "but I also find it hard to credit that a practicing physician is going to be out prowling around so late at night. Add together all the bits and pieces; it just doesn't feel right."

"Okay, then where are they getting their supplies?" asked Abe. He came back with a tray of fresh margaritas, passing them out as he spoke.

"I'm inclined to feel it would be more productive to try for the source of his other equipment. That set of irons he used on Harve, for instance. They sound to me like English shackles, with Hiatt cuffs. And that being the case — especially if he just got them and was trying them out, we might get a line on where they came from. There aren't many places in this country that sell them."

"You want some cops to do the legwork?" asked Abe.

"I don't think most of these suppliers are going to give a cop the time of day," Bruce replied. "I've got Dennie working on it. He knows several guys in the business. Of course, as closeted as this guy probably is, he might be getting his stuff mail order, from out of state."

"Then he'd have to give an address," Alice suggested.

"Unless he's using a mail drop ... mailing service," said Abe, thoughtfully. "Now there's someplace where we could use a police team."

"Might be worth a shot," Bruce agreed. "I'm afraid, though, that we're going to have to make some waves before we get any answers."

"Well, this Simpson guy seems willing. Should we go to the media with it?" asked Abe. "We can't keep it buried forever ... and if they do kill someone we're going to get a lot of heat for not warning people ... not that it would do much good if people did know, but it sounds better if the department's made the effort."

"Why don't you get Fullbright to put those two detectives on it for a few days — the ones who initially interviewed Harve. They already know about the assaults, anyway, and they might turn up something. Those irons would make a fairly heavy package. Someone might just happen to remember it. If possible they might also check out that house in Silverlake. It's a long shot, again — probably not the same perp, but I'd like to know who leased the place three years ago. Smells like money, again, so who knows?"

"I think it's interesting," Alice remarked, "that they used tape over the victim's eyes instead of putting a hood on him in this hot weather."

"Yes, also that they seem to have given up when he resisted so violently," Bruce agreed.

"Or they wanted to get him back before the girl got loose, or before someone found her," Alice added. "Or ... doesn't it sound to you as if they might have some concern not to do some permanent damage to their victims?"

"I have to admit that this is the most puzzling aspect of the whole thing," Bruce agreed. "He obviously doesn't want to kill, but he has no qualms about kidnapping, rape, physical abuse. He has to be a really strange man, with a very complex set of standards. The abuse of his victims seems to be getting progressively heavier, but that could also be a reflection of their degree of resistance."

"He has to be a real nut case," Abe said grimly. "I just hope we can nail him before he decides to change his standards. Remember, rape has also been called 'incomplete murder.'"

The heavy wooden doors to the dining room slid open, and Rita, the Javitses' Salvadoran housekeeper, announced that dinner was ready. Alice took Bruce's arm, remarking as they moved toward the table: "We're going to do this again very soon, and next time it's going to be a foursome."

SIX

"Dr. MacLeod? This is Harve Simpson. I'm sorry to disturb you on a Sunday morning, but I've just thought of something."

Bruce groaned and looked up at the bedside clock — 10:30. *Guess it's late enough so I'm fair game. Should have been up an hour ago.* "Yes, Harve, what have you got?"

"Ah, I don't know if I should even bring this up ... kinda silly, maybe, but..."

"If it's really silly we can just forget about it later," said Bruce. "Why not let me be the judge?"

"Okay, you asked for it," Harve continued hesitantly, "but you remember I told you the 'Master' kept calling me 'asshole'? Well, ah, about four or five weeks ago I had a run-in — in traffic, you know. This big dude in a gold Cadillac convertible. He got real ticked off at me 'cause I laid on the horn and called him 'asshole' when he was hoggin' the road and wouldn't move over. Afterwards, he followed me for better'n a block, and I thought he was gonna run me over the side or something. Then, with all these stories about nuts with guns shooting people over traffic arguments ... I took off as fast I could and lost him."

"That's all?" asked Bruce.

"Yeah, that's it," said Harve.

"Well, thanks, Harve. I'll ... I'll make a note of it."

"Yeah. Sorry to have disturbed you, Doc, but you did say to let you know if anything came to mind."

■ ■ ■

Bruce had purposely arranged Frank's appointment for late Monday afternoon, then had asked his patient to stay for a drink and some "gourmet leftovers" — which Dennie had prepared especially for the occasion. Although he suspected that Frank must realize something less incidental was afoot, each had played his part in the supposedly casual conversation that had followed. They had become so comfortable together after nearly two months of therapy, the subterfuge was not difficult for either.

Now, as the two men sat close to each other in the darkness of the gazebo, looking out over the twinkling lights between Beverly Hills and the beach, their conversation was proceeding in starts and jumps, neither completely at ease any longer. Frank sensed the uncertainty in Bruce's demeanor, and did, in fact, suspect the reason for it. It reminded him of the first time he'd kissed a girl, wanting to do it, but afraid to make the move. *But she wanted me to do it, just as I want Bruce to say ... what I think he wants to say. At least, I think I want him to say it.*

"I guess the only way to do this is to tell it as it is," said Bruce at length. "So, at the risk of sounding blunt and unemotional about the whole thing ... well, I'm terminating your sessions because I'm ... attracted to you."

"That's all?" asked Frank. Bruce's statement had certainly not caught him off guard, except that he hadn't expected Bruce to state his case so candidly. Yet his own response was also inadequate, and he knew it as soon as he spoke. But despite the warm surge Bruce's words caused within his loins, despite the urge to acknowledge his own reciprocal desire, he could not bring himself to do it. He had never in all his life admitted more than a casual interest in another man. But more, for the first time in their relationship he sensed his being in a position of ascendancy ... power. If he admitted his true feelings, Bruce would be back in control. Of course, he had left the door open for this to happen by his admissions a week ago, although that might be construed as a moment of vacillation, of weakness. To repeat such sentiments now would be tantamount to a commitment.

"That's all. Unless ... Dammit, Frank, you're smart enough to know what I'm saying to you." Bruce had allowed him plenty of time to say something else. He hadn't, and there was now a touch of annoyance in the other's voice. But this provided the necessary stimulus — that and the sense of total privacy provided by their surroundings. Frank leaned across the space between them and placed one hand on his companion's knee. "Are you saying that you'd like a toss in the sack with me, or are you hinting at something more?" Frank asked softly. The fact that the constriction in his throat prevented a more strident response was lost on neither of them.

"I'm saying that I think I'm in love with you, Frank," Bruce replied honestly. "I'm saying that I've had fantasies involving the two of us ... in a relationship that is certainly more than a quick toss in the sack." He paused, then cleared his throat, wishing he hadn't quit smoking, feeling a tension that had evaded him for years. "I don't think I can put it any more plainly than that. I know I'm not saying this very well, and I'm not making a properly romantic moment out of it, but I want you to understand the situation for what it is. I know what I'm asking of you, but in spite of that remark you made last week I'm not sure you're ready for it. I ... I don't like to put myself in the position of seducer, and I don't want to place you in a situation that's so uncomfortable that you ... maybe feel compelled to do something you don't want to do, or to do it before you're really ready."

"It's sort of a 'last chance' situation, then, isn't it?" Frank replied. "I mean, if I'm not coming for my sessions, and if I don't say something now..."

Bruce placed his hand over Frank's. "That's why it's been so difficult for me," Bruce admitted. "By terminating the sessions I'm cutting off a contact I don't want to lose. But, even if you have, uh, reciprocal feelings ... well, I know you might still be reluctant to admit them, or give in to them, regardless of what you said to me last week."

"You've thought about this a lot, haven't you?"

"Of course I have. Frank, I'll tell you, I haven't felt like this toward anyone in a long time. You know I'm not going to bullshit you." He felt his companion's hand stir slightly beneath his own. Gradually it turned, coming palm up to meet and grasp Bruce's fingers as he returned the pressure. Frank rose slowly to his feet. "I don't know where this is going to end, Bruce. It's all so different for me, against..."

In the next moment they were pressed together in the dim interior of the wooden shell, their bodies driving one against the other, lips seeking, locking in intense exchange. For each, it was the release of a terrible emotional burden, a surrender to the desire that had lain unacknowledged, forcefully denied. Each for his own reasons had done this. Now the curtain seemed to be rising on an entirely new horizon. And this brought a tremendous sense of relief, as well. They might be forced to display some false façade for others, but within their own private world there need no longer be any secret, any denial of their true desires.

Yet the outside world still existed, and as Frank felt his body yielding to their mutual desire, a part of his mind refused to let go of reality. He had a budding career that had been his life's ambition, and this relationship could easily spell its demise. And his family — his parents, his brother. What of them? How was he going to tell them? For several moments these thoughts continued to struggle against the swelling pressures of his lust. But Bruce was holding him, working his fingers between their bodies, unfastening the buttons on Frank's shirt.

A warm hand caressed his chest, riffling the hair between his pecs. The cloth had been pushed back onto his shoulders, and he now felt it sliding down his body ... a cool stirring of air across his back, then Bruce's hands displacing it, warming his skin, pulling him forward into a frantic embrace.

They were both naked to the waist, their lips locked again in unrestrained contact. It was so strange to kiss another guy, a man, to feel the roughness of his day's growth of beard instead of the flaccid smoothness of a woman. So different, so overwhelming. He felt Bruce's mouth draw back, the face coming into partial focus as their bodies moved slightly apart. Then the warm moistness of the other's lips touched his nipple, the tongue probing, teeth grasping gently, holding, pulling, bringing him to the verge of pain, then backing off. No one had ever done this to him before. He had never realized the depth of sensation a man could have in that part of his being.

He was reeling, almost dizzy. All the extraneous fears and anxieties were momentarily banished. He wanted everything that was happening to him, and more. He wanted to experience the totality of this physical exchange, and whatever the consequences he would deal with them later. Bruce's hands were unbuckling his belt, opening the buttons on his jeans, pulling the denim free of his waist. It was a moment of wild abandon, unrestrained passion — standing in the open, concealed only by darkness from the multitudes who moved about those distant lights, who drove the cars that swooshed along the boulevard only a few hundred yards away.

Then they were both completely naked, working their feet free of shoes and socks, standing together, balancing each other. Tentatively, Frank ran his hand down Bruce's body, felt the hard wall of his abdomen, traced a path through the thickness of his pubes, felt the base of his cock, hesitated as he touched its solid, springy tension. Again, a new dimension. To fondle, caress the genitals of another man ... to do it willingly, not in fear, not forced as he had been a few weeks before.

The recall made him pause, brought back a flash of the revulsion he had felt in those other moments. But since that time his own fantasies had altered the original perceptions ... then the other fantasies ... of Bruce in a condition similar to this, but less ... not outdoors, not naked in this esoteric setting. The reality was even more exciting than he had been able to imagine. And the maniacs — the ones who'd forced him, raped him ... even his memory of their mistreatment had been altered in the camera of his mind. Somehow, the pain and humiliation seemed less important, less the dominant theme of his memories. In retrospect the sexual contacts were now more poignant, more thrilling. He knew that Bruce shared their tastes in sex ... but not the unrestrained selfishness of taking another against his will. With Bruce it would be different, even more exciting than those few moments during his captivity when he had been compelled to commit the acts he knew now he had secretly desired, but compulsively denied.

He held Bruce's penis in his hand, stroked it, felt the velvet skin slide smoothly over its hard, distended core. He played his thumb across the crown, sensed the responding tremor in his partner's grasp, strong hands holding his upper arms, pulling them together until their cocks were touching, rubbing across each other, projecting into one another's groin. He continued to hold Bruce's sex in the curve of his palm, reaching for his own organ in the darkness. Then he brought the heads together, slid his foreskin over the other's projecting, unshielded shaft, joined them for a moment in the darkness.

"Are you ready to go inside?" Bruce asked. His voice was husky, and Frank could define the twin pulse beats against his fingers. He relaxed his grip and felt Bruce slide free. His own body was trembling — not from cold. All about him the atmosphere was warm, the air, Bruce's towering form, his own desire, lust, craving.

Suddenly, Frank was fighting back tears. He wrapped his arms around the larger, more heavily built form of his companion. His mouth now sought the contact, and it was at *his* volition that they hung together, a hard, passionate contact. Finally, as their lips parted, he forced his voice to become steady. "This is the first time in my life that I've been able..."

"I know," Bruce whispered.

"...to express it ... physically, to admit..."

"Let's go inside." Bruce urged him forward by the pressure of his arm about Frank's torso, guiding him through the shadows, shrubs and leafy branches grazing their nakedness.

■ ■ ■

Later, a long time later, they lay in the lassitude of mutual satisfaction, resting against the steps in the shallow end of the pool. Cool water lapped around their necks as their bodies swayed in the semiweightlessness, touching and drifting apart.

"How are we going to handle your friends?" asked Frank, after a protracted period of silence.

"Which friends?"

"You know, the police commissioner and his wife. You said you wanted me to meet them, but they know you've been treating a ... rape victim. They'll know it's me, won't they? I know you said they're the only ones, other than Dennie, but I'm still a little ... shy about the whole thing."

"Abe and Alice are so involved in their own games, they won't give it a second thought," Bruce assured him. "And they sure as hell won't blab it around."

"What games are they into?" asked Frank. His hand slid across Bruce's thigh, grasping him in a tentative gesture that had been so totally foreign only a few hours before. He felt the water-shrunken flesh respond to his touch, which encouraged him to retain his hold.

"They're into SM games," Bruce told him plainly. "Het stuff, of course, but they understand male relationships, respect them ... certainly seem to respect me. At least, they're about as close friends as I have, after Dennie."

"Hum." Frank leaned his head back, resting on the pool edge, never relinquishing his grip on Bruce's lengthening penis. "And is that where you'd like us to go next ... into some kind of kinky action?"

"If you think you'd enjoy it. I don't want to hurry you, though, don't want to force you." He leaned toward Frank's body, bringing himself into partial contact along their sides. The exchange of warmth contrasted with the coolness of the water, and a second later they were tightly grasping one another, feeling the pressure reigniting them.

"But I thought force was the name of the game," Frank whispered. "Wouldn't you like to force me, tie me down and make me do whatever you want?"

"Yeah." Bruce's lips crushed down on his, and Frank felt his body slipping deeper into the water. He held his breath as his head went under, and they both came up spluttering, laughing together, each still enthralled at the experience of their physical contact. A thin crescent moon had risen just above the treetops, casting a faint silvery glow over the area.

"Oh, Bruce!" came Dennie's voice from the shadows by the house. "I'm sorry. I didn't mean to disturb you, but I thought I heard someone out here." He advanced a couple of steps, then seemed to realize who it was in the pool with his friend. "Is that you, Frank?"

"Yeah, it's me."

"Well, it's about time! I thought you guys were never going to get it on."

Bruce felt Frank's hand tighten on his own. "It's okay," he said softly. "Has to be okay."

"I know." Frank released his hold and propped himself up, sitting on the second step so that his upper body was out of the water. "What time is it, Dennie?" he asked.

"Close to two o'clock. Our meeting went late down at the Center. Oh, by the way, Bruce, they want to set up a new group session if you can handle it ... whatever night you're free — for guys who are HIV-negative and are having trouble handling their guilt, or whatever."

The casual attitude on the part of both the others had a quieting effect on Frank, the very naturalness of their relationship and lack of concern about their own or anyone else's sexual preferences. It was something new to him, but it seemed less than foreign ... comfortable in a way. He drew closer to Bruce, not in any sense of defiance, but simply because he knew he could do it, and that it wouldn't matter, that his open display of affection would be totally accepted.

Bruce slipped his arm around Frank's shoulder, and for a moment Dennie seemed uncertain. "Ah, I'll leave you guys alone if you like," he said, "but I was hoping to have a word with Bruce before he went to bed."

"We've already been to bed." Frank laughed, proud of his ability to take it this lightly.

"I can see that," Dennie replied. "Anyway, congratulations. I hope it's going to be worth the wait for both of you."

"It already has been," Frank replied, surprising everyone — most of all himself. But he was happy, almost giddy, certainly more at home in this setting than any other he had been in since coming to the West Coast. He couldn't understand it, and for the moment he really didn't care.

"Look, I won't impose on you two lovebirds for very long," said Dennie, "but, Bruce, I've been thinking about that call from Harve Simpson this morning. You know, if this perp is as nutty as we think he is, why couldn't an argument in traffic set him off? And Harve said he was a big guy. You really think it's not possible?"

"I guess anything's possible," Bruce replied, "but we've got so many long shots already."

"Maybe," Dennie agreed, "but I kept thinking about it, and I figure if it did go down this way, then the big guy would have to check out Harve's address. Maybe that's why he followed him for that extra block — to get the license number. And that means he had to get the data from DMV. Don't you suppose they keep records of requests like that?"

"I think they do, but it's not on their computer. It isn't something I can tap into, anyway."

"What's this all about?" asked Frank. "You think the 'Master' went after someone because of a traffic hassle?"

"Why not?" Dennie responded. "Shit, they're out there shooting one another over freeway incidents. Why couldn't a traffic hassle trigger a nut like this to pick the guy for a sex victim?"

Bruce and Dennie continued their discussion for a minute or two, while Frank slipped lower in the water, his own thoughts cutting off their conversation. "Bruce," he said finally, "this whole thing's so crazy, but ... I had a peculiar incident a while back. I'm trying to think just when, but it must have been a month or less before ... before they grabbed me."

"You get in a traffic squabble?" asked Dennie.

"No, it was in that new bistro in Beverly Hills."

"So, tell us what happened," Dennie urged. He pulled up a lawn chair and sat beside the water, crossing his legs and taking out a cigarette.

"Well, it didn't seem like anything at the time, but Rufus took me to dinner at the restaurant. We were supposed to discuss a movie deal with this young producer. But the guy was kind of a flake, and I was sure he didn't have the backers he needed. Rufus liked him, though, so they got into sort of a drinking bout. Rufus can really put it away, you know. Anyhow, we were there for maybe two and a half, three hours, and when it came time to pay the bill this phony producer stalled until Rufus picked up the tab."

"What condition were *you* in?" Dennie asked.

"Oh, I was okay," Frank assured him. "I'd only had Perrier before dinner and a couple of glasses of wine with the meal. And it's a good thing, because Rufus was in no shape to drive. That's what caused the trouble. We left after the so-called producer was gone, and on the way out Rufus tripped and almost knocked over a table. One of the men sitting there — a big guy, by the way — he gets up, madder'n hell, called Rufus a bunch of names, including 'fat kike son of a bitch.'

"So Rufus wants to haul off and hit him, and the other guy's all ready to go for it. I stepped in and dragged him out, although I was real pissed about it, too. I didn't like what he called Rufus. Still, I tried to calm them down, but that didn't satisfy this other guy. He was wearing a light-colored slacks suit, and some wine had spilled on it. He was really sore, so he followed us to the door, still yelling at Rufus, but then finally at me for ... Jesus! I ... he called me a Spic! Then he took a swing at me and I decked him. He must have still been sitting there on his ass when they brought the car around — my car, you see, because I'd picked Rufus up at his office. I purposely didn't look back at the guy, so I'm not sure what he was doing. The manager and at least one waiter had come outside by then, too, and they were trying to calm him down. I don't know if he got the license number, but he sure could have."

"I wonder if they'd remember who it was," mused Dennie.

"If he used a credit card..." Frank began.

"It would take an official police inquiry before they'd give out the information," Bruce reminded them. "But it's beginning to sound promising. Can you remember who else was at the table?"

Frank leaned back thoughtfully. "There was a woman, middle-aged, very made-up with a big black beehive hairdo. Sort of hard-looking. I particularly remember her, because she tried to pull the big guy back. Then there was a kid, I think, young, kind of handsome guy in his early twenties ... and a girl, I guess. Yeah, a girl about his age. I didn't get a very good look at her, or at the kid either for that matter. It was all going so fast, I don't think I'd recognize either of the younger ones."

"But you'd know the big guy?" This from Dennie.

"Yeah, I think so. But it's been, what ... three, maybe four months. I'm not real sure, but yeah, probably."

"Can you picture him in your mind?" asked Bruce.

Frank sighed. "Sort of," he said. "Let me think about it. Right now, though ... if you'll excuse us, Dennie, there's something I have to show Bruce." Underwater, he took hold of his friend's hand and guided it into his own groin, where his renewed desire was manifest.

■ ■ ■

"Sure. They're all kept on what they call 'Form 70s,'" said Pete Jackson. He was in the outer office, taking Bruce's call at the phone on LeRoy Holmes's desk. "But you're right. They don't put them on the computer, and I'm not sure how long they keep them — a few months, at least, I'd think."

LeRoy set down two styrofoam cups of coffee and went back to pick a donut from the community tray. Jackson watched him concentrate on the limited selection remaining. "But you know, Doctor, the DMV has something like a hundred and seventy offices in the state, and ... Well, locally there's ... let's see: Hollywood, Culver City, Santa Monica, Van Nuys ... Sure, if Commissioner Javits gives the word they can do it. How many names are we looking for?" He grinned to himself, expecting Bruce to indicate only the two known victims. "Three?" he said in surprise. "Did your secret source decide to come forward? ... Sure, they can keep it confidential." LeRoy was back with one glazed and one powdered-sugar donut that he set on the desk beside the cups of coffee. Pete placed the receiver back in the cradle.

Wonder what brought the other guy around, he thought. *And why DMV records? This amateur sleuthing is getting just a little out of hand ... commissioner cooperating, using police personnel, but no official file open on the case. Something's going to hit the fan if they don't all start playing by the rules.* Absently, he picked up his coffee and immediately scalded his lips. Holmes was occupied dunking his glazed confection in his cup. "LeRoy, you ever have to hunt through DMV Form 70s to find someone?"

"Sure did. Takes forever. You know how many requests those guys get? Hundreds — thousands. It was worse than the time I had to rut through library checkout slips. And half them muthers don't write so good. Like tryin' to read a doctor's prescription."

"Which office would be the most likely to handle requests from Westwood or Bel Air?" He frowned as he tried to dunk his donut, and it left a sugary film across the surface of his coffee.

"Culver City," Holmes replied. He had been concentrating on his own breakfast, and only looked up when he answered the lieutenant's question. He was puzzled by the expression of concern on the other's features. "Somethin' wrong?" he asked.

"Just this shitty donut you picked out for me," replied Jackson, but there was something much more serious plaguing his thoughts. In spite of himself he couldn't help liking Bruce MacLeod, although the guy was surely queer. And, like most policemen, Pete Jackson was normally contemptuous of queers. But the idea of his handling this investigation, almost in the role of a ranking cop — that *did* bother him. He could see the rationale behind it, assumed the chief knew what was going on. But it wasn't right.

"Sure there isn't somethin' bugging you?" asked LeRoy.

Jackson forced a smile. "Nah, nothing really. It's just some things ... well, sometimes they just ain't fittin', Miss Scarlett. They just ain't fittin'."

■ ■ ■

"That guy was sure pissed, Dad. Why'd you pick him, anyway?" The young man stretched lazily on the big bed, watching his father as the older man worked a tie under his stiffly starched collar. "He was good-lookin' enough, but we never had one fight like that."

"We fucked up," replied his father, turning now to face him. "It's what I've told you before, only I didn't stick to my own rules. That's the only way we can lose the game," he added. "We didn't check out that house closely enough — didn't know the woman would be there."

"Yeah, well, it's a good thing we had the chloroform along. That was good planning, wasn't it? Made everything work okay." He twisted his slender body against the black-and-white pattern of the lower sheet, pushing back the other coverings. His dad liked that, he knew, being able to look at him naked on the bed.

"It wasn't good planning," insisted the older man. He leaned forward, checking the lay of his curly salt-and-pepper hair in the mirror, smiled at the reflection of his son behind him. He turned then, forcing his face into a more serious expression.

"But the woman could have been a disaster. You know these he-men types aren't likely to file police reports. But the cunt might have, if she'd gotten free before we came back. She'd a'been hysterical, and we'd have had to leave him somewhere besides his house. The bloodhounds would have been on the scent for sure."

"Someone's going to cop out eventually, anyway," observed the boy. "It's gotta be just a matter of time, don't you think?"

"Maybe. But, you know, I've got a feeling the guy who'd know for sure would be that shrink. If the cops don't want to make it official, they might just use this guy. After all, that Jew Javits sent you there right off. They've used him as consultant on a batch of cases, and I think he's written some things for the FBI. Think you could handle him again?"

"I don't know, Dad, he's a real sharp man. When I get in that office with him, I don't know. It's like I'm in a tennis game with a pro, and me the beginner. He asks questions that you don't expect, and when you think he's going to follow up — and you've got the answer all ready for him — he goes on to something else. Then, in case he misses something, he makes a tape of the session. He can play it back again and again."

The big man sat on the bed, allowing his hand to stroke the inside of his son's thigh — an almost absent motion, yet one calculated to rouse the boy's desires. "You can handle it, son," he said evenly. "I know you can take on anyone, just like me. Remember, you're part of me. Keep that in the back of your mind. We're more than just a father and son." His fingers played with the young man's pubic hairs, curled them around the tips, palm pressing down on the tumescent cock. "Besides, isn't it time to have another AIDS test?"

"Not yet," whispered the boy. He wished his father would throw off his clothes, forget about his meeting, and take him down to the Room. He swallowed hard. "But, I guess I could make like I'm anxious about it. Or you could call him. If you lay it on thick enough he'll probably suggest I come by." In his mind's eye he thought of Dennie — big guy, very like his father ... younger, a little better-looking, with his close-cropped hair and beard. That first day, when he'd stripped off at the pool, he'd thought ... hoped really, that he could provoke some response. But Dennie had acted like he didn't see anything in the other's actions. *But that's how a straight man's going to act ... not pay any attention if another guy runs around naked. That's how it is in locker rooms and gyms, probably in the service. Nobody thinks twice about one man being naked in front of another. I'd sure like to see him naked! Big hands and arms, probably got a big cock. Christ, Dad'd kill me if he knew. But I'm queer, really queer, not like Dad.*

He watched his father leave the room. *Then what is Dad, really? He hates queers like he hates niggers and Spics. What he's doing now, what he's done with me ... that's queer, but it's not the same ... somehow it's not. He doesn't go to fag bars and wear clothes that are either effeminate or exaggerated butch. He doesn't have queer friends, not except for me. And I am his friend, his best friend, the only one he really trusts. Nobody else knows anything about him, really, no one except me.* He hugged himself and twisted again on the bed, hand stealing down to his crotch, where his passion still displayed itself. *I wish Dad would lay off these other guys for a while, though ... take me downstairs and really give me some of what he gives them ... hasn't done that since we first set the place up, and he wanted to try it out — and that once, with the first guy, when he tied me up against him and whipped us both.* He slipped naked off the bed, gripping his risen sex as he moved to the window. His father's car was gone — the Mercedes this time. And the gardener's truck had left as well. It was Thursday, help's day off. He was alone in the house. He grinned to himself and picked up his keys from the chest, padded across the room and down the stairs to the basement, to the secret room, *their* room, that no one else in the world knew existed ... well, except for the doctor. But he really didn't count. He was ancient, and he was Dad's oldest friend — not real close, though. Not like Charlie.

And that was the most important aspect, after all. He alone shared the totality of this secret with his father. He alone was the true object of the great man's affection. No one else mattered a damn to him. These others were just bodies to be played with, used, and later tossed aside. They shared these almost sacred moments, neither betraying the other's trust. They were lovers, although his father would never call it that. But they were. They were welded together in their passion and their sharing of this secret place, and all that happened there.

That doctor friend of Dad's had been asked by to watch a couple of times, had shown them how to use the rubber stuff and the needles, but he had never shared in their activities, and had only been there on the mutual invitation of the two of them. In that respect he was no more than another piece of equipment, a necessary asset to their adventures. Only Charlie and his dad shared it all, shared every aspect of their lives — no secrets, one from the other.

■ ■ ■

Bruce moved from one of the big leather chairs in his office to the other. The afternoon sun had shifted, and with it the light pattern in the room. He had been trying to read the book that one of his fellow doctors had given him — the volume that had created such a stir at the Center ... an AIDS memoir, written by the surviving partner after the death of his lover. *Beautifully written, certainly touching. But it misses the point in a way ... aside from the disease itself, the biggest problem these guys had was whether to attend a black-tie party or not, or which of seven bank accounts they should use to pay the bills. Most of the guys I work with are struggling to maintain some semblance of human dignity, trying to keep a roof over their heads. Just getting enough to eat, and the big bucks it takes to pay for their medication ... especially if they're trying one of the experimental things that aren't on the prescription lists. But it hits all segments; each guy has his own set of problems. This is how it was for this particular pair of lovers, and after all the guy wasn't trying to tell the story of the whole community. All very real for each...*

In a way, their story is closer to my life space than otherwise. I'm not poor, either, thanks to Abe Javits. If an HIV infection should ever become a problem for Frank or me, that's how it'd be for us ... not the scrounging these poor kids go through at the Center. Frank and me, he thought. *God, what an incredible difference that little phrase is making in my life!*

He put the book aside with a sigh, and turned his attention to the tape player, where he had one of Charlie's tapes on the spindle. *Worried about his HIV test again. Can't seem to convince him he has to wait it out. Tough at his age, though ... tough at any age, but any adversity is going to be strange to a kid like this. Has the world by the tail, unless this fucking disease becomes a factor — just about the only thing that could knock it all into nothing ... like it has for so many others.*

He wound the tape back and started it again, listening to the conversation for the umpteenth time. "Something's just not right, kid," he muttered. "Why can't I quite believe you?" The somewhat whiny voice droned on from the speaker: "...tied my cock and balls up with rawhide..."

Bruce sat up and tapped the "stop" button, wound the tape back: "...with rawhide..." *Now, how did you know that, you little shit? Your hands were tied; you couldn't see. How did you know it was rawhide, not just a piece of clothesline? Did you guess? Did one of them say they were using rawhide? Interesting. Are you playing games with me, kid, or was it just a guess?*

He wound the tape back and took it out of the player. *Maybe I'm going a little balmy. Kid's probably trying to remember all the details he can ... just assumed it was rawhide and stated it as fact. After all, why should he lie to me?* Why indeed?

He checked his watch. Just time for a quick snack before his next patient. Charlie Stuart's problem would have to wait, and he psyched himself up for the impending session. Middle-aged man with a young, sexually demanding wife. And the poor bastard couldn't get it up anymore. *Nothing physically wrong — wife just puts too much pressure on him. Some counselors would tell him to take her across his knee and show her who's boss. Might solve the whole problem, at that. Wonder how that suggestion would go over in the somber atmosphere of the session.* He laughed to himself, trying to picture the expression of shock on his patient's face if he ever suggested something so outrageous. He continued into the kitchen, where Dennie had left him a sandwich and glass of milk.

■ ■ ■

"Dr. MacLeod! Hi! Pete Jackson, here."

"Well, hi yourself, Pete Jackson here. What's up?"

"You sound pretty chipper, Doc. Somebody give you a shot in the ass?"

Bruce laughed, wondering if there was a double entendre in the policeman's remark. "No," he replied, "but I just helped a patient get it up for his lovely wife."

"You're a genius, Doc."

"I know. All in a day's work. But you sound a little chipper yourself."

"Well, I got some good news and some bad news," Jackson told him. "The dicks drew a blank on the mailing services. Nobody remembers a big guy receiving a heavy package. That's the bad news. Good news: they start at the Culver City DMV office first thing tomorrow morning."

"What's so good about that?" asked Bruce. "They haven't got anything, yet."

"The good thing is, they gotta do it, not me," Jackson returned lightly. "But I thought you'd be happy to know that the commissioner got it cleared, so the legwork is actually in process. God knows how long it's going to take, or whether they'll actually do any good."

"You sound doubtful," Bruce remarked.

"As you said yourself, it's a long shot," the detective reminded him.

"Well, let me know if they find anything," said Bruce.

As he hung up the phone, Pete Jackson's façade of levity melted away. *Acts like he has a right to all this stuff. 'Course he does, 'cause the brass says he does. Well, maybe they're right. He does seem to be working his ass off on the case, and he's smart — no denying that. Yeah, maybe they're right. Leastwise, I hope they're right. Maybe it takes one to catch one, but I'll be damned if I'm going to report to some civilian. Whatever I get from now on goes strictly through channels, then they can tell him, if they think he oughta know.*

SEVEN

Bruce was at his computer, where he'd been hacking until the screen was starting to blur in front of his eyes. Frank had long since given up his stance behind the chair, watching the series of letters and digits that seemed always to end in either "access denied" or "syntax error." Because the machine was located beside Dennie's desk, in the hall outside Bruce's office, the big man had wandered like a displaced refugee until he decided to join Frank in the backyard.

"Our genius is still at it," he said, settling onto a chaise beside Frank.

"Why's he having so much trouble? I thought his friend Abe got him all the access codes."

"He's got the police codes, and apparently the FBI access codes he already had are still good, but he's after records of corporate filings. Things that are supposed to be available for public perusal, but they make it as hard as possible to access them." Dennie looked across at Frank's trim body, glistening from the tanning cream, white patch around his waist and loins gradually darkening to match the rest of his midsummer coloring — darker still, his sun-swollen cock and deeply suspended testicles that fell casually across one thigh. Dennie forced his gaze to travel to a higher spot on the sculptured perfection of his best friend's lover.

"Last I looked, he was working on something called Sportsplan General, A.G., some kind of European corporation," Frank replied. His eyes were closed beneath his sunglasses, but he could sense Dennie's interest, secretly enjoyed it. The initial sense of distance he had felt for this closest of Bruce's friends was beginning to dissipate. There was no justification for jealousy, he realized, except that the two of them had shared so much, had done so for such a long time. But they certainly had never been a "couple," and Dennie seemed just as open and honest with him as Bruce was. More than this he recognized the big man's genuine pleasure at the relationship. There was no rivalry between the two friends, he realized, just a genuine respect and sincere regard — love? *Like brothers,* he thought, *deep and lasting. Only hope our kind of love can last as long, become as solid.*

"He hit on the Sports-whatever last night," Dennie said. "It's apparently the holding company that owns the American corporation, which in turn used to own that house where the creep took his hustlers to work them over ... what, four years ago? Pete Jackson's guys tried to check the old rental records, but nobody remembers, and the files have been conveniently lost. The cops are also looking for the reporters who did the original story in the gay newspaper, but one of them's apparently dead, and the other's back east someplace."

"How 'bout the DMV records?" Frank asked.

"Nothing on that, yet, but I've got a feeling that Jackson, or Jackson's boss, is dragging his feet. Those two hot-shot dicks were supposed to have starting sifting the records a couple of days ago, so you'd think there'd be something by this time — a negative report, if nothing else."

"I'm surprised they've let Bruce go it alone this far," Frank returned. He pulled the back up on his chair, and took his glasses off to look more directly at Dennie. "Cops are always so jealous in guarding their territory, but Bruce seems to have a way with them."

"Bruce has a way with everyone," Dennie laughed. "When I call him a genius, I'm not really kidding ... and they know it. He's turned out a lot of good stuff for them, and the top brass have insisted on keeping him on a retainer arrangement. So, in actuality, he *is* working for them. And on a case like this, where even the cops don't want the story in print ... or even in an official file..."

"It's us closet cases, I guess," Frank sighed. "Funny, you know, I can't really think of myself as gay ... but, I am ... yet I'm not."

"You love Bruce, don't you?" asked Dennie softly.

"Yes, no doubt of that."

"But you can't think of yourself as a swishy faggot, or identify with the stereotypes you see on TV or in the flicks. You're like Bruce, if you stop to think about it. No one would pick him out as gay if he took any real pains to hide it. He's the classic example of a brilliant guy who just happens to prefer men to women."

"Yeah, I know all that," Frank told him, "and I've already told myself everything you've said. I don't really care, I guess, as long as I don't get knocked on my ass because of it. Trouble is, I've seen several other athletes who decided to 'come out,' only to lose everything they worked for. And actors? Since that Rock Hudson mess I think people are more aware than ever, and maybe taking a closer look. As happy as I am to have found Bruce, I can't help but worry. Take Rufus, for example: what do you suppose he's going to say when he finds out?"

"You're his bread and butter, kid — or at least part of it. I have a feeling he'd fight like hell for you. In fact, in your shoes he's the first one I'd tell and let him advise me how best to handle it, from the professional side." He sat up as he spoke, slipping off his shirt. "I'm starting to sweat," he added.

"Why don't you just lay it all bare? I won't attack you," Frank said, grinning.

"I should be so lucky," Dennie muttered. "No, Bruce scheduled that little shit-bird Stuart kid to come by for a talk this afternoon and I've got to look like the proper receptionist when he arrives."

"He's the one with the right-wing father?"

"Yeah. Now there's a 24-carat asshole for you! You know, he's bugged Bruce a couple'a times about the HIV test, and he acts like he's much more concerned that his son doesn't come down with a 'fag disease' than whether the kid's actually in danger. That's one who'd shit a blue brick if he thought his baby boy was being treated by a queer therapist."

"How 'bout the kid? I thought you liked him. At least from the couple of remarks Bruce made..."

"Oh, he's a hot little number. No doubt about it, but he's square, square, square. Although — and Bruce tells me I'm full of shit — but, you know, I had the feeling that he was prick-teasing me the first time he came by. He stripped his clothes off and went into the pool with hardly more than an offhand invitation. Then he stood there drying himself, toweling off his prick like he was polishing the crown jewels. It's a good thing I had my pants on, or he'd have seen how effectively his little strategy worked — if that's what it was."

"Just your type, huh?" Frank slid gracefully to his feet, stretched, and reached for his towel, knowing his own equipment was hanging full and loose, enlarged by the sun's heat. He wondered if Dennie would think he was prick-teasing, like Charlie. "Well, if Junior is coming by, I'd better get out of the way," he said. "I've got a couple of errands to run, anyway. And I have to go home and change clothes. Bruce is taking me to meet the Javitses tonight."

"Yeah, he told me," Dennie said. "You'll really like them, especially Alice. She's a sweetheart. You'd never know she was a Top, but maybe that's what makes her so effective ... the contrast, I mean."

"Well, Bruce is a Top, too, isn't he?"

Dennie also got up, and started rubbing himself dry. "I think you'll probably find that out for yourself soon enough," he said.

As the two men were about to head into the house, Frank suddenly turned to Dennie. "Hey, one more question," he said, laying his hand on the big man's arm. "When you and Bruce talk together you always say 'SM,' but most people say 'S and M.' Is there a difference?"

Dennie grinned, the suggestion of levity rumbling deep in his throat. "Them as knows the score say 'SM,' because most guys into the scene are either or both. The great unwashed — the uninitiated — they say 'S&M,' because they think you've got to be only one or the other." He laughed aloud, then, and clapped Frank on the back. "If you're lucky, babe, you'll learn the great truth on your own." Still laughing softly to himself, he continued into the house, leaving Frank in a state of momentary bewilderment. *And Bruce talks about games we're forced to play,* he thought. *Here's another gambit I've got to learn ... or do I?* Realizing that he was still standing like a naked statue in the yard, he quickly wrapped the towel around his waist and followed Dennie inside.

■ ■ ■

CLINICAL TAPE #4: Stuart, Charles I., IV (excerpt)

Therapist: Charlie, I want you to understand that as much as I enjoy your company, I really don't think there's all that much we need to work on. Not unless you're worried about something more than what you've mentioned.

Patient: I am having some trouble, trying not to worry about maybe getting sick. I wake up at night sometimes thinking about it, and I can't get back to sleep.

T: Have you discussed it with your father?

P: I've tried to, but he keeps telling me not to worry, just like you do. But then, in the next breath he's asking me if I feel all right, and telling me I ought to call you for another test.

T: But I explained to him it's too soon to tell. What the test picks up are antibodies that your system produces to fight the virus. We have to wait long enough for this to happen.

P: That's the whole problem. That's why I'm so worried.

T: It's just one of those things you can't do anything about. You should be having safe sex with everyone, anyway. As long as you do that, you won't pass it along if you do have it —

which I doubt — and you can also be reasonably assured that you won't get infected by someone else.

P: But what if I do have it?

T: Charlie, that's something to worry about when, and if, you know. But even if you do turn out to be positive, by the time anything starts to show up there'll be more protocols available than we have today. It won't be like it has been for people who've gotten it in the past, or even for those who are sick now.

P: Yeah, but it would just kill my dad.

T: Our concern here — and your concern — has to be for your own health, not what your father or anyone else thinks about it.

P: I wish I could really believe that. Uh, Doctor MacLeod, are they any closer to finding the guys who did this? If they'd just get them and make them take a test...

T: I think the police have some leads, finally, but I don't know just how close they actually are.

P: What'd they find out?

T: I don't really know, Charlie. I'm not that close to the investigation.

P: There is an investigation, then.

T: Oh, I'm sure there is — has been, at least unofficially, since you went in to see Mr. Javits.

P: Well, it'll be a relief when they get 'em.

T: Charlie, there's something I'd like to ask you about a comment you made, the first time you came to see me.

P: Sure, Dr. MacLeod.

T: When you were describing what the rapists did to you, you said that they wrapped rawhide around your genitals.

P: Did I? I don't really remember, but I ... I think that's what they did.

T: But why rawhide? What made you think it wasn't just some kind of rope?

P: Gee, I don't know, Doc ... Oh! I think one of them said something, like ... yeah — the big guy. He'd told the other one to get some rawhide, and then a couple minutes later they were wrapping it around my nuts. So, I just assumed it had to be that.

■ ■ ■

Frank had finished his errands, then gone home to clean up and change his clothes. He had been particularly careful to select a subdued, masculine ensemble — dark brown slacks with a simulated military cut, a tailored beige shirt, and dress boots that reached to midcalf, under the slacks. He wore no jewelry except his class ring and a plain gold wristwatch. No cologne, just a touch of very lightly scented after-shave. He used an Old Spice stick deodorant that one of the studio girls had given him in a Christmas gift pack, one he'd never used before. Although both his athletic career and his present occupation required that he meet a great many people, he was inexplicably nervous. This would be his first experience, being introduced to heterosexual people who would know he was gay ... if he really was gay.

It was such a strange sensation for him — as if he had decided to explore a new pathway, and the gate behind him had suddenly slammed shut. Yet the thought of Bruce buoyed him, excited him even in his nervousness. That was the key to the whole dilemma, he told himself. *As long as I've got Bruce, I can face almost anything. After close on three months of trying to tell myself I wasn't attracted to him, now I'm so drastically in love I couldn't change it if I wanted to. And it's not only physical, although that's great! Jesus, he's such a beautiful man — face and physique like some Greek statue — really hard body ... keeps it up with all those sit-ups and push-ups every morning. But he's so much more ... a really, genuinely nice guy. He loves me, loves me like I do him ... or I hope he does. I pray this isn't just for the sex. But he's too sophisticated for that ... Commitment, that's the word everybody's using these days. He hasn't said it, but I know it's on his mind ... or I hope it is. I'm making a big change in my life; in a few days I'll be too committed ... won't be able to go back ... don't want to go back ... don't think I want to go back. Worry, worry. That's me, old worrywart, and all because I'm doing what I want to do, and I'm so happy about it I can't believe it's for real!*

He called Rudy and let him relieve himself before settling the Lab into the front seat of his car — a yellow Nissan convertible. He'd decided to treat himself to the short drive with the top down — something he often avoided doing, because it always messed his hair. *But now that I've admitted to myself — and soon to a great many others — that I'm queer, I've got to stop worrying about having every hair in place. Somehow, gayness should be a more natural masculinity, unless I want to play it like some picky fairy. But I'm not that, and neither is Bruce — nor Dennie, nor any other man I can really respect.*

Strange way to come out, though ... falling for my therapist after I've been kidnapped and raped ... whipped by a pair of maniacs, and now I get a hard-on waiting for Bruce to do the same thing to me ... but not the same, really. Respect for limits; that's the way Dennie put it. Mutual, like any other kind of sex. Can't see myself in all that leather drag, though ... Bruce either, when it comes to that. But Bruce would look hot in leather, somehow ... not with all the chains and crap, but ... Jesus, down boy! I'll arrive with a tented crotch. Dennie'll think I'm in heat ... which I am. Never this turned on by anybody, man or woman ... never.

He made the drive in less than half an hour, pulling into the circular lane of asphalt in front of Bruce's house just before seven o'clock. Getting out, he paused to put the top up, assuming that Bruce would want to take his Mercedes. If Frank left the Nissan open, the seats would be wet by the time they got back. He had almost finished, when Rudy bounded up the short flight of stairs to the front door just as the portal opened. Then he was all over the young man who stepped out. Dennie was immediately inside, speaking to their departing visitor, who did not seem the least perturbed by the big Lab's enthusiastic greeting.

The young man's face was averted as he leaned down to pet the dog, and for a moment a flicker of recognition flashed through Frank's mind. Then the kid was facing him, and the impression vanished. As they passed, the youngster smiled and said, "Hi," then continued on to his own black Triumph sports car, which was parked ahead of the Nissan. Frank paused to watch him, almost certain that the kid had projected just a split second of recognition, and Frank still had the lingering impression that he'd seen him somewhere. *Just another pretty face, I guess. Seen one, you've seen 'em all. Or maybe he recognized me from the TV series. Hard to be anonymous when you're a star.* He was chuckling to himself as he went inside, Rudy still cavorting around him. "And you behave yourself while we're gone, Buster," he said. "You mess up Uncle Bruce's house, and he might not have any more goodies for either of us."

■ ■ ■

They were on the coast highway, Bruce patiently holding back his speed as the opposing traffic crawled along, and several sheriff's cars zipped past them, hunting for offenders. Frank could not help glancing at him, watching the even features in profile as his lover concentrated on maneuvering the car. *Lover ... that's really what he is ... the guy I love. Such a strange sensation — admitting to myself that I love another man. But he's also kind of distant, like his mind's on something outside our own space.* Frank had been almost amused when he had first seen how Bruce was dressed, considering his thoughts of a few minutes before. But he was too aroused by the effect. Bruce was wearing a pair of beautifully fitted leather pants, dark brown — almost the same shade as Frank's slacks, but cut like a pair of Levis. He had a matching vest, over a full-sleeved white shirt that might have been part of a costume from *The Three Musketeers*. The dark hair on his chest poked out from the rawhide lacings that lay loosely fastened across the front. It *was* a costume, Frank realized, but effective ... really effective.

"Was that the Stuart kid coming out when I arrived?" he asked at length.

Bruce nodded. "Yeah, his old man's been after him again to make sure he hasn't picked up a fag disease."

"The guy must be a real nut case."

"I guess. The kid isn't any mental giant, but I think he'd function better if Daddy'd leave him alone. Of course, he's spoiled as hell."

"It's funny. I had the feeling I'd seen him before, but I can't place him."

"He was on TV," Bruce said. "Back when they were picking the Olympic ski team. He was interviewed a couple of times, but he got chopped in the tryouts."

"Could be, but I don't remember seeing that coverage." He sat silently, thinking, trying again to place the kid's face. "It'll come to me eventually," he said. "From what Dennie told me, he's maybe a little more observant than you're giving him credit for being. You think he suspects the situation? The gay business, I mean, that he might be looking for a little action?"

"Hard to tell," Bruce admitted. "I get the feeling he's not telling me everything, but it's probably because the old man has him buffaloed. I'm trying to avoid getting into a real counseling situation with him, so I haven't done much probing in our sessions."

"You don't think he's played, then? With guys, I mean?"

Bruce reached across and caressed Frank's thigh. "I doubt it. Even if he wanted to play, he'd be too terrified of King Charles, the elder. You're the only one they've converted, so far." Although he said this lightly, and despite the pressure of his fingers against the rising lust in his companion's crotch, his words struck a discordant note in Frank's mind, caused him a moment of uneasiness. *Funny ... first time he's ever said the wrong thing to me. Wonder if he's so preoccupied he didn't think about it. But it proves he's not infallible. But he's so self-assured, so comfortable in being exactly what he is ... no pretense, doesn't need to pretend. God, I hope I can be more like him as time goes on. Just the touch of his hand, driving me crazy!* "If you don't stop that, I'm going to greet your friends with an unsightly stain," he said.

■ ■ ■

"You *think so,* but you're not sure! Christ, Charlie, how can you not be sure, one way or the other?" Charles Stuart III glared angrily at his son across the formal dining table.

"Dad, I'm sorry, but you got to remember I didn't get a very good look at him. It was dark when we went into his house, and he had the hood on all the rest of the time. The only place I really saw him was in the restaurant, and that was only for a couple of seconds."

"And you didn't get his name?"

"How could I? I just passed him on the stairs on the way out. I couldn't very well turn around and introduce myself."

"No, I guess you couldn't. But if he's going to see that shrink, too, it means the bastard knows a lot more than he's letting on to you."

"Maybe I could go back, set up another appointment and ask who the guy was. He's an actor, after all — if he's who you think he is. It wouldn't be out of place for me to have recognized him and be curious."

"I'm not sure you could pull it off, Charlie. I think we've been pressing our luck as it is, especially if that really was Frank DeSilva you saw going up the steps. And why so late in the day? Does MacLeod have sessions that late? On a Friday night?"

"Oh, I don't think he was going in for a session. He was too dressed up, more like he was going out someplace."

"How 'bout the doc? How was he dressed?"

"Just pants and a shirt, like he always is, but he cut me off right on the dot, because the big guy came in and reminded him what time it was. I think he was already heading to his room to change when Dennie saw me to the door."

"Well, we're going to have to find out," said the older man. "Let me think about it."

■ ■ ■

"We're getting a little pressure," said Abe, "but I think it's going to work out for us." He, like Bruce, was sitting on a bar stool, while Alice and Frank were behind them, huddled together on the sofa, laughing and whispering together.

"What'd you do?"

"Well, from my conversation with Fullbright, I knew he wasn't happy to have all this going on with no official sanction — especially after that kid came in and raked him over the coals. So I beat him to it; I went in to see the chief."

"How did he react?" asked Bruce.

Abe emitted a little snort of a laugh. "Handling the chief is a bit like herding a bull in rut. He likes to believe that he's on top of everything, which he usually is. But he's got certain ... limitations, and fortunately he's aware of them. Has enough sense to rely on other people, if he trusts them."

"Does he trust you?"

"More or less," Abe replied honestly. "Remember that hassle with the city council last year? The appropriation for police and fire pensions? That's when I went behind the scenes and called in a few favors. I did it without consulting the chief beforehand, but I let him find out afterward. He's never said anything, but he's been my pal ever since."

"The Byzantine intrigues of city hall."

"Be that as it may," Abe said grandly, "the Old Man's not afraid I'm going to shaft him, so he listened. I laid it all out for him, and stressed our concern not to see the department placed in an embarrassing situation. Fortunately, he also likes you. In fact, I think he's a little afraid of you, because he knows you've got contacts in the bureau. Anyway, to make a long story short, he asked what I thought he should do, and I told him to let you work with Captain Fullbright. That means you'll get Pete Jackson, too, because the captain's so dependent on him."

"It'll also keep it confined to that one division, where some of the investigators already know about it, anyway," Bruce suggested.

"True, but there's just one ringer," Abe said ominously. "The chief was adamant that we not keep it under wraps so that the media yells 'cover-up' somewhere down the road."

"What's that going to mean?" asked Bruce anxiously.

Abe leaned against the bar, absently watching his wife in her animated conversation with Frank. "It means we're going to go public when we reach a point where we can no longer justify the secrecy as 'proper investigative cover.'"

"In other words, all my assurances of confidentiality to my patients get tossed out the window?" He also turned to watch the others, his concern for Frank now his foremost thought.

"There's no way the department can make your records public," said Abe reassuringly. "But we have one victim who's willing to stand up and be counted. And I've saved the good news for last..."

He turned back to face Bruce, his expression one of impish delight. "The DMV records," he said.

"So tell me!" Bruce urged.

"They turned up a request for Frank's registration. It was made by an outfit called Bel Air Executive Search, and the reason given was 'routine records verification' — about as innocuous as it can get. So, when they tabbed that they went back and checked all the requests from this same outfit — just in the one office, of course — then went through the stuff they hadn't looked at before. In addition to a more recent request for info on Harvey Nicholas Simpson, they found thirty-six others. They only went back as far as September of last year, though. There didn't seem much point in going back further unless and until we make some sense out of this much data."

"What's the next step? Can they find out who these people are?"

"They've already done it. By eliminating the women, the older men, several guys whose pictures and physical descriptions made them of unlikely sexual interest — plus the obviously legitimate clients — they narrowed it down to eight Caucasian males — a couple with Hispanic surnames — all between the ages of twenty and twenty-eight, all residing in or around the west side. If this outfit is our rapists' source of information, these eight would be the prime targets."

"And the next step ... interviewing them? That'll take a more delicate touch than the police battering ram."

Abe nodded agreement. "They decided to use one of the rape counselors."

"A woman?" Bruce's concern was evident in his expression.

"Yeah, I had some reservations about that, too; but Fullbright decided to send her out with a male partner — on a trial run. They'll contact the first guy tonight, and see how it goes. I know the gal, and she's pretty hep. We can be sure it's going to be tough getting any of them to talk, certainly now when they probably think it's an unpleasant experience in their past, buried and hopefully forgotten."

"Okay, we'll have to go with whatever the department wants," Bruce agreed. "If I can be of any help..."

"You know we're going to keep you right in the middle of it," Abe assured him. "In fact, I think the plan is to try to get the guy to come see you once they establish he's been a victim."

"In New York they'd give me a gold badge," laughed Bruce, inexplicably relieved not to have been cut out of the case by the internal maneuverings of the police department.

"Oh, one more thing," Abe said, touching Bruce's arm to keep him from moving to join the others. "That company that ran the DMV checks — Bel Air Executive Search. We didn't want to tip our hand just yet, so no one's gone in to find out who initiated the DMV requests. They're apparently involved in placing estate or property managers, finding contractors for large home owners, bringing in higher level domestic help — English butlers and the like. They have one office, run by an old harridan by the name of Rose Caldwell. That's as far as they dared to go investigating them locally. We did check into the ownership, though, and it's a strange one! They're a subsidiary of a European conglomerate of some kind — chartered in Liechtenstein, of all places — an outfit called..." He fumbled in his pocket for a slip of paper, adjusted his glasses, and read: "...Sportsplan General, A.G."

EIGHT

Frank had been aware of Bruce's increased preoccupation all of the previous evening, ever since he had the long conversation with Abe. Other than this, the dinner had been a smashing success. Alice was one of the most charming women Frank had ever met; in fact, he had found himself once again questioning his own sexual orientation. But that had ended when Bruce took him to bed, and this morning as he lay in naked embrace against his lover he knew — even more surely than before — that he was confirmed in his new role.

Despite the safety precautions that Bruce always took, their sexual exchanges were the most overpowering he had ever known ... and the most tantalizing, because he anticipated the inevitability of their experiencing an entirely new vista, a type of physical exchange he had so far experienced only as the victim in a scenario completely lacking in emotional reciprocation. So far, there had been only vague hints of this in Bruce's behavior, once in a while in conversation. The idea frightened him — there was no denying it — but the fear was mingled with such a high level of desire that Frank found his thoughts dwelling on the prospect, and his body responding with an undeniable craving. In every other respect, he was completely comfortable with Bruce. He trusted him without reservation, would dare almost anything with him ... or for him. For the first time in his life, he realized, he was in a relationship that seemed totally without doubt or reservation.

Yet, even during last night's height of passion, he had felt somehow detached, as if he were being excluded from an important part of Bruce's thoughts, as if the emotional bonds were compartmentalized and separated from the other part of Bruce's current area of primary concern. *There's no doubt he loves me, but for some reason he doesn't function exactly on my wavelength, not yet. Or maybe I'm not on his wavelength. Maybe that's something that has to develop over time. But I know his preoccupation has to do with the rapist creeps, and I'm certainly as involved in that as he is ... a damn sight more, when it comes right down to it. It was my ass that got reamed and whipped.*

Bruce stirred in his sleep, tightening his grasp on his partner, pulling their bodies more solidly together. They were abruptly face-to-face, and without pause Frank kissed him, feeling a response a moment later as Bruce began to waken. Then they were locked in a fierce, open-mouthed contact. He could taste the trace of wine from the night before, but even the suggestion of stale fragrances didn't bother him. If anything, the animal scents that had developed overnight only increased his lust.

He felt his body being twisted backward, forced down flat against the mattress, as Bruce's heavier frame pressed onto him, pinning him. His upper arms were held firmly in place as Bruce lifted himself high enough to work his head down to Frank's chest, where the pressure of his teeth began to stimulate the smaller man's nipples, driving him almost into a frenzy as the pressure threatened to cross the line between ecstatic pleasure and actual pain. But Bruce's legs were locked on either side of his, and escape was impossible. It was the first time he had sensed the thrill of being compelled, forced to accept the ministrations of this guy he loved ... so different from the other time, when he hadn't wanted it to happen ... at least most of it. He realized that, too, but his rising tide of desire swept the thought away and his body surrendered to Bruce's demands.

Later, as they lounged beside the pool with their coffee, Frank tried again to span the gap he saw developing between them. "You haven't told me what went on between you and Abe last night," he said.

"I know," Bruce replied languidly, allowing his fingers to trail in the water. "I'm caught — as they say — on the horns of a dilemma. You're becoming the major focus of my life. I'm sure you know that." He looked up at Frank, who perched on the edge of the pad where Bruce lay outstretched on his back. Both men were still wearing the shorts they'd put on before leaving the bedroom. Frank had collected Rudy from his bed on the service porch and taken him out to the street for his morning constitutional, and Bruce had known that Dennie would have someone with him. They did not want to encounter a stranger in the buff. But, so far, neither the big man nor his companion had emerged from the other side of the house.

"My problem," Bruce continued, "is sort of multifaceted. I know you feel entitled to be in on everything that goes on as far as these rapists are concerned — really getting to a point where you're going to be entitled to know everything that goes on in my life. But I'm still a shrink, and that level of confidentiality is like a priest's in the confessional. I'm also involved in a police investigation, and that's supposed to be secret. But more than all the rest, I want to be sure..."

"Sure of what?"

"Baby, I don't know — not with any degree of certainty — just how deep your anger goes over all that happened to you. I do know how I'd feel, and maybe I'm transferring some of that onto how I perceive your response. What I'm saying is, I don't want to take a chance on putting you in a position where you might do something dangerous." Rudy edged a little closer to them, and Bruce reached out absently to pull gently on his ears.

"What, you think I'm going to go after them if I can figure out who they are?"

Bruce shrugged. "Something like that," he said, but his tone was vague.

"Or you're afraid I might let something slip at the wrong time, in front of the wrong people?"

Bruce propped himself up on one elbow. "It isn't so much that I don't trust your judgment," he said reassuringly. "At this stage of the game, though, we don't — any of us — have all the answers. Any one of us could make a misstep, and if you should do it ... shit, I don't want you back in their hands, especially if they think you can identify them."

"Why should they think that?"

"If you pop up someplace, or if your name pops up someplace where it shouldn't, who knows?"

"You're certainly being vague about it," said Frank. "I don't see how I could compromise anyone, myself included."

"Let's take a 'for instance,'" Bruce replied, the familiar clinical tone in his voice, now. "Let's say we identify the general area where these guys live. I wouldn't want you driving around there, trying to spot something. Or we put enough pieces together that, on your own — maybe at three in the morning — something suddenly clicks for you, but you're not sure enough to call and wake me up. So, you go off on your own, and..."

"It'll never happen," Frank assured him. "Besides, at three in the morning I plan to be in easy calling distance — say, about six inches."

Bruce laughed, his serious demeanor shattered. "Make it eight, and I'll buy it," he said, his hand tracing the outline of Frank's cock along his left thigh. "Okay," he added, finally, "I'll make a deal with you. I'll tell you whatever I know as long as it doesn't violate either patient confidentiality or something the cops have that no one else is supposed to even suspect. Whatever I discover on my own is fair game."

Frank smiled down on him. "So, now what are you going to do about those eight inches?" he asked.

■ ■ ■

It was well past noon when Dennie emerged with his little friend — a young man with the telltale haircut and manners of a Marine. They puttered about in the kitchen while Bruce and Frank remained poolside, a minimum of amenities having passed between the two couples. Rudy was busy, making his way back and forth, cadging what tidbits he could from the breakfast table, but never staying very long away from Frank's side.

Dennie had just come outside with his friend when someone rang the front doorbell. The big man lumbered off to answer it, Rudy at his heels. This left Billy, the Marine, in awkward solitude at the far end of the pool from the others. The young man was wearing Levis and a red t-shirt, although it was getting uncomfortably warm under the late September sun.

"Feel free to take a dip, if you like," Bruce called to him.

"Thank you, sir," the youngster answered, "but I ... I don't have a swimsuit."

"No need to worry," Frank assured him. "We'll be skinny-dipping in a minute, ourselves."

The youngster blushed and shook his head, moving a bit closer to make it easier to hear. He was a pretty kid, whom Bruce assumed to be about eighteen, short and stocky, with muscular arms and a well-defined chest filling out his t-shirt, with the Marine Corps emblem emblazoned across the front.

"Sit down and join us," Frank offered, pointing toward a nearby lawn chair.

"Thank you, sir," Billy replied. He eased himself onto the white plastic, gripping the armrests as he did so, and in that moment Bruce picked up on the kid's problem. A small, telltale streak of red showed against his tan, sinewy biceps.

"There's no need to be ashamed of your battle scars," he said easily. "We've all had 'em."

The Marine blushed again. "Yes, sir," he said, but he remained seated.

Frank looked questioningly at Bruce, but before he could say any more Dennie was back with a handful of mail.

"Guy from a messenger service arrived along with the mailman," he said. "You got something by special speedy delivery." He handed Bruce a maroon-and-white mailer. "Come on, kid," he added to the Marine. "Let's take a swim." With that, he stripped off his shorts and sat down at the edge of the pool, dangling his legs in the water before gingerly lowering himself into it.

When Billy still hesitated, the big man grinned up at him and beckoned with his hand, glancing over at Bruce and Frank. "They won't mind," he said reassuringly. "They've seen it all before."

Slowly, the young man stood up, hesitated, then quickly removed his t-shirt. Bruce, still holding the unopened mailer in his hand, watched in amusement as the stripes of red across the youngster's torso became visible to Frank, who tried for a moment to look away. Then, when the well-reddened ass and back came into view, he blushed as deeply as the Marine had a few moments before. Once he was stripped, the youngster's hesitant mode vanished, and he dove headlong into the water, as if to hide the scars of his night's escapade from the others. Much to everyone's surprise, Rudy loped in right behind him.

Frank's eyes remained riveted on the splashing figures for several seconds, then he returned his interest to Bruce, who had now opened his letter and was reading it with evident surprise. He held two tickets in his hand. When he finished reading, he looked up with an expression of exaggerated amazement and handed the paper to Frank.

In a large, cultivated scrawl on parchment notepaper embossed with a full-color coat of arms:

Dear Dr. MacLeod,

I have to apologize for my abrupt behavior on the phone, but I know you will understand that I am motivated by a deep concern for my son's welfare. I hope you and Mr. Delong will be able to use the enclosed theater tickets, and that you will accept them as a small token of thanks for the efforts you have expended on Charlie's behalf.

(Signed) Charles Stuart III

"What did you get, Bruce?" asked Dennie, surfacing beside him. Billy was dog-paddling in the center of the pool, as Rudy climbed out at the shallow end, shaking himself.

"King Charles sent us tickets for the Music Center," he said, examining the pair of chits. "Jesus, they're for tomorrow night — in the center of the Founders' Circle." He extended the note to Dennie.

"Now, listen, you guys go ahead and go," he said as soon as he'd read it. "I've got some plans with Billy, anyway — for tonight and tomorrow." He handed back the dampened note.

Frank had been examining the envelope. "Funny," he said, "he sent this thing from the delivery service's central office — last night. See the time and date stamp on it?" He handed the envelope to Bruce. "He must have had a last-minute tinge of conscience."

"Either that, or he got a better offer and figured to use his leftover seats to make some brownie points with his kid's therapist. These have to be season tickets," he added, looking at them again. "Well, what do you say we do it up right ...

136

dinner at the Pavilion, and ... what is it we're hearing? Oh, Domingo conducting. Should be a good performance."

Frank remained silent for a few seconds. He was remembering the times he had been to various functions, seeing two good-looking men in each other's company, remembered the remarks he'd heard other people make, the things he'd thought himself. Bruce noted his hesitancy, but the cause escaped him. "You didn't mention any other plans," he said at length.

"No," said Frank, his features suddenly brightening. "No, I don't have any other plans. Dinner's on me."

He had just about resolved his previous spasm of anxiety, when Billy pulled himself onto the edge of the pool, resting his well-defined arms atop the coping. "Hey, Frank," he said, "you really look like a guy in that cop series — Washington something-or-other. Are you an actor?"

Before Frank could answer, Bruce perceived the fleeting shadow of concern on his features. He watched as his friend regained control and smiled at the young Marine. "Yes," he replied in a seemingly casual tone. "I did 'Washington Street Beat' for three seasons. Guess it's in reruns, now, isn't it?"

"Yeah," Billy responded eagerly. "You were really great! Gee, it's the first time I've met a real TV star!" He remained in place for a few more seconds, gazing at Frank in near adoration. Then Dennie called to him, and he ducked back into the water.

"It's the price of fame," said Bruce, forcing himself to sound casual, but well aware of the myriad thoughts that had to be coursing Frank's mind.

"I've got to get used to it," Frank replied with an almost grim set to his jaw. "I've made my choice, and if there's a price to pay ... well, that's the way it goes."

"And tomorrow night, when people see us together in the restaurant and in the theater?" Bruce urged. "A lot of them are bound to recognize you. Can you handle it?"

"I've got to handle it," he said firmly. "I've got what I want, and..." He glanced across the pool, noting that Billy was sitting on the steps at the shallow end, watching them. "...and I don't care who's lookin'." With that, he leaned across Bruce and pressed his lips against the outline of cock that showed clearly defined within the fitted shorts.

■ ■ ■

Charlie Stuart knelt on the floor of his van, parked on a side street below Bruce's house. The vehicle was concealed from any passersby on the adjoining road, but he still exuded the anxious sweat of fear. He was dressed in dark clothing like the hit man he liked to pretend he was. Adding to his fantasy was the set of picks he carried in his pocket, which his father had taught him how to use. Charles Iverson Stuart IV — "Cis" the kids used to call him. Well, he wasn't a kid anymore. And he wasn't a "sis." He was a man on a secret mission.

He had seen Bruce's Mercedes go by more than an hour before, and there had been two people inside. He could not see more than that, because of the tinted glass and the abbreviated glimpse he'd gotten. But if his father had been right, the house should now be empty. "Even if they don't use the tickets," he'd said, "they'll be out, because it'll mean they had something planned beforehand." All Charlie had to do was wait until it was completely dark, then drive up the entry, park in the shadows behind the shrubs, out of sight from the street. He would then have several hours, with no one to disturb him. He had a portable tape duplicator with fresh batteries, and two pocketsful of blank tapes. His father had bought it all the previous afternoon, and they had spent a long time going over exactly how it worked. Charlie could now do it blindfolded, or in the dark. He checked his flashlight, and decided it was almost time to move.

■ ■ ■

Sitting in the glittering, green-and-gold elegance of the Music Center Pavilion, Frank realized that he was actually feeling a sense of pride to be in Bruce's company — a far cry from the apprehension he had experienced earlier in the day, thinking about this first "public appearance." He had already been introduced to several of his companion's friends, and he had sensed the cordiality extending beyond Bruce, and seeming sincerely to include him as well. Glancing around the dining room, with its gleaming chandeliers and uniformed waiters, he noted at least half a dozen other male couples.

"It's fairly liberated, isn't it?" Bruce remarked, cutting into his thoughts.

It took Frank a moment to comprehend his friend's meaning, then he smiled and nodded agreement. "Do I offer you my arm when we go up to the buffet?" he laughed.

"I think I can make it on my own," said Bruce. "Better load up on the oysters. They're supposed to do wonders for your virility."

"You haven't been complaining up to now."

"Nothing is ever so perfect it can't get better," Bruce chided him. "Besides, from the way you were looking at Billy's battle scars yesterday, I thought you might — after you've properly wined and dined me — that we might ... um, try to deepen our relationship tonight."

Frank returned his smile, but he felt a knot tighten in his gut. He knew that he'd been toying with the idea, and the prospect excited him enormously. Yet there still remained that modicum of fear, and something more ... an inculcated social sense of ... something he couldn't name. He knew it was a line he wanted to cross, and knew that when it came right down to it he surely would. But in some way it was like one might feel standing on the edge of a pool of water, knowing it was cold, wanting to dive, yet still reluctant to make the final commitment. "We'll see," he said at length. "If you eat all your veggies, we might find you a little dessert."

"Are you okay?" asked Bruce unexpectedly.

"Sure," Frank assured him.

Bruce, sensing some anxiety in his companion's demeanor, misread the signs and assumed they stemmed from his concern over the public exposure. "You know," he said, "most people go through a regular routine of grooming their hair, doing a crash diet if they gain a pound or two, all sorts of nonsense — because they're so concerned with the impression they're going to make on other people. But in the end, the only person who's really aware of the little changes is the guy himself."

Frank looked at him blankly for a moment, before his mind shifted gears and he grasped the point his friend was trying to make. He grinned, dazzling Bruce with the beauty of his features — the sparkling green eyes against the sun-darkened skin of his face, white teeth, and sensuous lips. "What I'm thinking about, baby, has nothing to do with the public," he said. "But, yes, I think I'm ready for whatever you have in mind. Fuck the rest of the world!" Then his smile slowly faded. "I'm willing to take whatever risks I have to take in order to make this thing work between us," he added more seriously. "Just don't ... don't ever ... make me go it alone."

It was then Bruce's turn to shift his thought patterns, and his clue to laugh. "We may have been talking at cross purposes," he said, "but I'm with you on both scores. We'll play our games as the circumstances permit, and if you think I'm going to let you get away from me, now that I've found you ... well, don't even consider it. If there weren't so many people around, I'd show you in a little more dramatic fashion."

"First things first," said Frank, getting up and heading toward the buffet of hors d'oeuvres. He was experiencing another moment of light-headed pleasure, of glee. All the clichés about love and its effect on mind and body were edging at his thoughts, but they had never before had any real meaning for him. Now, surrounded by well-dressed people in an atmosphere of subdued propriety, he experienced the sensations that would have been more at home in the bedroom ... or in whatever space Bruce used for his more exotic sexual adventures. *Interesting that he missed the focus of my thoughts, a minute ago. Shows he's not perfect — just almost perfect, and that's enough for me. Always trying to reassure me. Made that remark on the way in.* "Look around you when we're seated," he'd said. "Try to imagine any of those proper people doing what you know damned well they do in their own bedrooms — and some things you couldn't even begin to imagine." The thought made him want to laugh as a very proper middle-aged woman joined him at the buffet, and his mind conjured up a most undignified situation for her.

He continued to smile inwardly, and to experience the warm glow of pleasure as he ladled several oysters onto his plate. He was so happy, there were no words to express it. And, he told himself, there's no need to hurry. This wasn't a momentary situation, where one had to grab the gold ring while it flashed within reach. He and Bruce had all the time in the world. This was starting out to be a perfect evening, and he intended to savor every moment of it: the restaurant with its fabulous food, the impending concert, and afterward ... each element another jewel in the crown of this perfect thing his life had suddenly become.

■ ■ ■

Charlie pulled to a stop just past the center of Bruce's drive, carefully getting out and silently closing the door. He carried his materials around the side, through the narrow gate into the backyard and pool area. He tried the door to Bruce's office, found it locked, and went quickly to work with his picks. It took less than two minutes to get it open. He lifted his gear and slid the panel back, ready to step inside when he found himself face-to-face with a black, wriggling shape.

Rudy had heard the noise and come to investigate, but it wasn't in his repertoire to realize he was supposed to guard the house. Besides, he'd seen this young man before, and he'd been petted by him. Instead of standing his ground, he bolted forward, causing Charlie a moment of panic. But once the dog was outside the young man slid the door closed behind him. There was an immediate sound of scratching on the glass panel, causing the amateur burglar a moment of desperate frustration.

Not knowing what else to do, Charlie slid the door back a crack, not enough to admit the dog. "Shut up!" he whispered. "Go lay down!" And to his surprise, the black form emitted a whine that might almost have been a sigh of resignation, and Rudy stretched out on the grass, head resting dejectedly on his front paws. "And stay there, you big-ass fucker!" Charlie reclosed the door, pausing to assure there was no further sound from outside. He then approached the cabinet where he knew Bruce kept his tapes. This proved a more difficult challenge than the door, and in the end Charlie had to force the lock. After that, it was a simple matter to locate his own and Frank's tapes, and to run them through his duplicator. Although his machine ran at several times the regular tape speed, recording all four tracks at once — two forward, two backward — it still took him over an hour to complete his task.

He was just replacing the final tape when he heard a door open somewhere in the far wing of the house. A wave of music flowed out momentarily, then stopped as the door was closed. He looked about quickly for a place to hide, Bruce's desk providing the most obvious sanctuary. He gathered up his materials and quickly ducked into the dark cavity between the heavy oak pedestals. He tried to keep his respiration under control, but his heart was a steady, whispering thud in his throat. He heard someone moving about in the kitchen, two rooms away. The doors were open, however, on both sides of the intervening den. Once reasonably assured that no one was going to enter the office, he crept backward, out of his hiding place, and peered across the desktop.

He had a narrow, vertical view of the kitchen, framed by the juxtapositioned placement of the two intervening doors. Whoever it was had not turned on the bright ceiling lights, but there was a dull glow from the panel above the stove. At first the only motion he could see was a shadow, then a brighter flash as whoever it was opened the refrigerator. He heard the snap and hiss of a beer can being opened, then another, and then ... Dennie!

The big man walked slowly across his field of vision, holding a can to his lips as he took a sip. And he was naked, except for a leather strap arrangement across his chest and around his waist. That was all Charlie could make out, before Dennie passed into the hall and started back toward the far side of the house, closing the hall door behind him.

Charlie's first impulse was to bolt, and he had actually taken a couple of steps toward the exit when he paused, aroused and drawn by what he'd seen. He fumbled the light from his pocket and checked his watch. 10:05. Final curtain was not until ten-thirty or so, and it would take nearly an hour for Bruce to drive home. Carefully, he piled his materials by the glass panel and slipped through to the hall door, leading off the far side of the kitchen. He opened it cautiously, crept through, and closed the door behind him.

This was a part of the house Charlie had never seen before, and the hallway was completely dark. He felt his way along, aware of a dim light around the distant corner. He could hear the music quite distinctly now, and also the dull hum of an air conditioner. He reached the corner and peered around. A soft, amber light leaking out from a partially open door illuminated the few final feet of hallway. After pausing to be sure no one could see him, he slipped across and approached the door.

There was a sense of motion, moving shadows upon the nearest wall, but the door was only open a crack and Charlie couldn't see any more than this. He stood helplessly for several seconds, desperately trying to decide his next move. He knew he should leave, make good his escape while he still had plenty of time. That's what Dad would tell him to do. But Dad wasn't here. He'd left this chore to Charlie, and it was Charlie's decision to make. He flattened himself against the wall that formed a right angle to the door. The portal itself was only about eighteen inches from the corner, leaving just enough room for Charlie's body. He squeezed himself into the restricted space, and gently nudged the door so that it swung inward a couple more inches.

He could still not see the center of the room, but he did catch a glimpse of Dennie's naked form, dark and sinister in the muted amber glow. The music seemed to swell now, a full orchestra playing some slightly discordant melody ... like the Richard Strauss his father sometimes used, but different, not quite the same. He had nearly decided to risk another touch on the door when he realized that the farther wall was mirrored. By repositioning himself a few inches, he gained an almost unobstructed view of nearly half the room.

The images were faint, softly diffused by the dim reddish light, but he could make out a bed, covered in some dark material, with heavy wooden posts at the four corners, these joined near the ceiling by equally heavy crosspieces. Suspended from these, kneeling on the bed, was a well-muscled young man. He was facing into the room, into the mirror. His arms were stretched wide above his head, secured by a pair of leather cuffs, these in turn clamped to chains that fastened onto the upper wooden frame. He was leaning forward, causing his upper arms and torso to reflect the light more strongly than the rest of his body, but the overall effect was one of powerful, restrained masculinity.

A moment later, Dennie's heavily muscled form obscured Charlie's view of the prisoner, but this only heightened the observer's fascination. The big man had always excited him;

watching him now as he acted out his role of Master was so poignant a fulfillment of his fantasies that he almost cried out. He wanted so desperately to enter the room that he had to blink back his tears. He was trembling, and despite the air-conditioned atmosphere of the hall, he could feel the sweat collecting across his back, where it pressed against the wall.

Dennie had given his captive a drink, and was now leaning into him, saying something that was lost in the swirling chords of the music. Then he saw Dennie's hand move down, grasp something, and pull it toward him, causing a moan of pain, or ecstasy, to escape his prisoner's lips. He heard the bound man begging: "Please, Sir! Yes, Sir ... Sir..." Another groan, and Dennie backed away, coming closer to the door, allowing Charlie a quick glimpse of line — rope or rawhide — connecting to the captive's genitals, pulling his body forward so that it arched outward from the bed.

Charlie held his breath, so close to Dennie that he was afraid his rasping intake of air might be audible. But the music rose to another crescendo, and at that moment Dennie moved forward again. Now giving way to fear, and terrified lest his desires overcome any semblance of judgment, Charlie slipped quickly down the hall, through Bruce's office. He paused only long enough to gather up his kit, then exited through the back door, retaining just enough sanity to ensure the lock had clicked into place. With Rudy prancing at his heels he made for the gate, latching it behind him, thus trapping the dog in the enclosed backyard. Once he was through this last barrier, he really felt the near-debilitating terror take possession of his body. On rubbery legs he tumbled into his van, quaking so badly he could barely fit the key into the ignition. He drove onto the street at 10:40, struggling to keep the big vehicle on an even course and speed.

NINE

Bruce's hand was just unsteady enough that he found himself fumbling to get his key into front door lock. Not since the night in the gazebo, when he and Frank had originally admitted their feelings to each other, had he been in such a state of overpowering arousal. They were now about to take this deeply significant step, and he was already questioning the way he had gone about it. It should probably have happened more casually, he told himself — simply begun as an unplanned diversion, initiated in the height of passion, without either of them thinking much about it ahead of time. Now the expectation was creating an unnecessary tension just beneath the surface of their mutual lust.

Frank was a few paces behind him, and as Bruce pushed open the door, he turned to let him catch up, for their bodies to touch and cling together in the darkness of the entry. He could feel the reciprocating thrust of desire through the layers of clothing, but he was also aware of a slight tremor through the other's being — much as he had perceived on that first night. But, again, a commitment had been made on both sides, and neither seemed willing to let the moment escape. Despite the underlying tension both were more than ready.

Inside the cooler interior of the house, they drew together again, reaffirming their mutual desires through the unspoken language of continued physical contact. Bruce deliberately prolonged the moment. As he continued to hold his companion in a tight embrace, he could feel some of the tension drain from the other's body, as if reassurance were passing like a viable current from his own being into that of his lover, while he himself absorbed and dissipated the negative particles.

When they finally moved apart, each stood quietly for a moment, trying to regain his equilibrium. Then Bruce laughed. "I left a good bottle of champagne in the frig," he said, starting toward the back of the house. "Let's take it in with us."

It took Frank another few seconds to recover, by which time Bruce was already in the kitchen. "Hey, is Rudy back there with you?" he called. "I better take him out for a minute."

"He's not here," Bruce replied. "Oh, wait a second; I think I hear him at the door."

Frank walked up as Bruce let the dog inside. "Funny," he said. "Didn't you leave him in the house?"

"He was in when we left. Dennie must have let him out," Bruce answered absently.

Frank was puzzled for a moment, then shrugged and went to get the leash. One point he'd made when first bringing the dog to Bruce's house was that Rudy would only be allowed into the well-tended backyard when they were with him, and then only after he'd been walked. When Frank had suggested this, Dennie had been the first to agree.

"Be right back," he said, heading for the front door with the big Labrador cavorting happily at his side. "I'll make sure he's drained for the night."

When they returned, the lights were on in Bruce's office. Frank looked in, curious. "What's up?" he asked. "I thought we were on the road to our grand adventure."

Bruce was standing by the door, an expression of dismay on his face. "I think we've had a visitor," he said. "I came in to check the answering machine, and found this." He held a small piece of black-and-gold plastic in his hand. "It was on the floor behind my desk."

"What is it?"

"It's a wrapper from a cassette tape — not one of the brands I use. And look!" He crossed to the storage cabinet, fingering the catch. "Look at this scratch. Someone's forced the lock." He pulled open the top drawer and fingered the rows of tape. "Huh, nothing seems to be missing." He opened the next drawer, where he kept tapes of his older cases, mostly terminated sessions. "Not here either."

Frank was at his side by then, watching in concern as Bruce returned his attention to the upper drawer. "If they left a tape wrapper, maybe they..."

Bruce extracted one of the plastic boxes at random. "Tape's still in it," he said.

Frank reached over his friend's hands and picked out one of his own cassettes, turning it over in the light. "Still here, too." He started to slip it back into place when Bruce grabbed his arm.

"Wait a minute." He took the box and opened it, pulling out the cassette. "Look, it's not rewound." He pulled out several more from Frank's section. "They're all the same," he said grimly. "Some asshole's copied them."

Frank regarded him with a puzzled expression. "If they were copied ... I mean, why would they copy just one side and stop. Your sessions go long enough that you'd use both directions ... maybe not all the way on the second side, but these are ninety-minute tapes."

"A high-speed duplicator does it all in one direction ... tapes the second side backward. When you finish, the tape is like this unless you rewind it to the start of the 'A' side." Bruce started pulling out one tape after another, leaving the ones that had been copied in a pile on the table. "All of yours," he said finally, "and all of Charlie Stuart's." He looked in puzzled thoughtfulness at one more he held in his hand. "But, for some reason, they didn't copy the one I did on Harvey Simpson. And nothing else seems to have been disturbed." He leaned his backside against the desk, rubbing his chin in thought. "Now who the hell would know to do this?" he muttered.

"Maybe we should check the rest of the house," Frank suggested. "See if anything's missing."

"Go ahead," said Bruce, "but you won't find anything gone ... I'd lay money on that. I'm going to check with Dennie." Rudy chose that moment to press his cold nose against the back of Bruce's hand. "Fine watchdog you are," he said, patting the furry head.

■ ■ ■

"So you were right," said Charles Stuart. He pressed the stop button on his tape player, cutting off the voices that had been resounding from multiple speakers in the grand salon. "He *has* been counseling the Spic. And they're both queers," he added. "That's an interesting point, isn't it? They're queer and they got the hots for each other. That's why you saw him going in the door, all dressed up after business hours."

He sat upright on the elegant white couch, staring with unfocused concentration at the twinkling city lights. The daytime heat was rising from the earth, taking the smog with it, leaving the entire vista clear, like a vast array of gems on a black velvet background. But the view did not even register on his consciousness. The fact that he had confirmed his suspicions now brought an entire new perspective to his thoughts. For the first time since embarking on his nefarious activities he had to face the very real possibility that he had somehow left a trail, however slight. That might be all it would take for a man of Bruce's intellect to challenge him ... Bruce plus whatever resources the police were expending on the investigation.

He tried to think of any place where he could have slipped up. There would certainly be no way for them to connect his activities of several years ago to his present game plan. He continued to think of it as that, a game wherein the better man — the master strategist — always won. No, he was completely dissociated from the preliminaries. The present, main event remained his only concern. He slumped back, closing his eyes and trying to enumerate the clues contained in the taped interviews.

MacLeod had to be aware of their using the tranquilizer on their subjects, but that source was untraceable — and a fine piece of planned misdirection. Should anyone trying to unravel the mystery conclude that a doctor could be supplying him, his use of an animal tranquilizer would surely muddy the waters of logical deductive reasoning. Nor could anyone possibly uncover the connection to the veterinary supply company, owned by Sportsplan General, A.G. And even if they did, they'd never pierce the corporate veils in Liechtenstein to the holding company in Zürich, to the American conglomerate. Then, there *was* a doctor involved — marginally. Old Doc didn't like the idea of using an animal product on humans, but he'd appreciated Charles Stuart's logic ... had gone along as he'd always gone along, because Stuart let him watch sometimes. That was the old man's game — voyeurism, and in his exalted position he couldn't trust anyone else to provide an outlet — a live outlet, so much more satisfying than some video porn.

But Charles Stuart wasn't happy about the question MacLeod had raised at the end of Charlie's last session ... that bit about the rawhide. But the kid seemed to have covered himself. *Sharp, that shrink, picking up on the kid's only slip.* He looked across at his son, feeling a rare sense of pride in this extension of his own being. *But Charlie handled him like a pro ... just like tonight. I needed him to do a job and he did it — no questions asked, just went in and got the job done. No slipups, no hesitation. Now I know part of their game plan, while they have no reason to suspect their secrets have been compromised.*

And what else might the bastard have picked up? Charlie threw him off with his description of the second man, so that's going to be nebulous. We purposely set the scene of Charlie's "kidnapping" miles away from any of the real ones. They'll never find the DMV inquiries, because they're all mixed in with the legitimate requests that Rosie's office makes every day. They only represent a few of the total we've done, anyway. Huh! I'd like to see 'em get anything out of Rosie ... hard-nosed as some Dachau matron, and so happy with her new girlfriend that I set her up with ... no, no chance of a leak on that end. No, the old Master's got his game plan well in place. Still...

"Charlie, did you see tapes from anyone else?" he asked at length. His son was sprawled on the floor at his feet, half asleep after listening to several hours' worth of clinical interviews.

"There were lots of tapes, Dad," he replied. "I didn't recognize any other names, but you didn't say to look. And I didn't always know the guy's name, remember? You said it might be just as well if I didn't know all of them."

His father returned to his own thoughts, not completely comfortable with his son's response. He should have gone himself, he realized. But it had seemed such a simple task, except that he should have made certain Charlie knew the other names to look for. But that would be seventeen guys, now, and the kid would never have been able to remember them all. He would have to have written them down, and if somehow the list got into the wrong hands ... he shuddered to even consider it. That would be the kind of mistake a lesser man might make. Not Charles Stuart III. But the very possibility of error, the fact that he could consider even the fractional chance that he had made a mistake ... it brought the first flush of fear into his gut. Until now, he had been blissfully unaware of what, if any, measures were being taken to find him. Now he knew that one man, at least, was after him ... knew he existed and wanted to find him out.

Crap, he thought, *no queer psychiatrist's going to outsmart the Master. I'll win, just as I've always won. I'll go along doing whatever I want to do, and the lesser men of this world will knuckle under, just as they have for generations.* He stood up and stretched. The quick recall of his conquests had aroused him, and he wanted relief ... more than just the routine vanilla fucking and sucking he usually enjoyed with his son. "Come on, Charlie," he said. "Let's go downstairs. I think you've earned a reward."

■ ■ ■

"Sportsplan General, A.G.," said Abe Javits. "It's a Liechtenstein corporation, as we already discovered. That means you can't break the seal, no matter who you're willing to bribe. But I've got a friend over there, in Geneva, who knows a lot of things he's not supposed to know. He's asked around in his personal circles, and we've got just a smattering of facts."

Bruce flipped his phone onto the speaker, so Frank and Dennie could hear the conversation. All three of them were sluggish from lack of sleep, especially Dennie, who had run Billy back to Camp Pendleton in time for his eight o'clock Monday morning roll call. "Okay, what do we know today we didn't know last Friday?" he said.

"First, the corporation itself isn't new. It was founded in the early thirties, possibly as a Nazi cover. You know they were prohibited from having — or buying — various armaments. That lasted until 1936, when Hitler told them to take the Versailles Treaty and shove it. But they were arming themselves on the Q.T. from ... oh, back in the late twenties, and this accelerated after the *Führer* came to power in '32. Nothing was ever proved, of course, mostly because I doubt that anyone looked very hard."

"So we're dealing with a bunch of neo-Nazis?" asked Bruce.

"Not very likely," Abe replied. "The corporation went into a sort of limbo during the war, and it wasn't until sometime in the late fifties, early sixties, that someone acquired it and started pumping money back into it. That much we know for sure. Now the rest is part speculation, part logical deduction: First, it appears to be controlled out of Zürich, but the paper trail ends there."

"Then we're not sure who owns them out of Zürich, and we have no idea how that connects to whatever else the Zürich outfit may own in this country that isn't directly controlled by Sportsplan, A.G. And that's all we've got?"

"So far that's it, except there's a rumor that Internal Revenue has been poking around the Zürich end. There've been too many large dollar transferrals out of Liechtenstein, and they figure there's got to be some fire under all that smoke."

"But we know they owned the management company that leased that house in Silverlake, plus the executive search outfit. Isn't there any way to find out what else they own over here?" Bruce asked.

"Not really," Abe told him. "I'm going to try to stir something up at the state Franchise Tax Board. They're after these foreign-owned companies, because the new unitary tax rulings give them a crack at a bigger tariff. Unfortunately, my sources there aren't too solid, and I can't make it an official police inquiry — not yet, anyway. If I do, I'm apt to tip off the owners, and it could all fall back on the department if we don't get something up front and official on the books pretty quick."

"How would you like to take a burglary report?" asked Bruce.

"Who? You? You mean you got ripped off?" There was genuine alarm in Abe's tone.

"Nothing stolen, just a batch of tapes copied ... Frank's and Charlie Stuart's," Bruce told him.

"When was this?"

"Last night," said Bruce. "King Charles sent us a pair of tickets to the Music Center — by private messenger service, no less — so Frank and I went. Dennie was home, but ... ah, otherwise occupied. When we got back a little before midnight, we found the lock broken on my file cabinet and several tapes that had been run, but not rewound."

"I smell a rat," said Abe immediately.

"Like?"

"Like Charles Iverson Stuart III," he said.

"But, why...?" Bruce broke off, the myriad possibilities suddenly competing for acceptance in his mind.

"You've been counseling his kid," said Abe. "And the guy's a nut, Bruce. I wouldn't put it past him to lure you out of the house, then send some thug in there to take copies of the kid's tapes ... just to satisfy Daddy's paranoia."

"But why Frank's tapes, too?" Bruce asked, but his mind was already racing toward another, impossible answer.

"If you're thinking what I'm thinking," said Abe, a twinkle of laughter tracing the edge of his voice, "I'd say forget it, at least for the moment. Nobody fucks with King Charles III."

"King Charles may very well have fucked with me," said Bruce. "Maybe I'll give him a call this afternoon, thank him for sending the tickets, and see if I can stir up a little response."

"Careful, Bruce," Abe replied seriously.

"Careful it will be," Bruce assured him as he pressed the button to terminate the call.

"You don't seriously think that ... that fascist, fag-hating pig could have anything to do with this, do you?" asked Frank.

"It seems pretty farfetched," he admitted. "But Charlie never did ring quite true to me, and ... those DMV records. His name never showed up there, did it? The search outfit never checked for Charlie's address, did they?"

"No, I don't think..." Frank pulled a sheet of paper from a file on the corner of Bruce's desk. "No," he said finally. "He's not on the list."

"But he was a victim," Dennie urged.

"He *says* he was a victim," Bruce corrected him.

Everyone remained silent for several seconds, each trying to sift the facts to reach some acceptable conclusion.

"Frank, when you came back last Friday," Bruce began, "...when you went home to change and brought Rudy back with you. You arrived about two seconds after Charlie Stuart left. Didn't you say you ran into him out front?"

"Sure he did," Dennie interrupted. "I was afraid Rudy was going to nip Charlie's ass, but he just tried to play with him."

"Okay, so Charlie saw you ... maybe recognized you. If he did, and he told his father..."

"But why?" Frank protested. "I still don't get it. You can't imagine that Charles Stuart could be involved in anything like this. Why, the man's one of the world's greatest bigots! He hates queers like he hates every other minority."

"Which only makes him a rich sickie, right?" Bruce paused to let a couple more thoughts solidify. "Of course, it might not be King Charles. What if Charlie's involved ... doing this with some other guy, and Daddy's tumbled to it ... trying to protect the kid?"

"And his own good name," Dennie added.

"Yeah, probably that more than the kid's welfare," Frank said bitterly.

"Frank, have you ever seen the old man? Do you know what he looks like?" asked Bruce.

"No," Frank admitted. "I've never seen him, not even a newspaper photo."

"Then what say we take a drive. He lives up on Mulholland. Suppose we drop in on him and thank him for a nice evening?"

"Wouldn't that be a little obvious, Bruce?" Dennie asked. "And, if he *is* involved ... maybe a little dangerous?"

"He's right," Frank agreed. "Can't we get a picture of him first? Remember, this is just the sort of thing you were afraid I might do on my own. Better stop and think, Bruce."

"Okay, maybe I'm being too impulsive," Bruce admitted, "but if he turns out to be the guy who had the scuffle with Frank in the bistro..."

"If he is," said Frank, "I'll have still another score to settle with him ... last night, remember ... all the things we didn't do? But seriously, Bruce, if Old Man Stuart sent someone to rifle your files, wouldn't he have sent a professional? Someone who would know enough to rewind the tapes, and not have to force the lock on your cabinet?"

"Unless he sent Charlie, or whoever it is who's playing games with the kid," Bruce replied. "We've got lots to think about. In the meantime, let's see if we can't get some shots of King Charles. I'd be real curious to see what kind of response that rape counselor gets from them, if she shows them to the other guys who were on that DMV list."

Frank shook his head, standing up and looking down at the other two men. "Bruce, you'll never convince me that Old Man Stuart is running around kidnapping young guys and raping them. Charlie, who knows? But from everything I've heard about Daddy, no way."

"Time will tell," said Bruce. "Right now I'm going to take a little nap before my afternoon sessions start. Want to join me?"

■ ■ ■

Allison Palmer had been a social worker before she became a police officer, and she was not completely sure she had gained very much by the change. Her current assignment, at which she was good — very good — hardly compensated for the fact that all the excitement and adventure she had imagined would be her lot as an on-duty police officer was simply not coming her way. However, her second motive for joining the force was certainly coming to fruition. She had turned thirty while still in the academy, and until this time it had seemed she was condemned to remain a spinster lady for the rest of her life. Although she liked men and got on well with them, she was always their "good buddy," seldom a bedmate. It wasn't her appearance, so much, although she was tall. She had a pleasant face, and a good figure. But she could not resist the competition. She was smarter than most of the men she met, and try as she would she could not help letting them know it.

Now, she was working with a six-foot hunk named Marty Martin, a sixteen-year veteran, which made him about five years her senior. And he was easily her intellectual equal. He also liked most of the same things she did: good jazz, ethnic restaurants, quiet weekends — a goodly portion often being spent in bed. He even wanted to marry her, which made it her turn to hesitate. As much as she liked and admired him, and however much she enjoyed feeling his substantial endowment buried within her body, she was not quite ready to marry a cop. And she wasn't quite sure she actually loved him — well, she *did* love him, but she wasn't *in love* with him, and that was quite another story.

As the unit's rape crisis counselor, she had worked with dozens of female victims, and had developed nearly infallible techniques for getting them to discuss their feelings with her. She even managed to get a fair percentage to file charges and actually get up on the witness stand to testify against their attackers. But she had never even met a male rape victim, much less been faced with the problem of getting a man to admit he had been victimized when he believed no one was ever going to know about it. That was the problem confronting her as she approached the neat little town house on the edge of Westwood Village. It was the home of Michael P. Rittenhaus, the second name on her DMV list. She didn't even want to think about the first response they'd gotten when she and Marty had gone to the door together. This second address had been obtained from the DMV the previous October, almost twelve months before. If Michael Rittenhaus had been the victim of rape, it was likely he had long since decided to relegate the memory to his collection of past, unpleasant memories.

Having persuaded Marty to stay in the car for this second attempt, she rang the doorbell and waited uncomfortably for someone to answer it. It was just after 6:30 p.m., and the subject's vehicle was parked at the curb in front of the town house. The guy had to be home. As she stood waiting for him to answer, she carefully framed the words she'd use to start their exchange. But this did not prepare her for the moment of initial contact.

She almost permitted a gasp to escape her lips when the door was opened by a startlingly handsome young man, dressed only in a pair of well-worn jeans. He was of medium height, but his slender body was all hard sinew and smoothly cultivated planes of muscle. He was beautifully tanned, with dark blond hair that was almost platinum at the ends, where it had been bleached by the sun. His eyes were near violet-blue, and his facial features were the type one saw in high-fashion commercials, seeking to convince potential customers that the perfume in question could seduce any gorgeous male. After a moment of silence, he grinned: "Well, what are you selling?" he asked in a bone-melting baritone.

Allison partially recovered her presence of mind and flipped open her leather identification case. "I'm a police officer," she said redundantly, "Officer Palmer, and we have reason to believe you might have information that could help us in an investigation." That had not been her intended introduction, but it was the best she could manage.

The young man stared at her, now obviously as nonplused as she had been. "I don't know what I could possibly know—" he began hesitantly.

"Mr. Rittenhaus," she said in her best 'trust me' tone, "I want to assure you that you are not a suspect in any sense of the word, and that you are not under any obligation to speak with me. But I would very much appreciate your letting me ask you some questions, to see if you can help us." She flashed him her softest, most helpless feminine smile, and he invited her into the house. He even offered her a drink, which she surprised him by accepting.

Once they were settled into comfortable chairs in his very informal living room, Allison came into her own. The initial shock of his appearance had finally worn thin enough that she was able to question him and to learn that he was a fairly successful model. In fact, he was currently starring in a series of TV ads being run by a major manufacturer of designer jeans. And, yes, now that he mentioned it, she *had* seen him, and frankly she thought he was even more handsome in person.

Mike Rittenhaus blushed politely at her compliment, and gave her another display of his white, perfectly capped teeth. "Okay," he said at length. "What do you think I might be able to tell you?" He maintained a seemingly unruffled attitude, except that he was chewing occasionally on his lower lip, and one bare foot was playing across the wooden rung of his chair.

"I'm afraid there isn't any way to put this any more delicately," said Allison sweetly, "but ... you see, I'm a rape counselor for the department, and..."

If she had turned the fire hose on him, she could not have produced a more salutary effect. Mike was up from his chair, almost upsetting his drink, and pacing. "How ... how the fuck did you find out?" The anguish in his voice was almost tearful.

"Let me explain what's happened," she continued softly, sensing that her subject was going to respond as she wanted, if she could just keep him talking — and if she could maintain control of their exchange. "Maybe if you understand the situation you won't be so upset ... won't need to be upset." She could see that he wanted to answer her, but she waved him a "just-a-minute" gesture, and he slumped back into his chair.

"We know," she told him, "that there are a pair of nuts who are kidnapping handsome young men and subjecting them to some very degrading situations. Their M.O. is generally to inject a narcotic of some kind into the victim, then transport him to a secluded ... ah, well, 'dungeon' I guess is the only word for it. After they finish whatever it is they wish to do to the man, they drug him a second time and the next thing he knows he wakes up in his own bed."

She stopped, waiting for him to reply. When he did not, she urged him gently. "Is that, basically, what happened to you?"

"You know, lady," he said in an almost angry response, "whatever happened to me really isn't anybody's fuckin' business. I never filed a complaint, and it's something I'd just as soon forget about."

"But that's just the problem," she continued in a reassuring tone. "We ... I don't want to put you into any kind of an embarrassing situation..."

"I'm already in an embarrassing situation," he responded loudly. "Here I've got some strange woman sitting in my living room, asking me if I got raped, and if the answer is 'yes,' to please describe the details."

"If you'd be more comfortable talking to a man..."

"I'd feel more comfortable not talking to anyone," he said, and anger was definitely beginning to underlie his responses.

"Mr. Rittenhaus, please understand that my idea was not to upset you, and nothing you tell me need be made part of any official record. But we do very badly want to catch these men, and anything you might tell us could very possibly help us do that. And I'm sure you'd like to see them caught, too, wouldn't you?"

"I'd like to see them strung up by their balls," he answered harshly, "but I don't want to be involved."

"But you are involved," she insisted.

"Not officially," he argued, "and just for your record, you can tell them that I denied having anything happen to me."

"All right," she agreed. "For the record, I'll put down that nothing happened to you. But just for my own information, if you'd just answer a couple of questions..."

"I can't describe this stuff to a woman," he protested.

"Then you *would* feel more comfortable speaking to a man," she suggested again. It was more a statement, now, than a question.

Rittenhaus stood up for the second time, sighed, and slammed a fist into the palm of his other hand. "Yeah, I guess I could tell something to another man — but not a cop, and definitely *not* 'on the record'!"

"If you'll agree to see him, I can arrange for you to speak with a professional, who has already spoken to several other victims."

"A shrink?" he demanded.

"A really bright, wonderful man," she replied reassuringly. "I know you'll like him, and you can't help but feel at ease in talking to him."

"I guess I don't have much choice," he agreed finally. "But, I'm ... I'm getting married next month ... to a girl from a very proper family. If word of this gets out!" He regarded her with such distress she had the impulse to take him in her arms and console him as she might a child.

"You won't have a thing to worry about on that score," she said instead. "Whatever you tell Dr. MacLeod will be as secure as if you told it to a priest in the confessional."

"I don't want to go down to the police station," he added guardedly.

"The doctor has a lovely home in Beverly Hills, not very far from here," she said reassuringly. "He usually sees his patients in his office there."

Mike Rittenhaus nodded unhappily, making an openhanded gesture of helplessness. "Okay, so now I'm suddenly a patient."

■ ■ ■

Frank took Rudy for a long walk, to the top of the canyon above his home, where the big Lab could have a proper run. It was late, close to midnight, and distant rows of streetlights glittered through the remaining wisps of smog and ground haze.

Frank lifted himself atop a stone retaining wall that had once enclosed the yard of an old mansion. The house had burned down during the depression years, and had never been rebuilt, although the scarred, naked earth on either side bore evidence of impending development.

He tore the wrapper from a fresh pack of cigarettes, feeling guilty as he did it, because he had quit smoking when he first started training for collegiate football. But on the drive back from Bruce's house he had stopped at a liquor store, and without really thinking about it had bought them as if it were a habitual act. Now, looking at the evidence of his weakness, he felt a surge of revulsion and impulsively threw the contraband as far as he could, down the brush-covered hillside.

Nervous as a whore in church, he thought, *but that's not the answer.* He gripped the stones on either side of his butt and tried to convince himself that he really had nothing to worry about. But a feeling of ominous expectation had crept into his being, and there was no way he could escape its depression. The theft of the tapes, or more accurately their contents, was not something he could dismiss lightly. Whether they were in the hands of Charles Stuart or some other unknown enemy, they represented a potential threat to everything he had achieved. Nor did the fact that the culprit probably had more to lose than he did — if the contents were ever made public — do much to alleviate the panicky fear.

Then there was the situation with Bruce. That afternoon they had gone into the bedroom together and had slept for several hours, trying to make up for the previous night, when they had stayed up discussing the implications of the burglary and attempting to deduce its possible ramifications. They had stripped off their clothes, as they always did, but both had been so tired there had been no thought of sex when they slipped under the covers.

Later, when Frank was still in a deep sleep, he had felt Bruce's hands repositioning his body, and awakened to find himself lying on his stomach with his friend's heavier frame settling down on top of him. He had moaned contentedly, alerting the other to his returning consciousness, and had made no resistance several minutes later when he felt Bruce rise up to kneel astride his ass, drawing his wrists together behind his back. He had known immediately what was about to happen, and he had experienced a thrill of desire at the prospect. In fact, when he felt the rope being wrapped around his wrists, his cock had responded with an immediate, almost painful erection.

"You okay?" Bruce had asked softly.

"A promise is a promise," he'd replied, wanting to say more, but strangely inhibited, as if fearful of admitting to the fierce, animal lust that was now all but overpowering his senses.

"You look beautiful," Bruce had whispered.

"You should see the other side," Frank answered.

Roughly, then, Bruce had flipped him over, laughing at the rigid projection, grasping Frank's upper arms to hold him in place as he dropped his mouth about the soaring column. He had tantalized him after that, nibbling at his nipples, setting small plastic-tipped metal clamps on them afterward, then more clamps on the genitals, causing Frank momentary spikes of pain, but always backing off when his captive began to show signs of distress or anxiety. It had been a sexual exchange over which he had no volitional control, but that he had somehow still guided by his internal desires, his responses seeming to communicate themselves in unspoken waves of thought into his partner's awareness.

Looking back on it, he realized that the empathy he had shared with Bruce had been so complete it was almost as if they had been thinking with one mind. But that was his lover's skill, he realized, an ability he had developed over long years of experience. How much resulted strictly from the rapport they had established between them was another matter. He would have liked to believe that this was the core of it, but he wondered. *Would Bruce have been as attuned to some other partner? Would he have known exactly when to push ahead, when to ease off? Maybe. But regardless, he was doing it with me. Not with anyone else, and that's really all that matters. If he learned on someone else's body — and mind — so what? Today he used all his skill and perception to make a ... a what? A fullness, a totality? Whatever, he made it with me and I have to admit I never responded to anyone like this before ... man or woman. Wonder if it might be like that with a woman ... with Alice. She's a Top, Dennie says. Hard to believe...* He tried to project himself into a scene with Abe's wife, but there was no accompanying response, no surge of desire as he felt when he thought of Bruce. *I'm converted,* he admitted half aloud. *I'm queer as a three-dollar bill, and I'm completely satisfied ... can't wait to try it again, maybe go a little further, do a little more, feel ... pain? The pain I felt today was real, no denying that, but it was sensual, too — sexy like nothing else I can imagine. If I just knew who had those fucking tapes! Jesus! No matter how great everything is on the one hand, there's always something on the other to fuck it up!*

TEN

"Dr. MacLeod? Sorry to call so late in the day. Please hold for Commissioner Javits."

"Bruce, how's your schedule?"

"Must be serious, Abe. Not even a hello?"

"Things are popping, kid. The chief's in a snit because you seem to have become the center of our investigation, but he can't figure any other way to do it. Frankly, I think if he had his druthers he'd take a long vacation and try to forget the whole thing."

"I'm surprised he's that concerned," Bruce replied.

There was a controlled chuckle from Abe's end of the phone line. "We've had time to do some more checking on that DMV list — just a credit verification on the names we pulled out as 'most likelies,' and there're a couple with D&B ratings — and none of the eight are in any line of work that should have brought them into contact with the executive search outfit. Our maniacs didn't restrict themselves to just the deserving poor. In fact, it looks like they purposely chose several young men who were otherwise beyond compromise."

"Are you sure that none of the eight could have gone to Executive Search as customers instead of contractors or potential employees?" Bruce asked.

"It would be highly unlikely," Abe assured him. "These are all young guys, all single, all living in circumstances that wouldn't put them in need of the company's services."

"So what's got the chief's balls in an uproar — other than having to use my services?"

"He can't make up his mind how to handle the secrecy issue. He knows if he blows the lid and lets the media get ahold of it, several of the victims — and their families — are going to be needlessly embarrassed — and consequently pissed off at him. On the other hand, he doesn't want to be accused of failing to adequately warn the public. It could be very damaging for most of these men to have their names published as suspected victims, as I know you understand. And it could get legally sticky if they deny being involved, then turn around and sue us for invasion of privacy. Then there's the problem of sexism. If any of the feminist groups get wind of it, they're going to ask how come we're so concerned with hiding the fact that some asshole's raping men, when we're so free and easy about reporting female rape."

"But there hasn't been a leak, so far?"

"No, not yet," Abe said. "Other than Harve Simpson — who's perfectly willing to go public — there's just the Stuart case ... still unofficial, of course. And I've already headed off King Charles for him, but he knows he'll have to face another couple of men with clout if we rattle the wrong cage. He's let it be known that he'd just as soon the potential hot potatoes get left to last in Detective Palmer's investigation, and he's threatened to cut the balls off anyone who leaks a hint to the media before he's ready to do it."

"So, what do you have for me?" Bruce asked.

"We've got another victim who's more or less agreed to see you, because he's bashful to tell his story to a woman, and he's scared of cops. I assume you'll do it. He's one of the DMV eight — the only one, so far, who hasn't slammed his door in the investigators' faces."

"Sure, I'll see him. How do you want to set it up?"

"It's going to be a little tricky. The department will have to pick up your tab, so technically you're working for us. But I've discussed it with the chief, and he agreed to let you make a report, omitting the victim's name. That way, you can assure him of a reasonable degree of confidentiality. Otherwise, though, we'll want a full transcript of your interview. I'm also sending along a list of questions we'd like you to ask — probably things you'd ask anyway, but this way it makes you part of the act."

"Did you set a time?" Bruce asked.

"This evening, if it's okay with you. We'll have Officer Palmer pick him up and bring him by, just to make sure he gets there. She knows she isn't going to sit in on the session, though. She's a nice gal — very bright and personable. I think you'll like her."

"Anything else I should know?"

"Just do a real low-key number on him. He's already spooked, and he's getting married next month."

"That's enough to spook anybody," Bruce retorted. "But I meant about your checking around the world of high finance."

"Oh!" There was the sound of rustling papers. "Yeah, I've done everything I can at this point, without violating the banking laws. Your Liechtenstein company has only a few direct holdings in this country — the property management and executive search companies that you already know about, plus a rental place out in the Midwest ... leases TVs, VCRs, computers, office machines — specializing in veterinary equipment. I can't see any relevance to the case at hand. But I'm now about 99 percent sure they're owned out of Zürich, and in turn from either New York, or more probably Delaware. Still no names, though."

"Have they gotten a line on the surviving reporter? The one who tried to trace the guy in the Silverlake house?" Bruce asked.

"He's working for one of the gay rights groups in D.C. Jackson placed a call to him, but he hasn't called back yet. I did get you a picture of King Charles, though. It's in the envelope with the list of questions, along with a half-dozen neutral photos. I assume you know not to just put his picture out by itself. Give anyone you question the whole stack, and ask if they recognize a face."

"Sure, I know the routine. Have you had any more thoughts on the Stuart situation?" Bruce looked up as Dennie edged the door open and gestured at him.

"My friend, I hope you're wrong. That's one mother I'd really prefer not to tangle with. If he should turn out to be the one, we'd need more than the usual evidence to convince a DA to take it into court. Oh, by the way, I didn't mention your little problem a couple of nights ago. Thought it might be just as well if, for the moment, no one knew your files had been compromised. But for Christ's sake, Bruce, make sure no one can get their hands on any more investigative material."

"I will," Bruce assured him. "You must have been pretty sure of my answer. Dennie tells me your boy just arrived."

"He's yours now, kiddo. Good luck. Oh, one more thing. The Silverlake house. We went back for a second run with the property management outfit. The house was sold over a year ago, and their records show it was vacant during the suspect period."

Abe hung up and Bruce motioned for Dennie to bring in his visitors. He stood up and came around his desk to greet them, extending his hand to Mike Rittenhaus as Allison Palmer introduced them.

"I'm not too sure what I'm doing here," Mike mumbled.

"Sure you are," Bruce said in a kindly tone. "You want to help catch these clowns, and you're here to talk to me about it instead of the police." Despite the friendliness of Bruce's manner, the underlying threat sent a shiver through the young man's body. But he did feel more comfortable, because somehow the setting implied a type of confidentiality he would not expect in a police station. Once Dennie had conducted the policewoman into the next room, his tension dropped another degree.

"All right, Doctor MacLeod," he said resignedly. "You've got me; what do you want to know?"

"First, Mike, I want to establish some ground rules, so we both know exactly where we stand. I guess you understand your own status — the victim of a crime, whom we want to protect. That is to say, I'll go to very extreme lengths to assure you aren't embarrassed. On the other hand, I have a couple of other clients who have also been victimized, and I want to make sure these rapists are stopped. So the questions I'm going to ask you are not exactly the same as I might ask if you were coming to me as a regular patient." He paused, then, to allow his subject to answer while he extracted Abe's list of questions from the envelope Allison Palmer had given him.

Surprisingly, the young man nodded quietly before fixing Bruce with a very hard expression in his eyes. "If I could get my hands on the fuckers," he said, "I'd literally cut their balls off — which is exactly what they deserve. Believe me, Doctor, I'll tell you anything I can to help you catch them. Just don't fuck up my life any more than they already have. And believe me, I did go through hell for weeks after it happened — crying jags, jumping every time the house creaked at night, the whole bit. I hate those bastards!" His display of vehemence had been so sudden, it actually caught Bruce off guard, but also pleased him more than he was willing to admit.

"If that's true, Mike, it's going to make it much easier. Understand, though, I am taping this interview, and I must pass on the relevant facts to the police."

"But not my name," he insisted stridently.

"Your name won't be in my report, but you know they already have you on that list they got from the DMV."

"I understand that," he replied, "but Officer Palmer led me to believe it would be deleted if the list was ever made public ... on condition that I cooperate with you."

"Well, if she told you that, I'm sure that's exactly what she'll do," Bruce assured him. It also occurred to him that an investigative reporter could easily put together the same list without help from the police, but he kept that thought to himself.

"So, do you just want me to start at the beginning?" asked Rittenhaus.

"Sure. Go ahead," said Bruce. "I'll interrupt if I need something clarified."

■ ■ ■

CLINICAL TAPE #1: Rittenhaus, Michael P.

Patient: I guess I ought to start by telling you that one thing the officer said wasn't right.

Therapist: How's that?

P: She mentioned that one — or some of the others had been drugged. That didn't happen to me. I parked my car in the underground garage at my apartment one night last October ... a

Thursday. I'd been out late, because I'd finished my first series of newspaper layouts for a shirt company, and I didn't have anything coming up for another couple of weeks. I got out of the car and started for the elevator, when a big guy in a black ski mask sort of thing, he steps out from behind a pillar and he jabs me in the ass with a stun gun. I don't know if you've ever seen one of those things work, but I felt like I'd been slugged by a prizefighter. I lost all control of my muscles, and I went down.

T: But you could still see and hear, right?

P: Sort of, but I couldn't move and I couldn't really focus my eyes. I know the big bastard caught me before I hit the ground. Then a second figure materialized, and he pulled my hands together behind my back, locked them with handcuffs. Then a piece of tape went over my eyes, and about that point I was starting to come back to life. I wanted to yell, but before I could figure out how to make the muscles work, they had a second piece of tape over my mouth. They picked me up, and they carried me ... not very far, and they dumped me into the trunk of a car.

T: You're sure it was a car, not a van?

P: No, it was definitely a car — a big one, I think. At least the trunk was big. Then they drove me around Robin Hood's barn — lots of turns and side streets, a short stretch that seemed to be on a freeway, and then more twists and turns. I guess they drove for about a half hour, but I had the feeling they didn't really go very far — just did it to confuse me. But I was lying on my side, and everything was dark, so I can't be sure. And, naturally, I was scared shitless. I couldn't imagine what the hell they wanted with me, and I kept thinking that they must have kidnapped me by mistake, or else they thought my girl's family would pay ransom for me. I didn't know anyone else who could.

    Finally, they pulled into a driveway. Now this, I can be sure about. The surface was brick. It felt like it in the car, and when I stepped out I could feel it under my feet. I was wearing canvas deck shoes, so that makes it even more sure. I'd tried to work the tape loose, but it was still tight over both my eyes and my mouth. They hauled me out of the trunk, and they walked on either side of me into a building, and down a long hall that had a very hard floor — like stone or marble, very smooth and there was an echo.

T: Could you judge their size, or body build, from their touching you?

P: Well, like I said, the one guy was real big — I'd say six-two or -three, at least. The other was maybe my size — five-nine or so. And the big guy was husky; the other one was sort of slender, I think. It was hard to guess their ages, because I never heard their voices, just whispers ... real weird.

    So, they walk me down this hall and I can hear them open a door, and then we go down a flight of stairs that have like that ribbed rubber stuff on them ... to keep you from slipping, you know. And they must have been narrow, because the big guy's ahead of me, the other behind. At the bottom, they take me across a cement floor to another door, and they shove me inside. And this room was really different. It must have been soundproofed, because there wasn't any echo at all, and the floor was padded — like vinyl sheets over some kind of foam.

T: Was there music?

P: Oh, yeah. It was light classical, or more a series of themes from famous symphonies and things, 101-Strings type of stuff. And it was fairly loud, so once that door closed I never heard any sounds from outside.

T: Did you hear any extraneous sounds when they took you out of the car? Or even when you were still in the trunk?

P: (Thoughtfully) Now that you mention it ... when they took me out I did have the impression of being outside, in the country. Crickets, maybe? I'm not real sure. There was a breeze, though, and the air was cooler than it had been at my apartment ... or maybe it just felt that way after my being in the trunk.

T: (After a lengthy pause) Now, I guess, is when it started to get rough. Would you like a beer, or a drink?

P: I am getting a kinda dry. A little bourbon and seven?

T: I'll have one with you. Try to relax, now, but do your best to take me through it step by step.

P: Okay. First, they put a rope around my neck. This must have been attached to a pulley in the ceiling, because they could make it tighter or looser without coming up and touching me. The big guy says — whispers — that they're going to take my clothes off me, and if I cooperate I'll get them back later. Otherwise, if they have to rip them off, I might find myself naked out on a road someplace. One of them comes up to me and unfastens my belt, and yanks my pants and underwear down around my ankles. I'd been to the beach — I guess I forgot to mention that — so I was wearing white jeans and a polo shirt.

I might have put up a struggle, but it didn't seem much use, and besides they had my pants down so fast I didn't have time to react very much. Of course, I still didn't know what they were after, so I wasn't as pissed as I might have been ... still scared, more than anything. But I'm standing there, hobbled by my clothes, with the rope around my neck and my hands still cuffed behind me, when one of them stands up in front of me — the small one, I think, and he yanks the tape off my mouth at the same time as he grabs me around the balls.

Of course, it hurts like hell when the tape comes off, but he's not too gentle with my nuts, either, so I really let out a scream, and without thinking I try to pull away. So suddenly I'm really off balance, like I'm being hung. Both of them have ahold of me, then, and they get me back standing on my feet. They whisper together, and one of them pulls off my shoes and all the rest that's down around my ankles, while the other says something about I'm gonna lose my shirt, after all, and he rips it off me ... has to cut it, I think, because the material was too tough to come apart.

Then the big one takes hold of my shoulders and starts giving me a little spiel, about my being there to amuse him, and how I'll be let go as long as I cooperate and do what he tells me, and don't try to get a look at him. He says he's going to use my body, but he's not going to damage it. He's going to cause me some pain, but nothing a big man like me can't handle — stuff like that. And while he's talking his hands start moving along my skin ... real creepy, like a meat inspector going over a slaughtered carcass. I was still so shook up I didn't say anything right away, although it was obvious the guy had to be queer, and probably a little cracked. And I kept thinking about how I'd fought these guys off ever since I came out here, and now I'm fucked — figuratively, at that point, but they changed that in a hurry!

T: You say you'd fought them off, meaning homosexual advances, I assume. Did you actually ever have to fight anyone?

P: No, but the entertainment industry is full of them and ... well, I *am* a model, so I'm bound to attract some advances. But I'm not such a big name I can afford to offend people, so I try to play it cool, "just say 'no,'" sort of thing.

T: So you haven't had a serious argument with anyone as a result of his making advances to you?

P: No.

T: How about a shouting match in traffic, or in a store, restaurant — not necessarily a gay-related dispute, but just a few hot words with someone.

P: Not that I can think of.

T: Okay. What happened next.

P: They made me have sex with them. The big guy worked his way down to my penis, and started playing with it. I told him to knock it off, and he just kept on going, started fingering my balls, too, and talking to the other one in whispers about ... about what I've got ... saying how it's not very impressive, and how it needs some help. Then they tie something around it, around the base of my cock and balls, some kind of rope, and they wrap it around and around my nuts.

T: Actually around the testicles themselves, or around the scrotum above them?

P: Yeah, above them, doing what he called "ball stretching," and he hung something heavy on it after he'd tied it off. The pain got really intense then, and it felt like he was cutting into my side ... just really hurt, and I was begging him to take it off.

T: Did you get angry, call him names?

P: I was angry, all right, but I was so afraid of him ... I didn't know what kind of a nut he might be, whether he'd just castrate me if I got too salty with him, so I tried to play along, hoping something might happen so I could get out of there. But, I guess I was really scared he might use that stun gun on me, and I'll tell you, that's something I never want to feel again! Remember, I was standing there stark naked, handcuffed, with a rope around my neck. If he hit me with that current again, I'd have been a goner.

T: Did you express any of this to him?

P: You mean how scared I was? Yeah, sort of; I guess I didn't put on a very he-man act with them. I figured there wasn't anything I could do to stop them, however they decided to use me. I just wanted to get out of there alive. You see, I've got a lot going for me, now ... did then, too, and I couldn't see giving it all up for the sake of telling off some shithead. You hear about this kind of thing all the time —

woman gets slashed because she screams at a rapist ... that kind of thing. I decided to keep my mouth shut and try to survive. I could see they'd gone to a lot of trouble to make it impossible for me to identify them, and that made it more plausible they might really let me go.

T: Had you ever had any kind of relations with a man before?

P: No. Oh, circle jerks in prep school, and I knew a guy in college who'd give me head once in a while. But I've just never been interested in other guys.

T: How long did they keep you, then, and what did they make you do?

P: I was there about one day. It was around midnight when they grabbed me, and close to three a.m. when they let me loose the next night. But right then, the big guy got pissed when I couldn't get hard for him, so he left all the bindings on my genitals and told the small one to work on it for me. He went down on me, and did everything he could to provoke an erection. Nothing he did worked, and I was trying to relax, because I knew something worse was going to happen if I couldn't perform. Then after a while, the big guy says the little guy is doing a lousy job, and that we both deserve to be punished.

    I couldn't see exactly what he did, but I guess he tied up the smaller guy like he had me, because the next I knew for sure, the small one is standing right up against me. His hands had to have been behind him, and I'm sure he was roped by his neck, too. The big guy took the weight off my balls, and used the rope to tie me to the smaller one's genitals. And he used something like a long nylon webbing around both our waists to tie us together. When he finished, we were pressed tight all along the length of our bodies, held by the belt and the rope around our cocks and balls. Then he whipped us.

   He took some kind of a heavy piece of leather, and he landed it across my back and ass, and every time we turned he hit me on the side, and he was hitting the other guy, too. I guess it's a good thing he had us strapped around the waist, because several times I tried to pull away, and so did the little guy, so we'd have torn our balls off otherwise. I could hear the little guy crying, and asking the "Master," as he called him, to take it a little easier, but that never slowed him. Then, without any warning, the little guy was kissing me. I couldn't see him coming, of course, so he had his mouth on mine before I knew he was going to do it. He drove my head back, trying to push his tongue between my lips. I wouldn't let him, naturally, but the "Master" must have seen what was happening, because he let me have a really hard one across the ass, and said, "Kiss him." And when I just kept my lips there, he hit me again and said, "Do it like you meant it," so I ended up really having to kiss the little bastard ... mouth open and all.

   See, this is why I couldn't talk about all that happened to me with a woman ... it's why I hope you're going to keep your word to me. I acted like a wimp, and I know it.

T: Maybe that's why you're alive to tell about it.

P: Maybe, but I still feel like a real shit, not putting up more of a fight.

T: Mike, I've talked to three others guys that this happened to, and so far you've come off the easiest.

P: The others fought back?

T: The punishment each of the others received was proportionate to the amount of resistance. The harder they fought, the more punishment they got. In a way, you played it as cool as you could have. Of course, you may also have been their first victim — or close to the first. They seem to have refined their technique a bit as they went on. It's possible they've also gotten heavier in their behavior as they progressed from one victim to the next. There's no way to be sure, but I really don't think you should feel guilty for trying to make it as easy on yourself as you could.

P: Maybe you're right, Doctor MacLeod. I'd sure like to think so.

T: So, where did they go from here?

P: The next thing they did ... once the big bastard had finished his whipping number, was to untie my neck, and make me crawl around on the floor. The big one had boots on — I don't think he was wearing much of anything else, but he made me lick them. Of course, my wrists were still cuffed, so I was kneeling with my face on the floor, with my ass up in the air, and every time he accused me of slacking off, he let me have it with his strap.

T: Was there any other conversation between the two of them, either while you were bound up with the little guy, or during this boot-licking business?

P: (Pause) Not very much. The small guy sort of faded out of the picture for most of this ... except ... yeah! You know, I'm sure he said something to the big guy while I was crawling around the floor ... called him "Daddy" once. Now I think back on it, I'm sure he said "Daddy, please," but I'm not sure what he was asking for.

T: So he had you down on the floor, making you lick his boots, whipping you. Did he say anything else to you? Call you any names?

P: He called me "slave" and "pig" and "fucking this and that." I'm not sure what you mean.

T: He seems to be quite a bigot, at least from the way he treated some of the others. He didn't call you "Kraut" or anything like that?

P: No. Oh, he did call me "pretty boy" a couple of times. And then, after he'd made me work on his boots for a long while, he told me it was "time I learned to suck cock, if I didn't know how already." I guess that's when I really started to beg him not to make me do it, because just the idea ... I just couldn't even imagine doing it. But he pressed the points of — I guess — that stun gun against my ass, while he was holding my head down on the floor by putting his foot against the back of my neck. He asked me if I wanted another shot of juice, and that scared me so badly I told him I'd do whatever he wanted.

"Well, the slave has shown you how to do it," he whispers, and he grabs a handful of hair to pull me up to a kneeling position. "It's too bad that Jewish doctor got hold of your dick," he tells me, "'cause I've got a little something they took away from you." Then he pokes me in the face with his cock, and I can feel the points of that stun gun right under my left nipple. I almost choked, but I took his penis in my mouth, and I tried to do what he told me. It tasted terrible, like a dirty jockstrap in a locker room. He had a big, very loose foreskin, and he made me lick up under it ... all very kinky stuff, Doctor. I really don't need to describe every motion, do I?

T: I think I get the picture. Was he able to get an erection?

P: Oh, hell, yes. He damn near strangled me with it.

T: Did he ejaculate in your mouth?

P: No. I'd begged him not to do that, so — sadistic bastard — he waited until he must have been very close, after he'd battered my throat raw. He just suddenly stopped, forced me to my feet and across the room, pushed me belly-down on top of a table. I tried to get loose, then, really put up a struggle for the first time, but it was too late by then. He just strapped me down, legs against the sides of the table, neck to something in the floor. He greased up my ass, and buggered me. (Spoken in very strained voice, cracking several times. Long pause.)

T: He hurt you, then?

P: (Sobbing) I can't help it, Doctor MacLeod; I'm so fucking ashamed that I acted like such a coward. Fucking wimp! I should have put up some kind of a fight, at least pretended like I had some guts. But instead, I just lay there and let him ... let him do it! And hurt me? You're fuckin'-A he hurt me! And when he finished, the small one jumps right on top. He was smaller, and after the big bastard he didn't really hurt me — not physically — but ... somehow, I felt even more degraded, because the big asshole kept calling him "slave," and I guess that made me ... what? The slave's slave? I never felt so dirty and humiliated in my life.

T: Did they leave you alone, then?

P: (Still sobbing) Yeah, for a while. They went out, left the music on low, and I tried to sleep, except I couldn't. It was all beginning to sink in then, what a shit I'd been, how I'd acted like a slave ... how I'd debased myself every bit as much as they'd debased me.

T: Then, when they came back, what else did they do to you?

P: Oh, basically, more of the same ... more whipping. He — the big one, made me suck off the small one. Said I owed him a good blow job. They ... well, Jesus, Doctor MacLeod, this is so embarrassing just to talk about, but they ... they bent me over that table again and they stuck a plastic nozzle up my ass and they ... they...

T: They gave you an enema?

P: Yes. And they washed me in some kind of a tiled area, with water coming from both sides. I hoped it would soak the tape over my eyes so I could get a look at them, but the water hit me lower, on the chest. And after I was clean, they went right back at it. Shoved me down on my knees. When one got tired, the other took over. I don't know how many times I was forced to ... to. suck their dicks. It was fucking hell! I kept choking and dry heaving, but that didn't slow them down. And they — at least the big one — he never got tired of trying to make me get a hard-on, and he kept whipping me because I couldn't.

T: Then after all this they let you loose?

P: More or less. They put my pants back on me, and left the tape over my eyes. They had me strung up by my neck when they took the cuffs off my wrists, and the big one held that stun gun hard against my balls — said he'd sear them off if I put up a fight. So, again, I stood there like a fucking dumb ass while one of them tied my hands behind my back with a rope. They walked me back to the car and put me in the trunk, drove for about the same length of time as before, and ended up back in my garage. They put me in my own car, and the big one told me they were going to cut partway through the ropes on my wrists. "It'll take you half an hour or so to work loose," he said, "and then it'll be up to you if you want to go whining to the cops." And they just left me there. I got loose in about three or four minutes, but by then they were long gone.

T: Think very carefully, Mike. Was there ever any particular sound, or smell you can remember? Did either one of them wear cologne? When you were in the car trunk, could you hear sounds, voices, anything?

P: No. I might as well have been in a coffin. The car was noisy — the engine, or whatever. And the road noise drowned out everything else. And I don't think either one of them used a cologne. One of them smoked, though ... the big one I think. Yeah, the big one smoked. I could taste it on his breath when he leaned close to tell me something.

T: And the small one didn't smoke?

P: If he did, I wasn't aware of it. And I should have tasted it when he kissed me, but I don't think ... no, I didn't taste it.

T: And you're absolutely sure you can't remember having a beef with anyone before all this happened?

P: No, I'm sure I didn't.

T: Have you seen a doctor? Been tested for possible infection?

P: Yeah, I have a friend who's an M.D. He's done a couple of blood tests — one just last week. I'm okay, at least so far.

T: Good. Now, take a look at these pictures. Have you ever seen any of these men?

P: (Long pause) No, I don't think so. Is one of them ... do you think one of them's the one?

T: I think one of them may be involved, but there's no proof, and he's very much of a long shot. You sure you never had words with any one of them?

P: Yeah, I'm sure. Is that it, Doctor MacLeod? It's getting kind of late.

T: That's all for now, Mike. Let's go join the others. You won't mind if I call you, though, if we think you can help?

P: No, I guess not. But be sure you're talking to me, you know; be discreet.

T: Always. And by the way, Mike ... You know, you don't need to be ashamed of the way you reacted. Being afraid in that situation was perfectly natural. Anyone would be. Your face — and your body — they're your fortune, so to speak. You were right to do whatever you had to do to protect your most valuable ... er, assets. And not being able to spring a hard-on for them ... well, that was a little victory for your side, don't you think?

P: (Hesitantly) Yeah, maybe ... maybe you're right. But I try not to think about it anymore. I'd convinced myself that it had to be the best way to ... to cure it in my mind, I mean. But, Doctor MacLeod, I can't forget it, and I want you to understand that I'm just pissed off enough right now — having it all dug up like this ... Well, if I can do anything to help you catch the miserable motherfuckers — without hanging my own ass out to dry in the process — I'll do it ... on the Q.T.

T: Thanks, Mike. I'll remember that.

■ ■ ■

"Shouldn't we move some of this stuff out, Dad? What if they get a search warrant and come in here?"

They were in the center of the Room, where Charlie was cleaning the vinyl surface, while his father made some adjustments to the pulley. They were wearing jeans and t-shirts, barefoot, sweating slightly in the fetid atmosphere.

"There's no need to worry about it," Stuart assured him. "They have no idea who we are, and even if they did there's not a fucking thing they could do about it. They'd be as helpless as one of those sniveling punks we've worked over down here."

Charlie looked up from his crouched position, watching his father with a worried expression on his face. "Dad," he said softly, "why don't you ... you know, try some of that stuff out on me again?"

"We really should get some air conditioning down here," remarked the older man. "Funny I never thought about it, but I'm not sure we can handle the mechanics ourselves ... maybe have some outfit run a duct into the wine cellar, and we could do the rest..."

"Dad, please!" He was almost whining, now, down on all fours in front of the bigger man. "Please, Dad. Do it to me. Show me you're still my Master — like you did a couple of nights ago."

"Charlie, come on now. All that's past between us. The other night was just an aberration, something I couldn't help doing. But I shouldn't have subjected you to it, and you know I went really easy with you. We're both Masters. You know, we can still enjoy each other upstairs in bed, but I don't want to degrade you like that. You're not some low-life punk, some pretty boy with no more than looks going for you."

"But, Dad — don't you love me?"

"Of course I love you. I've always loved you. Only now, I think it's time you start to take your proper place. You're not a boy anymore. I want you to start making some of your own decisions, take on the role in life that God intended for you."

"You mean, like come into the office with you?"

"Well, that too. But I ... I'm not sure how to explain it, Charlie, but now that I see you growing into genuine manhood, I don't feel the same way about you. Oh, I love you, and all that. But it's different now. It's heavily laced with respect — respect for you as another man. The idea of degrading you, as I enjoy degrading others ... that's simply not in the cards anymore. That's the reason it didn't work as well as it used to the other night."

"But it's always been just the two of us. It has, hasn't it, Dad? Like, there weren't any others for you ... men, I mean. There weren't, were there?"

The older man reached down and lifted his son to his feet, hugging him. "Of course not, Charlie. It's just you and me, the way I've always said it was ... just you and me, and these few punks we've brought in here together. We've shared everything, and we'll go on sharing. No secrets between us."

"If that's the way it is, Dad, okay. Just the two of us against the world!"

"That's right, Charlie; just the two of us."

ELEVEN

Bruce slumped in one of the big leather chairs beside his desk, trying to fit the pieces of his human puzzle together. Following the old statistical principle of the null hypothesis, he sought to make it anyone but Charles Iverson Stuart ... in effect, to form an equation that would reject the man as guilty.

"It's got to be him," he muttered at length. "It simply doesn't add up any other way."

It was now Thursday morning, the day after his interview with Mike Rittenhaus. He had drafted out a report, which Dennie was typing in the next room. Frank had gone off to meet Rufus over some kind of contract negotiation. For the moment, Bruce was alone except for Rudy, who was snoozing on the carpet by his feet. "If you'd just taken a piece out of that burglar, you might have solved the whole mess for us," he said, poking the sleeping form with his toe. Rudy, as usual, looked up with an innocent expression, tongue lolling halfway out of his mouth. "You dumb shit. What have you got to smile about?" Absently, he scratched the Labrador's ears, and went back to his contemplations.

Frank recognized Stuart's photo as being the guy he slugged in the restaurant. When I talked to Pete Jackson this morning, he said that Harve Simpson thought he was the same guy who had the verbal altercation with him in traffic that day. And there's a gold Cadillac convertible registered in Stuart's name. Score two for King Charles. And the reason Jackson had called was to tell me that the reporter who'd followed that creep into

Silverlake three years ago had also seen the picture and said it looked like the same man. That makes one positive and two "maybe" I.D.s, but only Frank seemed sure, and he can't afford to testify.

But what's it going to take to assemble enough facts for the cops to act? Stuart's a rich and very powerful man. Seems farfetched, even to me, and I'm just about convinced he's guilty. If he is, that means Charlie's also involved, and that — in turn — means that the little shit was conning me. Father-and-son team ... one of the classic gay fantasies, especially for SM guys. Means the great man's been getting it on with his kid, probably molested him in years gone by. I tabbed him as just a shallow, spoiled brat ... not too bright. Well, at least my professional judgment was right on that score. For sure, if he was the burglar — fucked it up all the way around.

So, if it is Charles Stuart and Son, what did he learn by getting his hands on my tapes? Knows that Frank has told me his story, and probably picked up on our mutual interest in each other. He probably doesn't give a rat's ass about all that. He'd also hear that his boy did a good job of bamboozling the brilliant psychiatrist. So he knows something about us, but we know he knows ... or ... I wonder. If Charlie, or whoever did the break-in didn't tell him how poor a job he did ... didn't mention the broken lock on my cabinet ... probably didn't realize he should have rewound the tapes, and didn't know he'd dropped that piece of wrapper ... In that case, the Old Man probably thinks he's in the clear, that nobody suspects him of being involved ... doesn't think we know about the break-in. So, he doesn't necessarily know that we know.

Brazen, conceited bastard! Probably thinks sending us those tickets would never connect him to the crime. Thinks he's smarter than everyone else, so fucking superior! Oh, I'd love to nail that bastard! The phone rang in the next room, and a moment later Dennie buzzed him.

"It's Alice Javits," he announced.

"Hi, Alice. I hope you're not calling to tell me you and Abe can't make it tonight."

"Oh, no, sweetheart. We'll be there. But I have a little smidgen that just can't wait. I haven't even told Abe, yet, so you're the first to know."

"Dish me the dirt, baby."

"Well, you know that leathermaker down on Melrose Avenue, the one who does all the custom hoods and harnesses?"

"I know him quite well," Bruce assured her.

"Yes, well, I rather assumed so. Anyway, I had occasion to drop in there this morning, and I showed him the picture of Charles Stuart, and guess what? He's almost positive it was the man who bought a custom lock-around-the-neck hood, about five months ago — a special design with no eyeholes, but with a mouth opening."

"One more little shovelful out of that grave we're digging," said Bruce.

"You have to admit, it all begins to point in one direction," she responded brightly.

"It certainly does," Bruce agreed.

■ ■ ■

Charlie Stuart sat cross-legged on the padded vinyl, his eyes roving the dimly lighted room. He was naked, preparing for one more of his masturbatory fantasies. His father was at his office, meeting some business guy for lunch. Charlie had the room to himself, alone with his collection of vivid memories. *So many good-looking guys, all getting their asses whipped. Dad giving them what I wish he'd give me. When I was a little kid, I was enough for him. Now he needs all these others. He loves me, he says, but somehow he can't seem to do it anymore ... started going easy on me months ago, much lighter than he did when we first started playing with leather and bondage. Says he can't stand to hurt me, doesn't want to degrade me. But shit, man, that's what I want! When I see him just whipping the shit out of some guy, it's all I can do not to shoot my load right there, imagining I'm the one getting it. It's a real turn-on for me, except I wish it didn't have to be like that, with some other guy involved.*

'Course, if Dad isn't going to do it for me anymore, I'd sure like to have Dennie take me on. Boy, that big hairy stud ... like what he was doing to that hunky guy the night I watched him. Bet he wouldn't be afraid I'd break if he whipped my ass for me. I'd love to tell Dad about it, but he'd be sore as hell if he knew I'd taken the chance of going down that hall. Better just

let him think Dennie went to the show with Bruce. Funny, Bruce is really a lot better-looking than Dennie — a real handsome dude, but he doesn't turn me on anything like Dennie does. Thinks he's so smart, but poor dumb little Charlie conned him right up to the eyeballs. Only thing, though ... the lock on that cabinet. I think I got it back so you really couldn't tell it'd been forced. But it was dark ... couldn't be sure. Wonder what he thought if he found it. Fuck, if I told Dad about that he'd shit a brick. Or ... maybe he'd get mad enough to do a real number on me. I wonder.

He stood up, stroking himself, proud of his soaring erection. *Wish we had a mirror down here, like in Dennie's bedroom. I'd like to see myself all strung up, flying on amyl, ready to shoot my load.* He pulled down a pair of chains from the ceiling, leaving them in the right position to go around his neck when he finished locking the other devices onto his body. *Yeah, got to talk Dad into putting up a mirror ... just far enough away that you can't be sure exactly who it is you're seeing. Then I could be any of them. They were all about my size. That's what Dad seems to like ... young guys about my height and build. Wonder why? Never seems to turn on to the others. Wonder how he picks 'em? I know a couple came off things he saw on TV, and he picked Frank because of that row in the bistro. But the others? And even Frank. Never wants to tell me how he gets their addresses, makes a big secret of it. He's got so many connections, but he won't say anything about them. Thinks old Charlie's too dumb to be trusted with the information.*

He had completed the bondage of his lower body by then: hard metal irons on his ankles, leather stretcher on his balls, harness around his chest. He moved a stool up close enough that he could reach it, keys and amyl, lube, the tit clamps he'd set once his neck chains were in place and his mind was floating on the fumes ... hard clamps, harder than he could take without the artificial stimulation. *Some day I'm going to lock myself up like this so I can't get loose, hang here in full bondage until Dad finally comes looking for me. Wonder what he'd do? Wonder how long it'd take him to think about coming down here. Maybe he'd punish me, then ... give me what I deserve for being such a fucked-up* kid. He took a deep hit of amyl, and dipped his fingers into the jar of lubricant.

■ ■ ■

"Bruce, there's no way we're going to go out on a limb on this one," said Abe Javits. "Charles Stuart is about as unassailable as the pope — more so, in some ways."

"But it's plain as the nose on your face that he's behind all this crap — probably the 'big guy' every victim has described."

Abe perched on the edge of his chair, surveying the small group of anxious faces: Bruce MacLeod, Frank, Dennie, and his own wife. "Look, I know each of you is thoroughly convinced that King Charles is our mad rapist. Off the record, I agree with you. But you don't have a shred of evidence I can take to the DA and get a search warrant, much less actually arrest him."

"But don't all these little pieces add up to one big whole?" Dennie insisted.

Abe shook his head, and started enumerating on his fingers. "You don't have diddly," he said firmly. "You've got him pegged as the recipient of an evil-tempered kid's insult on a public street. You have him giving tickets to his son's psychiatrist as a 'thank you' on a night when the shrink gets burglarized — and that's not even an official complaint. You have a gay reporter who *thinks* he saw him pick up some hustler four years ago, and despite the fact that you *believe* the hustler got roughed up, you haven't even got a written statement from him. And now, my wife tabs him buying a kinky hood, from a guy who *thinks* it looks like Charles Stuart in a photo. You have his son as an alleged victim, but that's also under wraps, so we couldn't use the information even if Bruce could prove he'd lied to him — which he may very well not have done. There isn't a single piece of evidence in this whole schmear..."

"Frank can definitely identify him in the restaurant," Alice urged.

"So, Frank can identify him as the guy he socked in the jaw. That's good enough to get Frank pinched for assault and battery, but it doesn't prove that Charles Stuart went out and kidnapped him."

Dennie moved into the kitchen to monitor the progress of their dinner. "What if Officer Palmer turns up something?" he called over his shoulder.

"So far, she's had four doors slammed in her face, plus a third guy who swears he's never been raped in his life. Her only success was with Mike Rittenhaus, and he doesn't really know anything — wouldn't testify to it, if he did." Abe spread his hands in a gesture of helplessness. "No, when it comes down to the legalities of the situation we have absolutely nothing to put in front of a DA. And you know as well as I do, it's going to be a much more impossible thing to get a judge to sign a search warrant — if that's what you have in mind — when it comes to Charles Iverson Stuart III, than if you were talking about some *schwartzer* drug peddler down in South Central."

"I agree that all we have for the moment is suspicion," Bruce said resignedly, "but instead of telling us how hopeless it is, let's try to figure out some way to bring it all together."

"I'm for that," Abe assured him. "But remember, Bruce, despite all this amateur sleuthing you're still not a police officer. I don't want you ... or any of you," he added, surveying the entire group with his gaze, "I don't want any one of you to dream up some scheme to try going out on your own to trap this guy. Not only are you apt to land in jail yourself, but you could get hurt. If he's as vicious as we all believe he is, I for one don't doubt he's capable of ... more-extreme violence."

"Abe," said Alice, speaking softly, as if from the background. "I have a thought, and I wonder if it might not help pull everything together."

Everyone watched her diminutive figure as she got up and took her place next to her husband. "Now, at this stage we have three men we know were victims of this pair. That's not counting Charlie Stuart, who may or may not be a victim. We also have the services of a leading psychotherapist available to us. Why can't we let Bruce put the three of them together in a sort of therapy group, try to do something like a brainstorming session. Maybe in a group, sharing their perceptions, they can mutually stimulate each other to remember some details that haven't come up, yet."

"I have a feeling that all you'd get would be another set of unproven suspicions," said Abe, "but like chicken soup, it probably can't hurt. What do you think, Bruce?"

The psychiatrist remained still, thoughtfully preoccupied. "The session," he began slowly, "might work if we also included Charlie."

"You can't do that!" Frank protested.

"No, you can't, Bruce! He'd learn almost everything we know, everything we're planning," added Alice.

"Not necessarily," Bruce replied. "What if we prep the other three — individually, so Harve and Mike don't know who's odd man out — and add in a few extraneous bits of fiction ... like our being on the trail of the guy — or guys — and we're just waiting from some additional identification ... from Europe, say," he continued, warming to his topic and beginning to speak faster. "What if we make it sound like we're on the verge of making an identification ... and an arrest."

"You're thinking to panic him, make him run to Daddy with some wild tale, as if the hounds were already snapping at his ass?" Abe suggested.

"Something like that," Bruce admitted. "If we could scare him badly enough, we might get through to Daddy, make him do something foolish — especially if — right now — he doesn't think we have any inkling of his being involved..."

"And imply that the cops are on the verge of uncovering the whole story," added Frank. "Yeah, I could go for that."

"And you wouldn't mind being part of the group? Being identified as a victim?" asked Abe.

"Well, why not?" asked Frank. "It isn't going to get newspaper coverage, and besides, if Charlie's the one who copped the tapes, he knows about me, anyway."

Again it was Alice's softly modulated voice that stopped the others' rapid conversation, and brought their collective attention into focus. "But before we do any of this, I think we should defer to Bruce's professional expertise. Bruce, I'm sure that by this time you've formed some kind of profile of this man. What are we really dealing with? Is he a maniac, or a split personality, or ... what?"

"You want the full lecture?" he asked, amused at the sudden rapt attention coming his way. "Well, for starters, let's assume it really is Charles Iverson Stuart III. If it is, we already know quite a lot about him, so we only have to speculate on the rest.

"For openers, he's a big, fairly good-looking man in his early fifties. He's fabulously rich and politically powerful, and he uses his position in a really ruthless fashion. Overtly, he's an arch conservative, maybe more ... maybe a secret contributor to some dingbat right-wing groups."

"I think we can assume that to be a fact," Abe interjected. "I've seen some of the police intelligence reports on his activities."

"Fine," said Bruce. "Now add what we assume to be true about his covert sexual behavior. He's a homosexual, but he refuses to acknowledge it — even to himself, in all probability. He likely sees his criminal conduct as the logical expression of power — power that he perceives as his by right of his innate superiority. The fact that his victims are male is further justified, because overcoming and dominating a male is a much more decisive display of superior force than could ever be the case with a woman, since he likely perceives women as weak and more or less defenseless. The fact that he is attracted to men instead of women is likely ignored in his own theorizing, and so buried in the morass of his twisted logic that he never even considers it."

"Or he justifies it, on the basis of something like the ancient Greek or Persian traditions, that permitted a warrior to capture and enslave an opposing soldier in battle?" Frank suggested.

"Possible," Bruce agreed. "This is all pretty wild speculation at best, so any of it could be true, or be pure garbage."

"No matter how you cut it, though, he's a very sick man," Abe warned them. "The fact that he apparently has never killed doesn't make him incapable of it."

"I think there's a reason for his not killing," Bruce said. "In addition to his assumption that most of his victims would never come forward, especially if they can't identify their assailant, I think it's just another case of his proving his own superiority. He may well perceive all of this as a game, with himself as the star performer ... so good he can afford to work with a handicap, a little on the idea of a big-game hunter going after his prey with a bow and arrow instead of a firearm.

"Of course, the handicapped hunter still kills his prey, but that's all part of his particular game. I think King Charles would go to great lengths — has gone to great lengths — not to take a life, but not because of any moral considerations. He'd kill if he had to protect himself. But he sees himself as so clever and so successful in what he's doing, he doesn't need to kill. If it actually came to a situation where he had no other way out, and was forced to murder someone to protect his identity, he'd probably do it; but in that moment, he would consider he had lost the match."

"Then the real trick is for us to shake his belief in his own superiority," Alice suggested.

"You mean, like putting him a position where he thinks he has to kill someone?" Frank asked.

"You do that, and you'd better be faster on the draw than he is," said Abe grimly. "Pushing him into that corner could very well trap him ... with your bleeding corpse in the trunk of his car."

"You'd have to unload his gun, so to speak," said Alice, "then trick him into trying to shoot you."

"I don't think he'd use a gun," said Bruce unexpectedly.

"Why's that?" asked Frank.

"Just a feeling, really. Call it intuition, but my sense of the man is that: Number one, he wouldn't want to kill you quickly. He'd rather watch you suffer for a while. And two, despite all his right-wing activities he's never been involved with the gun lobbies. My guess is that he doesn't perceive a firearm as his surrogate penis. A knife, maybe, but most likely a whip or a rope ... or some other SM fetish device."

"You mean he'd prefer to beat someone to death, rather than shoot him?" asked Abe, a true look of distress on his features.

"That, or maybe slow strangulation — some situation where he could watch his victim struggle through his final desperate moments," said Bruce. "But," he added with a bitter laugh, "it's only a guess. Remember, I've never actually met him ... just spoken to him on the phone, and read whatever I could find written about him. But, although I'm hesitant to try explaining it, I do have a theory — a sort of general theory about SM men, and I think it may be relevant, here — to Charles Stuart."

"That's a come-on if I ever heard it," said Abe, laughing.

"Tell us, Doctor."

"Hum, all right. This is still a bit nebulous. I've never tried to write it out, and organize my thoughts the way they should be for a proper presentation, but here's the rough draft:

"We know that, within male-to-male SM circles, the bottoms outnumber the Tops by a wide margin. Estimates range all the way from two-to-one, up to ten-to-one. More than this, we know that there are very few exclusive Tops. That is to say, most Tops will play the opposite role in the proper circumstances — not all Tops, but most. On the other hand, there are many bottoms who simply can not function in any other capacity. In further substantiation of this — and over the years, I've counseled a fair number of SM guys — it isn't uncommon for an exclusively functioning S to have M fantasies, but rarely, if ever, the other way around.

"Now, based on all this, I think I see the outline of a pattern. I would theorize that the M, or masochistic, component in SM men is the more consistent of the two. That is to say, that whereas most SM-oriented guys have some of each element in their basic personalities, the masochistic component is most consistently going to be in place. For many men who always play the Top role, their pleasure is coming to them vicariously. The enjoyment of their bottom's suffering is actually taking place because they subconsciously perceive themselves sustaining the pain. For one reason or another, they can't personally assume this subservient position, but they can experience it this way.

"Assuming some validity to all of this," Bruce continued with an almost apologetic expression, "if we apply the theory to King Charles, what do we have? Here's a man with all the wealth and power that it's possible for a human being to possess — or almost all. What if this M component is functioning within his psyche? Isn't it possible that he wants to sustain some pain? That he would really enjoy getting exactly what he's dishing out, but can't overcome the emotional resistance to the role?" In response to a couple of incredulous looks from his listeners, Bruce went on: "Think about some of the more-vicious serial rapists and killers you've read about. They've written on walls — sometimes in blood — 'Please stop me,' or otherwise asked to be caught and punished. Ted Bundy, for instance, deliberately went to Florida to commit his final crimes, because he knew they had the death penalty and actually applied it."

"Are you saying he wants to be caught?" asked Abe.

"I'm saying that he may find the risk of exposure very exciting, and while he'll do everything he can to outsmart us on a logical, intellectual level, he may have subconsciously left some clues. Remember Oscar Wilde's famous quote: 'It was like feasting with panthers; the danger was half the excitement.'"

"But he *has* left clues," said Frank. "We know who he is; we just can't prove it."

"And maybe that's exactly the way he wants it," said Bruce.

"Subconsciously," Frank added.

"Yes, subconsciously," Bruce agreed. "But let me carry this on to the next level of my theory. Up to now — except for the divergence into the realm of sex criminals — I've been speaking in general terms about men who are involved in what we might call 'normal SM' — that is, a sexual situation in which the two partners are working in tandem to produce the physical and emotional satisfaction that each is seeking. That's a very different animal from the rogue killer or rapist. He isn't a sadist in any sense that we can understand, not in terms of a mutual sexual exchange.

"The man we're after, and who we now assume to be Charles Iverson Stuart III, isn't going into his sexual bouts the way we do — hoping to achieve a grand and glorious lift, both for ourselves *and* for our partners. He's in a category similar to — but not identical with — any number of mass murderers and kidnappers we've all heard or read about. In effect, his crimes are not so much an expression of sexual lust, per se, as they are displays of aggression — and hostility. And, I think in his case, we might include the element of power needs."

"My God, Bruce, the man has all the power anyone could want," Alice objected.

"Ah, but you see, he doesn't," Bruce replied. "He perceives himself as all but omnipotent in almost every other facet of his life, except this one area. *He can't take just any person he wants and force that person to submit to him sexually.* You know, we've been joking about him, calling him 'King Charles,' but I'd be willing to lay money on his really perceiving himself as some sort of king."

"And kings always had serfs and vassals, at least in the classic days of kings," Abe remarked. "I'm beginning to see your direction, except I don't see how this makes him a man seeking to be caught and punished."

"I think that's the unique part of his particular complex," Bruce replied. "On the one hand he sees himself as the great ruler, but he also has the whole background of learning and education that all the rest of us have. He knows — again subconsciously, at least — that what he's doing is illegal. He may not perceive it as wrong, not for him. But he certainly knows it's against the law."

"But he perceives himself to be above the law," said Frank.

"He does," Bruce agreed. *"But the law is a rule of the game.* He feels superior to all the rest of humanity, and to their laws. Yet he knows that the rest of humanity, by and large, abides by the rule of law. For this reason, his opponents — us in this case — are bound by these particular rules. He can't have a proper contest with us unless he also has rules to restrict his behavior. But he's not willing to accept those that are made by men he considers inferior to himself. So, he makes his own rules, but once he's made them he *must* abide by them.

"And every game, even if the teams are decidedly mismatched, must allow for a forfeiture of something, even if it's next to impossible for one of the contestants to lose. And after several matches, with the stronger side always winning, the game can become blasé, boring for the victor. That's when it becomes necessary to give the stronger side a handicap. The thrill then becomes worth the effort, when there's a chance — however minimal — of losing."

"You're saying that he doesn't really want to be caught, but that he wants the excitement of the possibility," Abe suggested.

"That's exactly what I'm saying," Bruce agreed. "And then the underlying masochism that has to be present in his basic personality becomes a factor in all of it."

"I'm not sure I followed all of that," said Frank, "but I think I understand the general concept. I hope you're not saying that he could get off on an insanity plea once we nail him."

"I doubt that's ever really going to be an issue," Abe replied. "It's doubtful he's ever going to come to trial."

"Bullshit!" Frank responded with a startling display of anger. "He's committed a series of ... of heinous crimes, and he's got to pay for it."

"Well, let's see what comes out of Bruce's little séance," said Abe. "Maybe I'm wrong. I hope I'm wrong."

"I'd really hate to see all this come out in the Sunday supplement," Alice said. "It would reflect badly on all of us."

"Maybe someone'll nut him first, and save our having to expose him," Frank added harshly.

"Sick, sick, sick," said Dennie, emerging from the kitchen. "And on that joyful note, kiddies, dinner is served."

■ ■ ■

Glancing around him at the small group of men, Charlie Stuart felt the pulse quicken against his temples. Three of the men he and his father had kidnapped and abused, plus Bruce MacLeod and Dennie Delong. In all, it comprised the most astounding group of handsome studs he had ever seen in one place in his life! Not even the best collection of surf bums could compare to this. *And I've had more than half of them, had my mouth around their cocks ... my dick up their asses, watched 'em getting their butts whipped. And I've seen Dennie in action, too. Briefly, but still ... Bruce, the only one I haven't seen naked, even. Wonder what he's got. Wonder how he'd look in one of Dad's harnesses, strung up and ready for my attentions. Wouldn't be so smart and sassy, then, I'd bet. Wonder if he'd fight us, or give in like that first guy, sitting over there, now, looking so cool and composed, not like he was when Dad and I worked him over, whipped his ass and fucked him ... crying and begging us not to hurt him, not to mess up his face...*

"Okay, gentlemen. I really appreciate your taking the time to come by, but I'm sure this is just as important to you as it is to anyone. Just to set it all in perspective, the four of you," nodding at Charlie and his companions, "are all victims of a very sick pair of men, who have been secretly terrorizing young guys all over the west side for the last year or so."

"How come the others aren't here, too?" asked Harve Simpson. His freckled face was very red, almost as deeply colored as his hair.

"Looks like you've been out in the sun, Harve," Bruce remarked. "But to answer your question. We know who most of the others are, and we have people working with them. We just felt that this was a more manageable group. You see, the police have come up with a number of leads, and they seem convinced they'll have the perpetrators' names in a few days."

"Then why do you need us?" asked Mike Rittenhaus.

"Knowing who it is may not be enough," Bruce explained. "It's even possible that whoever is doing all this has his blackroom hidden off someplace where we won't be able to find it. And that's a piece of evidence we'd really like to have. Each of you has been there, and we'd hoped that by getting you to discuss your experiences you might stimulate some memories between you that would give us a better clue as to its location."

Charlie felt his pulse quicken again, but this time the whispering beat in his neck was not from sexual excitement. Even his cock felt shriveled as fear began to take possession of his senses. His first impulse was to bolt from the room and race home to warn his father. But he knew he had to remain, to hear everything, and then report it. He wiped his clammy hands on the legs of his jeans, and tried to focus his attention on Bruce.

"Let's go over the basic facts as we know them," he was saying. "First, our chief perpetrator — the one you've all referred to as 'the big guy' — didn't just start with this round of rapes and kidnappings. A few years back he worked the streets in Hollywood, and lured a number of hustlers into a house he had access to in Silverlake. Before this, he may have been doing similar things with call boys, but we have no firm evidence of that. We're convinced, though, that the smaller one is his son, who may have been too young during these earlier phases to have been involved."

One of the others was asking a question, but Charlie hardly heard him. He had never even suspected that his father had done anything like this. *A few years ago.* That would have been when he had assumed he alone was the object of his dad's passions. And he certainly had been old enough — eighteen, nineteen ... plenty old enough! Now, it seemed, he had been duped, betrayed! He blinked back the tears and forced his face to remain impassive, although he could feel a subtle trembling in his jaw.

"A couple of reporters from the gay press caught onto what he was doing in Silverlake," Bruce continued, "and they printed the story. Unfortunately, it served to scare the perp away, but didn't stir up the interest it should have in the major media."

"Did they trace him down? Rental records, license number?" asked Harve.

"Not at the time, but they're backtracking now," Bruce told him. "They also have one of the hustlers, who's agreed to identify his assailant. We've also got a couple of fingerprints that the reporters lifted from the house. They'd been kept stored away until now, but we're expecting a report back from the FBI any time." From the corner of his eye he saw with some satisfaction that his little tale was producing its desired effect on Charlie. The kid had huddled down in his chair, and so far hadn't said a word. He hoped the others would keep to the script.

"It sounds to me like we're after a guy with a few bucks," Mike suggested, right on cue. He glanced around at his companions, knowing only that one of them was suspected as being involved, but not knowing which. Bruce was happy he'd decided to do it this way. Both Harve and Mike were too emotional to put on a proper act, to keep some negative attitude from showing in their interactions with Charlie. The others knew, of course, so it was up to them to act their parts.

"I'm sure the guy is very well heeled," Bruce responded. "In fact, we're checking out some leads in Europe right now, in a little country called Liechtenstein. You may never have heard of it, but it appears that our perp has some business interests there, and used his subsidiary companies as cover for some of his activities."

"I've never heard of it," Harve replied. "Where is it?"

"It's a tiny principality between Austria and Switzerland," Bruce continued easily, speaking slowly, and maintaining his unobtrusive surveillance of Charlie Stuart. The kid had gone white as a sheet, even seeming to have lost his tan as he listened to the casual discussion of things he had been aware of only in a peripheral way. He had seen some papers on his father's desk with the little country's name in the letterhead. But even this disturbed him less than the thought of his father picking up strange kids while he had lain home, alone in bed, eagerly waiting for his dad to return. He felt used, the first probings of anger beginning to prickle beneath his skin.

"So, what I'd like you guys to do, now, is to take turns describing what happened to you — all with the understanding, of course, that what is said here does not leave this room. I don't have the tape recorder turned on, and I'd like to stay out of the discussion as much as possible. Frank, why don't you start, and then we'll go on to someone else. And if someone says something that doesn't seem quite right, be sure to speak up. The whole purpose here is to sharpen your recall. If you happen to remember something as being different from the way someone else remembers it, that may just remind another guy of something he's forgotten."

■ ■ ■

"Dad, Jesus Christ, Dad! Listen, they're just about to nail us!"

"Easy, Charlie. Calm down. No one's got any idea..."

"Yes, they have. They know we live on the west side, that we're father and son, and they know about your connections in Lichen-whatever it is in Switzerland."

"Liechtenstein? What did they say about that?" Charles Stuart had been lying in bed, watching an old movie on cable, waiting for his son to come home and report on his meeting. He had harbored no great fear, nor expended any time in worry over the outcome. Now he used the remote control to silence the images on the screen, as he turned his attention to his son.

"They said you used to pick up hustlers and take them to a house that was owned by a company in ... that place, and Dad ... Dad, did you really do that? Pick up street kids when I was a teenager, do things with them? And they said you maybe used call boys before that. You never told me. I thought ... I thought, after Mom left ... I thought, you know, just you and me. You always said, just you and me." He started to cry bitter tears, and this moved his father to a greater degree of compassion.

"Settle down, now, Charlie, and tell me exactly what they said. You know I always loved you more than any street punk. They were just a convenience, so I could do things I didn't want to do to you ... heavy things that you weren't ready for. Now stop the crying, and tell me what they said."

TWELVE

A strong Santa Ana wind, bringing with it the dry desert heat, had made the backyard almost oppressively warm. Bruce and Frank, sitting in the darkness after the meeting had ended, were both too keyed up for sleep, and each for his own reasons had been stimulated by the discussion. A three-quarter moon hung low on the horizon, casting a tenuous glow over the heavily landscaped patio. Neither man had spoken for several minutes, until Bruce stood up and started to remove his shirt. "Too hot," he muttered. "I'm going to take a dip." He looked down at his companion. "Want to join me?" he asked. "This weather's going to break in a few days, and we might as well enjoy the pool while we can."

Without speaking, lost in his thoughts, Frank stripped. Then he was standing naked beside the larger form of his lover, again reveling in the sense of wild abandon he always experienced when they moved about in the open, unclothed, as they had at the beginning of their sexual relationship. The hard, well-defined contours of their sweat-moistened bodies were momentarily displayed in the near darkness until they slipped over the smoothly rounded edge and into the pool.

They paddled about for several minutes before Bruce glided backward toward the side, reaching his hands above his head to grasp the convex lip. Frank moved up beside him. "Okay, Bruce," he said softly, "your little scheme is fermenting, and you've done everything you can for the moment. How about a little time for me?"

"That's a good idea, baby." He lolled backward, resting his head against the rim. "But what was that little confab you had with Harve and Mike after Charlie took off?"

"Oh, we just decided to compare notes while we had the chance. I had an idea, then ... I don't know ... But Bruce," he added, his tone abruptly more somber, "Abe's right, isn't he? The cops aren't ever going to nail Charles Stuart. I mean, no matter how many little pieces of circumstantial evidence we dig up, it'll never make a case that some DA is going to be willing to take into court, will it?"

"It's beginning to look that way," replied Bruce, unhappily. "He's confused the issue so thoroughly there's no real proof — only a series of suspicious incidents. And he's just too unlikely a criminal suspect, certainly for this type of crime ... too respectable, too overtly conservative ... too many influential friends, too much money. I'd say they would almost have to capture him red-handed, actually kidnapping a guy. If he's smart — which he is — he'll simply fold his tent and slip quietly away."

"Is that what you intended should happen when you invited Charlie here, tonight?"

"We're sending him a message: 'Quit now, or get caught.' I know it's lousy to think that he could get away with all he's already done, but it's better than having him continue, and maybe do more damage than he has already."

"And this little extra tidbit you dropped, about the bastard getting it on with call boys before he started on the hustlers. What made you say that?"

Bruce laughed deep in his throat. "I was watching Charlie," he said. "I saw his face when we mentioned the hustlers, so I just put a little icing on the cake."

"An additional touch of the sadist?" asked Frank. He pushed off slightly from the side, treading water, punctuating his words with little puffing sounds as he maintained his position in front of Bruce.

"I'm not optimistic that any of this is going to accomplish much," he admitted, "but each bit of additional friction can help bring it to an end."

"Well, that's what the three of us were talking about ... the hopelessness of the situation." Frank sighed. "I guess we've just got to do what we've got to do, and get on with it. But,

Bruce, what if he does stop for now? There's no guarantee he won't start up again in a year or so, and what do you think he might do then? Is there a possibility he might do worse than he has this time?"

"I can't answer that," Bruce admitted.

"But you see the pattern. The first time — at least the first time we know about — he picked on hustlers and tricked them into submitting. This time, he's actually been kidnapping guys and forcing them to submit. Isn't it possible he might start killing them on the next go-around?"

Bruce sighed. "I don't know," he said.

"But it's possible."

"Possible," he agreed.

"So, what do think we ought to do?" asked Frank.

"There isn't anything we *can* do," Bruce replied unhappily. "We've set a few things in motion. We'll have to see how they work out. Abe's on top of it. He'll make the move when he sees an opening — a warning that'll scare him off permanently, I hope."

"And in the meantime, you just retire from the case?" He drifted back against Bruce's side.

"For the moment." He traced the outline of Frank's arm with his hand, an absent gesture, but one that conveyed his feelings more adequately than words. "The best thing to come out of all this..."

Frank leaned forward and kissed him. The contact began to dissolve the mood of frustration that had possessed them both, but there was some tiny element in the contact that was different. Bruce sensed it, but passed it off without further thought.

"So, what did you have in mind for us?" Frank asked. He maneuvered himself closer, allowing his body to slide against Bruce, utilizing the contrast in temperature between his skin and the pool water to produce the desired effect. "We've never had a real scene, not like the one I thought we were heading into when we came home from the Music Center. Don't you think it's time?"

"I thought you were worried about that no-shirt scene you have coming up ... didn't want any marks on your skin. That's why I've been playing such light games with you." He stroked the sleek, finely delineated surface of his companion's slender body. "Do you really want to get heavier?"

Frank responded by pressing down more firmly, forcing Bruce's back against the tiles. "I had another idea," he said, his impish grin lost in the darkness. "I've been talking to Dennie, and he told me that brown leather — like you wore the other night — he said it sometimes had a special meaning."

"Oh? And what might that be?" asked Bruce innocently.

"Well, it seems that it might mean a guy who wears it has some more ... ah, ambivalent interests than a man who wears strictly black. And ... after your lecture on the masochistic component in SM men ... well, I thought of a way that wouldn't fuck up *my* skin for the shoot."

Bruce laughed, letting his legs float upward to grip Frank around the hips. Then, as his companion moved slightly aside, his body broke the surface. This allowed his dick to display itself above the water — not really erect, but definitely tumescent. "Has it really come to that?" he asked. "My sexy little novice, suddenly deciding to be Top?"

"Isn't that the way it should be?" asked Frank. "All the ambiguity of the situation coming full circle? The guy who's so dominant in real life submitting in SM sex? That's part of it, too, isn't it?" He pulled himself hard against Bruce, then slid his body back on top, so that his weight descended as much as his buoyancy in the water would permit. "And, you know what else occurs to me? We don't have to worry about AIDS anymore. You tested Charlie, even though it was supposedly too soon, and he's negative. Since Daddy's probably been fucking him for years, he'd almost have to be infected if Daddy was — right? So I'm home free, and we know you're okay..." He saw the glimmer of concern on Bruce's face. "All right," he continued, "we'll keep playing it safe for a while. But if you're game," he added in a whisper, "I'd sure like to try it my way."

"It's what you really want?" Bruce whispered hoarsely.

"Yeah," Frank told him. "Maybe just this one time, but ... well, it's ... can I call it 'important'? Maybe that's too strong, but it's become something I've thought about ... a lot, and ... well, maybe I need to prove something, to myself if not to anybody else."

■ ■ ■

Although he had acquiesced with a mixture of apprehension and involuntary anticipation, the scene was going much better than he had expected. Frank was displaying an amazing degree of imagination, even sensitivity, as a Top. *Of course, love plays a part in this ... always does.* His hands were bound behind his back with cotton rope. He was face down on the bed now, secured by neck and ankles, his body aflame — outwardly from the punishment Frank was giving him, inwardly from the realization that they had achieved a high point in their relationship ... it was a balanced mutuality, neither solely Top or bottom. Frank was running his hands over his captive's body, testing the warm glow across the back and ass, occasionally reaching down, between the imprisoned thighs, to grasp and tantalize the thrusting hardness. The room was illuminated only by a red night-light, and soft symphonic music was coming from the wall speakers. Despite the implied or simulated violence, there was a sense of calm, unhurried exchange that both of them felt.

Somewhere, far in the background, Bruce heard a car enter his driveway. The knowledge registered deep in the recesses of his mind, but it had no relevance to him ... *probably some trick of Dennie's* ... had no effect on the exchange he was enjoying. He wanted to feel the solid weight of Frank's body come down on his own. He anticipated the warmth, the brief spasm of pain, the final sense of penetration and ultimate joining of their physical beings, the emotional climax after prolonged moments of sensual pleasure.

But abruptly Frank had moved away from him. He was standing in the center of the room, as if anticipating someone's arrival. "What's wrong?" Bruce whispered.

Frank motioned him silent and moved to the door, opening it a crack as he listened. Then Bruce could hear, too: voices rasping softly in the corridor, a suggestion of agitation in the speakers' tones. Frank stepped into the opening, his naked body blocking any view in or out.

"Dennie, what's the matter?" he asked, and with that he moved into the corridor, outside Bruce's range of hearing.

The big man's footsteps moved closer. "It's Charlie Stuart," he whispered, "just came around rapping on my window. Seems he's had a row with Daddy and came here to see me."

"Frank, let me up," Bruce called.

His friend looked back into the room, shaking his head. "No," he said softly. "Not yet." Then he had moved completely into the hall, pulling the door closed behind him.

Bruce could hear the continued murmur of verbal exchange, but Charlie Stuart's voice was too soft to be recognizable. Dennie's deeper tones were also inaudible, and Frank's whispered responses did not register at all. Bruce lay in helpless anxiety, trying desperately to hear, not wanting to call out to the others ... not totally comfortable to think of them finding him in his present condition. But he was becoming desperate to know what was happening. He would have forgotten about his own situation and shouted if Frank had not slipped back into the room.

"What's going on?" he demanded.

"Just an old trick of Dennie's — got kicked out by his roommate and came running to Daddy." Frank had forced Bruce's head back onto the pillow, where it was impossible for either to see the other's face. But his story seemed to find acceptance.

"It's not the first time," Bruce muttered. Frank could feel the captive body relax into its previous state of near lethargy, and he forced himself to resume the sensual stroking. Then, gradually, the continued physical contact took possession of his senses, and he picked up the pace. He tangled his fingers in Bruce's hair, forcing his face around far enough to reach his lips. He kissed him deeply, with a warmth and passion that extinguished his anxiety in a warm surge of lust.

■ ■ ■

Bruce had several patients scheduled for the morning and early afternoon. Although he was a shade off his top form as a result of the scene that had lasted into the wee hours, he managed to cope without any difficulties. In fact, he became so preoccupied with the harried schedule as to remain oblivious to the goings and comings in the rest of the house. That his lover and his best friend had conspired to deceive him did not register until he completed his final session. Once Dennie had shown the woman out — a wealthy Bel Air matron with a penchant for shoplifting — Bruce got out of his chair and stretched. He was hungry, he realized, having had only a sandwich around one o'clock, that Dennie had brought him at his desk between patients. It was now after four.

He went into the kitchen and started rummaging about in the refrigerator. He glanced out into the backyard, but there was no one by the pool. Dennie had gone into his own room, he supposed, because the house was completely silent. He took a wedge of cheese from the compartment in the door, and was looking in the cabinet for a box of crackers, when he heard a sound that made him pause, straining to listen. Silence. He shrugged and returned to his quest, when he thought he heard it again — a muffled cry? He couldn't be sure. Still listening, he cut a few slices of cheese, and then it came again. Definitely a human voice. He moved to the door leading into Dennie's wing. It was closed and he paused, not wanting to intrude on his friend's privacy. Then he heard it again.

Dirty old man! He's had that kid strung up back there since midnight ... never let on all day. Played it really cool! Curious now, he went into the front hall and looked out the window, wondering if he'd recognize the guy's car. To his surprise, he saw Charlie Stuart's small black Triumph — and in front of it, Frank's Nissan. Now really puzzled, he moved down the hall to his own bedroom, opening the door to discover Rudy snoozing on the made-up bed. But no sign of Frank. Thoughtfully, he returned to the kitchen and munched on his cheese and crackers.

He could not understand what was going on, and finally — despite a reluctance to violate the unspoken agreement between himself and Dennie — he opened the door to his friend's quarters and started down the hall. This time he clearly heard the snap of leather against flesh, and the unmistakable response of a bottom blubbering into his gag. The door stood half open at the end of the corridor, and much as Charlie had done on the night of his bungled break-in, Bruce wedged his body into the corner of the hall to survey the interior of the room.

A young man — presumably Charlie Stuart — was spread-eagled in a standing position, bound to the frame that formed the foot of Dennie's bed. He was facing away from the door, but the small, tightly compacted body was all but unmistakable. Dennie, now stripped to the waist, was standing behind him with a doubled belt in his hand. And Frank was reclining on the bed, wearing just his black Speedo, watching the captive's struggles with an expression of unconcealed satisfaction.

"What the fuck is going on here?" Bruce demanded.

All three occupants of the room seemed momentarily frozen in place, although each had turned in his direction — Charlie straining to see over his shoulder. Then Frank was off the bed and at his side, and Dennie stood in sheepish silence in the center of the room. Charlie merely looked away, sagging in his bonds as if in silent surrender.

"Would one of you tell me exactly what the fuck is going on here?" Bruce demanded again.

"It's a long story," Dennie answered softly,

"I can see that," said Bruce.

"I think we'd better step outside." Frank gently took hold of his arm and began guiding him down the corridor. Dennie started to follow.

"What about the kid?" Bruce asked.

"Let the little asshole hang there," Dennie replied. Then, pulling the door closed so his prisoner could no longer hear him, he added, "He's happy as a pig in shit."

"Well, I'm not!" said Bruce. Now that the surprise was past, he could feel anger building as his mind began to structure the myriad possibilities. "I want to know what you guys have done," he added. While puzzled by Frank's presence in Dennie's scene, his concern was focused elsewhere.

Bruce had continued to lead the group down the corridor, and at the doorway he started automatically for the patio.

"Let's go into the den," suggested Frank. "It's too hot outside."

Biting his lower lip to stifle the thoughts coming to mind in frightening proportions, Bruce nodded agreement and they all settled into the leather chairs around the coffee table. Frank made a couple of unsuccessful attempts to start the conversation, and Dennie took over after several seconds of strained silence.

"Charlie had a falling-out with his father," he said. "We talked for a long time last night, and he told me the whole story."

Bruce started to interrupt, but Frank placed a restraining hand on his forearm. "Let him tell the whole thing first," he said softly. Bruce glared angrily at both his friends, but acquiesced and allowed Dennie to continue.

"Now I know you're the master shrink, Bruce," he said, trying to inject some banter into his account, "and you think the kid's not very bright. Well, maybe he's not, but his old man's a lawyer and I guess some of that rubbed off. Anyway, he understands the hearsay rule pretty well, and he made it clear that what he said to me wasn't going to be repeated to anyone else. Apparently, that means it can't be used in court. Is that right?"

Bruce nodded. "I'd have to ask a trial lawyer, but I think he's probably right. If he denies — later on — that he ever told you anything, I don't think they'd be able to get it in at a trial, at least not against his father."

"Okay, that being the case, here's what he said happened. He went home after the meeting last night, and he told his old man everything we said — just like you assumed he would. But what none of us thought about was how upset he was going to be when he found out that Daddy'd been tricking with hustlers three or four years ago. Then you made that extra comment about call boys. That really set him off, because ... well, he was jealous. Daddy was his lover, and I mean the kid really had a case for the old man. And from what Charlie said, I guess King Charles didn't realize it, either. He doesn't think of himself — or Charlie — as queer, you see. He just never realized that the kid could be in love with him."

"But why ...?" Bruce began.

"I guess he's had the hots for me — at least he says he has — since that first day. Remember, I always thought he was prick-teasing me when he stripped off and went for a swim, then stood there drying his cock in front of me. So, when Daddy got mad during this ... fight, discussion ... whatever, the kid ran out and jumped in his car and after driving around a while he came and rapped on my window. Says he never wants to see the old man again, and..."

Dennie paused, and Frank finished for him. "He wants to be Dennie's slave. Says he'll be the houseboy, do anything that any of us tells him ... as long as it's all right with Dennie."

Bruce sighed, rubbing his chin in thought. "And King Charles has no idea he's here?"

He was perplexed when neither of his companions responded, and as he glanced from one to the other he realized that there was still more to be told. "Does this silence mean that Stuart *does* know where his kid is?" he asked.

Dennie shook his head, obviously uncomfortable and unwilling to speak.

"All right, Frank, you seem to be in the middle of this. What else happened?"

His friend took a deep breath, and looking down at his intertwined fingers, he began in a barely audible tone: "Last night," he said, "when the meeting broke up and Charlie took off, Harve, Mike, and I had a little discussion." He looked up sharply, his green eyes flashing brightly as he seemed to gain some inner strength. "See, none of us agreed with the idea of letting those fuckheads off with a warning, letting that bastard Stuart walk away from it, just by closing down his operations for a while — and it would just have been for a while. You agreed with that, yourself! Once everything cooled down, it would have been business as usual, maybe with a little different twist. That wouldn't have been right, Bruce!" Although he tried to sound angry, there was a decided aura of anxiety, almost pleading in his tone.

"Are you telling me that those two guys...?"

"They'd already figured it out," Dennie interjected. "When Charlie took off, they both knew who he was."

"That's when Harve pulled me aside," Frank continued. "He and Mike would 'take care of the situation,' he said. All we had to do was make sure ... make sure you wouldn't interfere, wouldn't tumble to it and call the cops."

"*We*'?" asked Bruce, looking from one guilty face to the other.

"Yeah, Dennie and me. He loaned 'em a few things they'd need and we were..."

"So you were both in on it. And..." He felt a sinking feeling in his guts, as the truth came down on him. "So, the two of you conspired with the other two. They went off to ... do God-knows-what to Charles Stuart, and you, Frank ... you put on that big act for me, got me to let you play Top, just in case the phone rang or ... Jesus H. Christ!" He slumped back in his chair, the surge of anger giving way to near-despair as his mind began to grapple with all the possible scenarios. "Do you guys have any idea what you've done? If those two maniacs ... Oh, shit! If they went after Stuart ... they might very well have killed him! Do you know where that puts you — puts all of us?"

"It wasn't an act, Bruce." Frank was on his knees beside Bruce's chair. "Please, baby, believe me. It just came at the right time."

Bruce pushed him away and stood up. He went into his office and looked up the Stuart phone number, angrily punching the digits into his desk phone. After it rang a good ten times, he dropped the receiver into the cradle. He stood silently for a moment, trying to collect his thoughts. He felt a terrible sadness, mingled with a mounting fear — a terror, such as he had never felt before.

He returned slowly to the den, tempted to pick up the phone again and call Abe Javits. *No, not yet. It's my mess. I've got to sort it out first.* "Dennie, go let that animal loose. We'll have to bring him with us."

■ ■ ■

They had taken Dennie's Buick, because all the other cars were two-seaters. But Bruce was driving. As they passed through the open gates of the Stuart grounds, the sun was low on the horizon, casting long shadows across the red-brick driveway. Charlie, who had been silent for most of the drive, sat beside Frank in the backseat, and from the desultory conversation passing between his companions, had gathered enough insight into the purpose of their trip to begin expressing himself. "...and they might have gotten me, too," he was saying. "Dad wanted to send me to get the van after I told him what all you guys had said at the meeting. But I was so pissed off at him, I told him to move the shit out of the dungeon, himself. I never wanted to see him again. And I took off." He started to sob, as he had been doing periodically ever since leaving Bruce's house. "You aren't going to call the cops, are you?" he pleaded.

No one answered him, because the others would normally have deferred to Bruce; but at the moment he was not feeling very much in command. Frank had tricked him, he realized, had purposely set up the scene so that he would be bound and helpless if anything should go wrong. If Harve and Mike Rittenhaus had gone after Charles Stuart, Frank had known about it ... Dennie, too. And that would make them just as guilty as the actual perpetrators, whatever the nature of the crime. That was something he'd have to work out later. But despite Frank's complicity in the attack, and regardless of the fact that their relative roles in that evening's scene may have been a ploy, he knew there had been an underlying sense of sincerity. Frank was an actor, but no one was that good! It still angered him, or more accurately hurt his feelings — or wounded his ego — to think that it had been occasioned by a plot, and more so that he had fallen for it!

He braked to a stop by the front door, and Charlie led them at a run through the marble hallway to the basement door. Not a sound came from the lower level, no hint of motion, just the glow of subdued lighting. Bruce followed the youngster down the stairs and onto the padded floor. A single spotlight illuminated a naked figure sagging in helpless suspension in the center of the room, his hands locked to a pair of chains that spread his arms wide apart, and that were in turn locked onto large eyebolts in the ceiling. Despite the leather hood that left only his mouth uncovered, it was obviously Charles Stuart III.

Bruce rushed forward and unfastened the buckle that anchored the hood about the victim's throat. He tossed the leather covering aside and felt desperately for a pulse, sliding his finger along the clammy skin until he found a pressure point on the neck. As he did so, the figure emitted an anguished groan, and the leg muscles made an attempt to reposition the body weight. For a man of his age, Stuart was in remarkably good shape, although the years had left him a little soft about the middle, and the hair on his chest was gray. But his physical strength had apparently sustained him through his ordeal. He struggled to get his feet under him now, relieving the pressure on his wrists. In the bright glare of the spotlight, his body displayed evidence of heavy abuse. Hardly a square inch of his skin remained unmarked, and a puddle of fluid was drying about his feet: urine certainly. Bruce could smell it. But his punishment had been very heavy, and the trickles of blood from his lacerations could well have contributed to the dark, congealing mass.

"Take me down," he gasped. "Please, get me down before anyone else sees me like this."

Bruce examined the chains and realized that they were locked in place, both around the wrists and to the eyebolts in the ceiling. "Charlie, where are the keys?" he asked.

The youngster dashed across the room, rummaging around at the base of a pegboard rack. "I can't find them," he called back in desperation. "Oh, God, do you suppose they took them away?"

"I hope they did," said Frank. He had taken Bruce's place in front of the battered form, and yanked the head up by its hair. "You arrogant, fucking bastard! I hope they put you up there so you never get down. I'm just sorry you're not hanging in the rotunda at city hall."

Bruce tried to pull him away, but Frank's fury had mounted as he spoke, and he shook his friend's hand off his shoulder. "It looks like they took care of this, too," he gloated, hefting the captive's genitals in his hand. Bruce had been so intent on trying to free the man's wrists, he had failed to notice that Stuart's assailants had done a wicked job of binding his cock and balls. There were several chains locked around, each fastened with small padlocks. "I suppose the keys are missing for these, too?" he muttered.

"Under ... under the chains," gasped the prisoner.

Bruce tried to displace the metal to see beneath the gleaming loops, but it was too dark, and he wasn't sure what he should be looking for. But he realized that there was definitely something wrong with the testicles, something more than would be accomplished by a few loops of chain, or any other device with which his SM experience had acquainted him. The whole sac was purple, almost black, the contents swollen far beyond any normal dimension.

Charlie had moved up to him by then, and also tried to see. "Oh, shit!" he gasped. "They found that thing Dad bought in

Texas last year. Doctor MacLeod, you've got to get it off him!"

Bruce looked at him, puzzled. "What is it, Charlie? What's under there?"

"It's a thing from this," he said, picking up a chrome pliers-like device from the corner, where the assailants had apparently thrown it. "They sell it to ranchers to ... to castrate animals. See, a rubber band–like thing goes here, and it stretches it out, and snaps it down. It makes everything turn black in a couple of days, and then the nuts just fall off. You got to get it off him!"

"Charlie, look again and see if you can't find the keys," Bruce told him. Although there was a note of urgency, even desperation in his tone, he was fully aware of the irony. He was also grateful that Harve Simpson had shown the degree of restraint that he apparently had. Charles Stuart was still alive, and Bruce would have bet against it. *But Rittenhaus was with him, probably held him back. Wonder which one used the gelding kit. Harve, I'd guess. Mike probably couldn't figure out how to work it.*

"I can't find the keys," Charlie whined from behind him. "But wait a minute! I've got ... here!" He reached into the bottom of a chest and extracted a leather packet. "Dad showed me how to use these. Let me see..." He fumbled out a pick and shoved the tip into one of the locks on his father's wrists.

"Think we should call the paramedics or something?" Dennie asked.

"No!" pleaded the bound and beaten figure. "Please! Don't call any officials. Charlie," he gasped, "please ... call Henry Winslow. Get him up here, please, Son."

The lock popped open, and Charlie went to work on the other, keeping at it in silence, not answering his father.

"Henry Winslow, the surgeon?" asked Bruce.

"Yes," rasped the prisoner. "He used to be chief of staff at St. Martin's ... good friend. He'll come."

"How long has that thing been around your nuts?" Bruce asked.

Stuart gasped and tried to swivel his head to face him. "Too long," he whispered. "It was one of the first things they did." The second lock came loose, and Bruce steadied him as Charles Stuart slumped onto his knees.

"What made you think you could get away with this?" Frank demanded. He was standing just behind Bruce, who was supporting the older man as Charlie probed at the locks around his genitals.

"I did get away with it," he rasped.

Bruce called to Dennie, who grabbed Frank just as he was about to throw himself on his defeated antagonist.

"Just how much you got away with remains to be seen," said Bruce, as the first chain dropped free. "But I'm willing to bet you've paid a fairly substantial price." He looked down at the darkened, swollen testicles. "If we get you to a hospital, you might be able to use these again. Otherwise..."

Charles Stuart looked up at the three men standing above him, and made a grim gesture with his lips, which might have been a smile. "Just get Henry up here," he gasped. "No one else. None of us wants the media circus that would put all of our names in print," he added. His voice, while harsh and raspy, had already regained a modicum of command. "You're MacLeod, aren't you?" At a nod from Bruce he continued. "So you're a doctor. You'll do whatever you can for me, until Henry gets here. But you won't call the cops and you won't take me to a hospital. That's my deal. Otherwise, we'll all have a lot of questions to answer — including those two punks you sent up here in ski masks to revenge yourself. If I lose my balls, that's my forfeit in the game. I'll pay the price, but I'll keep my silence. And so will you, because you don't want it out any more than I do."

■ ■ ■

"Can you believe that guy?" said Dennie. "He'd rather lose his balls than face a little publicity and a few years in the slammer." He was sitting in one of the chairs beside the Stuart pool. Frank was with him, and Charlie hovered in the background. Bruce was still in the upstairs bedroom with Doctor Winslow and his patient.

"He'll keep his nuts, all right," said Frank grimly. "...in a jar of formaldehyde."

Charlie knelt on the cement beside Dennie's chair. "What... are you going to do about me?" he asked lamely.

"What do you think we should do, Charlie?" Dennie asked.

215

"I don't know," he replied, glancing uncomfortably from one man to the other. "I guess I'm as guilty as Dad."

"Maybe we ought to cut your nuts off, too," said Frank harshly.

Charlie hung his head, causing his long blond hair to fall across his face. "Maybe you should," he replied softly.

Bruce came out of the house, shirt plastered to his body by sweat. He hunkered down beside the others, sitting on his heels. "I don't know exactly what I should do," he said. "I'm not a surgeon, so I can't really argue with Winslow. He won't remove the band, because he says there's already gangrene, and if he lets the blood flow out of it, the old man's going to die of blood poisoning."

"So he's castrated," Frank observed grimly.

"Heavy price," Dennie growled.

"Isn't that exactly what he deserves?" said Frank.

"You know it is," Dennie agreed.

"But it's not exactly ethical, is it, Bruce?" Frank added. "It puts you in a spot you don't want to be in." He slipped off his own chair and came down beside his friend, placing an arm across his shoulders. "But my body was one of those that he abused. He kidnapped God knows how many other guys. He ought to face the death penalty, with all the nasty publicity that goes along with it. Instead, he's making us play by his rules again. He..."

"Do you want me to call the cops, paramedics?" asked Bruce.

Frank was silent for a moment, sensing that for the first time in their relationship he was truly in command. Bruce would abide by his decision. "Are you going to forgive me for what I did last night?" he asked. He could sense Charlie's motion, as the youngster looked up at them questioningly.

Bruce seemed to see Charlie for the first time. "I'll leave it up to you," he said, addressing the younger Stuart. "In my opinion, your father's going to lose his testicles no matter what we do, but your friend Winslow, regardless how good a surgeon he may be, is working without proper equipment. That's what your old man wants. He's adamant that we not call the police or paramedics — or have him taken to a hospital. He's also going to lose partial use of his left hand, but Winslow says he can save it ... not have to amputate it. You're his nearest relative. You decide."

"If Dad doesn't want it, that's the way it's got to be," replied Charlie softly. "He told me, when I went upstairs with you, he told me not to call anyone. Said he'd lost the set, and if anyone found out about it, he'd have lost the match. Of course, as far as I'm concerned, he can go fuck himself. And I already told him that. But the rest is up to him, and he's made his mind up to it."

"Dennie," Bruce said, "take that little shit downstairs and whip the bejeesus out of him."

The big man hesitated. "Are you serious?"

"Sure. I don't see any reason to shed crocodile tears over King Charles's balls. And before we leave, we ought to break out some champagne from the old bastard's cellar and celebrate. But right now, Frank and I have a few things to discuss." Bruce's tone had been harsh, although none of his listeners could be sure if it was bitterness or sarcasm that colored the quality of his voice. "Hasn't all this made you a little horny?" he added, his tone colder still, as if he were finally merging his own sense of righteous retribution with that of his companions. "Little Ass-Wipe, here, says he wants to be your slave. If you want him, take him. He isn't good for anything else, and it's the only way he's going to get punished — and it might as well start in his old man's dungeon, on top of the old man's crusty gore."

Dennie muttered a few unintelligible words, then stood up and started toward the house. Charlie, head still bowed, followed at his heels. Once they had gone inside, Frank turned and stared into Bruce's eyes. "This has been a really rough day," he said softly, "and I know you have every right to be pissed at me. But..." They were kneeling on the cement deck, facing one another, their bodies almost touching.

Bruce pulled him forward, crushed Frank's body against his own. They kissed in an exchange of such desperate hunger that all other questions became momentarily unimportant. "I don't know how I'll explain all this to Abe and Alice," he sighed at length. "I just hate the idea that King Asshole might have won."

Frank shrugged. "He hasn't," he whispered. "How can you even suggest it? And a few days from now he'll know it. He'll never enjoy this again," he added, running his hand over Bruce's crotch. Then he slid the sweaty shirt off his friend's shoulders. "Once the shock wears off, he'll know he's lost the game. We're the winners."

"Not really," said Bruce. "I've got a better picture of his twisted psyche now, and by his standards ... by his rules, it's at best a stalemate. He's lying up there with his nuts ripped off, a paralyzed left hand, and probably going into shock. But he isn't going to die. Remember my 'M component'? All he's lost is a heavy forfeit in his game, but he hasn't broken his own rules. On the other hand, I'm down here with my prick poking into your belly, ready to slide into his pool and have sex with you ... me, a doctor, who's sworn to protect life and limb. But I don't want anyone to know about this, not any more than he does. So in that sense I'm violating *my* oath, violating *my* rules. Don't you see? I've compromised my sworn set of ethics, violated the rules of my own game in order to preserve *his* rules."

"So, in effect you're saying he's beaten you? Bullshit! You tracked him down, and made it possible for two of his victims to take their revenge on him. And without a pair of balls he'll never play his games again. I'd say that's a victory."

Bruce sighed. "I don't know," he said. "If we're talking about it as a game, he hasn't really lost. And that's how he perceives it."

"Will you be able to live with it?" asked Frank seriously.

Bruce nodded. "Yeah. It may take a while, but I'll get over it."

"But he won't," Frank insisted. "And we've still got..." He looked questioningly at his companion. "...both the equipment and the will to use it. We do, don't we?"

Bruce wrapped his arms around the slender body of his lover. "We sure do," he whispered.

EPILOGUE

The little restaurant was crowded, with white-jacketed waiters hustling from table to table, giving the impression of rendering the type of service one is supposed to receive in a Beverly Hills bistro.

"That's the table where King Charles was holding court," said Frank, pointing toward a spot near the front door, "and that's where he shoved Rufus," he added, indicating another table several feet away.

"Well, let's hope you don't have to punch out any unruly patrons tonight," said Alice Javits. She leaned toward her husband, pinching his leg under the table. "We're all going to behave like civilized ladies and gentlemen."

"Well, Bruce, I'm glad to see that you two have made it through the most difficult period," said Abe, and at his friend's questioning glance, he added: "This is your six-month anniversary, in case you haven't kept track."

"So that's the special occasion," said Bruce. "I wondered what you meant when you called."

"Oh, that would be enough to celebrate, just by itself," said Alice, "but I think Abe has a little more to tell you."

"Should we wait for the champagne, or do we want it right now?" asked her husband, so pleased with himself Bruce knew he didn't want to wait.

"Let's have it now, while we're all cold sober," he replied.

"Well," began Abe expansively, "you remember our conversation after the night of the nutting? How concerned you were that King Charles might have won the game?" At a nod from

Bruce he continued: "Well, I'm pleased to inform you that, as a result of our investigations — plus a few bits of information obtained and dropped by my friend in Geneva — I have it on the best authority that Charles Iverson Stuart III is just about to be indicted by the IRS. And, they're going to nail his ass to the wall!"

"How does that affect our game?" Bruce asked.

"They're going to put him in prison, dear," Alice explained.

"Just going into the Big House is going to be bad enough, but can you imagine the hell he's going to go through when they give him a physical?" added Abe. He laughed aloud. "Medical observation: no testes. The story will be all over the joint in less than an hour."

"I'm not sure..."

"Bruce, look: You think you lost the game, because you weren't able to control your own people. Right? But, when you stop to add up the pluses and minuses, he lost his most trusted subordinate, the only person in the world he had any true regard for. And it's a real, total loss, not just a momentary defection. Dennie still has his slave, right?"

"Right," said Frank. "The little fucker's become our most devoted houseboy."

"Okay, that's loss number one," said Abe. "His son is now an admitted homosexual, and in willing voluntary bondage to his arch enemy. For the moment, the great game player is sitting all alone in his big, fancy house with nobody for company, and no nuts even if he wanted to buy a little companionship. Add to that the blow that's going to fall on him in a few days, and Daddy's on the path to the worst hell he could possibly imagine."

At this point, the waiter arrived with a bottle of Dom Perignon, which he ostentatiously opened and poured into four fluted crystal glasses. As soon as he departed the table, Abe lifted his glass. *"L'chaim!"* he said jovially. "We offer a Yiddish, gay, SM toast to the world's greatest bigot — about to become better known by a federal prison number — a true loser!"

"I'll drink to that!" said Frank.

"And so will I," Bruce echoed after only a moment's hesitation, and they all clinked their glasses.

Other books of interest from
ALYSON PUBLICATIONS

LEATHERFOLK, edited by Mark Thompson, cloth, $20.00. There's a new leather community in America today. It's politically aware and socially active. This ground-breaking anthology is the first nonfiction, co-gender work to focus on this large and often controversial subculture. The diverse contributors look at the history of the leather and S/M movement, how radical sex practice relates to their spirituality, and what S/M means to them personally.

STEAM, by Jay B. Laws, $10.00. San Francisco was once a city of music and laughter, of parties and bathhouses, when days held promise and nights, romance. But now something sinister haunts the streets and alleyways of San Francisco, something that crept in with the fog to seek a cruel revenge. It feeds on deep desire, and tantalizes with the false and empty promises of a more carefree past. For many, it will all begin with a ticket to an abandoned house of dreams...

BROTHER TO BROTHER, edited by Essex Hemphill, $9.00. Black activist and poet Essex Hemphill has carried on in the footsteps of the late Joseph Beam (editor of *In the Life*) with this new anthology of fiction, essays, and poetry by black gay men. Contributors include Assoto Saint, Craig G. Harris, Melvin Dixon, Marlon Riggs, and many newer writers.

BI ANY OTHER NAME, edited by Loraine Hutchins and Lani Kaahumanu, $12.00. Hear the voices of over seventy women and men from all walks of life describe their lives as bisexuals. They tell their stories — personal, political, spiritual, historical — in prose, poetry, art, and essays. These are individuals who have fought prejudice from both the gay and straight communities and who have begun only recently to share their experiences. This ground-breaking anthology is an important step in the process of forming a community of their own.

THE ADVOCATE ADVISER, by Pat Califia, $9.00. The Miss Manners of gay culture tackles subjects ranging from the ethics of zoophilia to the etiquette of a holy union ceremony. Along the way she covers interracial relationships, in-law problems, and gay parenting. No other gay columnist so successfully combines useful advice, an unorthodox perspective, and a wicked sense of humor.

THE ALYSON ALMANAC, $9.00. How did your representatives in Congress vote on gay issues? What are the best gay and lesbian books, movies, and plays? When was the first gay and lesbian march on Washington? With what king did Julius Caesar have a sexual relationship? You'll find all this, and more, in this unique and entertaining reference work.

THE GAY BOOK OF LISTS, by Leigh Rutledge, $8.00. Rutledge has compiled a fascinating and informative collection of lists. His subject matter ranges from history (6 gay popes) to politics (9 perfectly disgusting reactions to AIDS) to entertainment (12 examples of gays on network television) to humor (9 Victorian "cures" for masturbation). Learning about gay culture and history has never been so much fun.

GAYS IN UNIFORM, edited by Kate Dyer, $7.00. Why doesn't the Pentagon want you to read this book? When two studies by a research arm of the Pentagon concluded that there was no justification for keeping gay people out of the military, the generals deep-sixed the reports. Those reports are now available, in book form, to the public at large. Find out for yourself what the Pentagon doesn't want you to know about gays in the military.

BETTER ANGEL, by Richard Meeker, $7.00. The touching story of a young man's gay awakening in the years between the World Wars. Kurt Gray is a shy, bookish boy growing up in a small town in Michigan. Even at the age of thirteen he knows that somehow he is different. Gradually he recognizes his desire for a man's companionship and love. As a talented composer, breaking into New York's musical world, he finds the love he's sought.

I ONCE HAD A MASTER, by John Preston, $9.00. In these intensely erotic stories, John Preston outlines the story of one man's journey through the world of S/M sexuality, beginning as a novice, soon becoming a sought-after master.

ENTERTAINMENT FOR A MASTER, by John Preston, $9.00. In this second volume of the Master series, John Preston continues his exploration of S/M sexuality. This time, the Master hosts an elegant and exclusive S/M party. To prepare for the festivities, the Master recruits volunteer masochists who are to instruct and entertain the Master's three guests.

THE LOVE OF A MASTER, by John Preston, $8.00. What could possibly follow the elegant S/M party in John Preston's last book, *Entertainment for a Master?* Certainly not the reclusive life his hero had been living in the mountains of New England. Now the Master surveys his world, wondering how he can feed his needs. There's always the city with its erotic underground, or the secretive Network with its willing sexual slaves. But it would be so much more ... *interesting* if he could discover the dark sexual dreams of one of the young men around him who might be looking for *The Love of a Master.*

THE LITTLE DEATH, by Michael Nava, $8.00. As a public defender, Henry Rios finds himself losing the idealism he had as a law student. Then a man he has befriended — and loved — dies under suspicious circumstances. As he investigates the murder, Rios finds the solution as subtle as the law itself.

HOT LIVING, edited by John Preston, $9.00. The AIDS crisis has closed off some forms of sexual activity for health-conscious gay men, but it has also encouraged many men to look for new forms of sexual expression. Here, over a dozen of today's most popular gay writers erotically describe those new possibilities.

FINALE, edited by Michael Nava, $9.00. Eight carefully crafted stories of mystery and suspense by both well-known authors and newfound talent: an anniversary party ends abruptly when a guest is found in the bathroom with his throat slashed; a frustrated writer plans the murder of a successful novelist; a young man's hauntingly familiar dreams lead him into a forgotten past.

SUPPORT YOUR LOCAL BOOKSTORE

Most of the books described above are available at your nearest gay or feminist bookstore, and many of them will be available at other bookstores. If you can't get these books locally, order by mail using the form below.

Enclosed is $_____ for the following books. (Add $1.00 postage when ordering just one book. If you order two or more, we'll pay the postage.)

1. _____

2. _____

3. _____

name: _____

address: _____

city: _____ state: _____ zip: _____

ALYSON PUBLICATIONS
Dept. H-89, 40 Plympton St., Boston, MA 02118

After December 31, 1992, please write for current catalog.